A GUEST AND HIS GOING

The many readers who enjoyed P. H. Newby's 'Egyptian' novels, *The Picnic at Sakkara* and *Revolution and Roses*, will remember the eccentric and patriotic Muawiya, who has now been invited to London as a guest of the British Council.

At a time when the maritime powers are busy inventing the Canal User's Association at Lancaster House, Muawiya jeopardizes Anglo-Egyptian relations further by appropriating a car and driving it furiously (unlicensed and uninsured) until it is smashed up in Park Lane. He eludes the police; takes refuge in the Egyptian Embassy; emerges from sanctuary to give a party; publicly debates the motion 'All men are brothers'; and finally orates at Speakers' Corner in Hyde Park.

Muawiya with his lunatic logic is only one of many strands woven into a story that is none the less serious for its light-hearted telling.

By the same author

A JOURNEY TO THE INTERIOR

AGENTS AND WITNESSES

MARINER DANCES

THE SNOW PASTURE

A SEASON IN ENGLAND

A STEP TO SILENCE

THE RETREAT

THE PICNIC AT SAKKARA

REVOLUTION AND ROSES

TEN MILES FROM ANYWHERE

A GUEST AND HIS GOING

a novel by

P. H. NEWBY

London
JONATHAN CAPE
& THE BOOK SOCIETY

THIS EDITION ISSUED ON FIRST PUBLICATION BY THE BOOK
SOCIETY LTD., IN ASSOCIATION WITH JONATHAN CAPE LTD.
JUNE 1959

© 1959 BY P. H. NEWBY

PRINTED IN GREAT BRITAIN IN THE CITY OF OXFORD
AT THE ALDEN PRESS
ON PAPER MADE BY JOHN DICKINSON & CO. LTD.
BOUND BY A. W. BAIN & CO. LTD, LONDON

CHAPTER ONE

A WOMAN and three men, one of them dark-skinned, crunched down the drive of a once red but now soot-dyed house in North London and were just approaching the gate when a large man appeared from the rhododendrons.

'So glad to catch you up.' He waved a boneless hand northwards, in the direction of the Crematorium. Leading the party on to the pavement he took up position under the board which said HELVETIA SCHOOL OF ENGLISH FOR FOREIGNERS. 'This suburb is difficult to get away from. No taxis, and they're very expensive anyway, as you must have learned. Golders Green station is a good ten minutes' walk. Let me give you a lift in the car. Take you wherever you like. I'm free for the evening.'

The rest of them looked surprised. The young Egyptian had not set eyes on Napier Hillingdon before they had been introduced over tea that afternoon but he could sense that this was uncharacteristic behaviour. It was not just a matter of popping out from behind a lot of bushes. There was a more fundamental oddity, and Muawiya was pleased. The courtesy visit to his old teacher had been disappointing. Mrs Perry *said* she remembered him in Cairo but she was so cool that Muawiya was sceptical. Not even an Englishwoman was cool to the man who had saved her husband's life, and he did not care to remind her of the circumstance. Professor Perry remembered him very well, of course. He asked after other students and wanted him to stay for dinner, but he too seemed less pleased than he might have been.

No doubt they were all angry over the nationalization of the Suez Canal. That was the trouble with English people these days. They could never disentangle politics from personal relationships, and Muawiya was saddened to think how much more statesmanlike he, an Egyptian, would have been in Perry's position and how far below this standard Perry was falling. Perry ought to have mentioned the possibility of cutting off Nile water at the Uganda frontier, sent out for more cream pastries and insisted on his staying the night. But the British temperament was no longer what it used to be.

'We're only going to Hampstead,' said the young man from the British Council who was supposed to be looking after Muawiya during his stay in England.

'Run you there in a couple of minutes.' When Hillingdon took his seat at the wheel of the 1938 Morris the near-side of the vehicle lifted in a snarl to reveal its tyres. 'You ever been in an English pub, eh? I know you Moslems are against alcohol but you could have a lime-juice. You can't understand England without knowing what goes on in a pub.'

'I'm not against alcohol,' said Muawiya. 'Before I go back to Egypt I hope to obtain exclusive representation of a Scotch whisky distillery.'

'You mean in Egypt?'

'All intellectual and military Egyptians like whisky.'

'You mean you want to import whisky into Egypt?' said the young man from the British Council.

'And gin.'

'But I thought you were a journalist.'

'I'm that as well.'

Still there was this feeling of surprise in the air. First Perry and then his wife shook Muawiya by the hand when he had taken his place in the car, but their eyes strayed speculatively to the back of Napier Hillingdon's head, rather as though he were normally kept locked in a sound-proof room, had been let out for the day and was showing disturbing signs of sanity.

Water from the soaked trees pattered on the roof of the car. The greyness and coldness of the evening cut the parting short. Hillingdon, too, was unaccountably impatient to be off and Muawiya had scarcely time to invite the Perrys to a party he was giving (he would telephone and make all arrangements) before they were grinding down Meadway in a direction roughly opposite to the one they should have been taking.

'I think I must tell you, Mr — '

'Muawiya.'

'Moo-āh-wee-ah! I think I must tell you that I am making certain inquiries. Don't be alarmed! I'm just a private citizen. As soon as I clapped eyes on you this afternoon I realized you were just the fellow to help me. Now you, sir, Mr — '

A thumb was jabbed over his shoulder in the direction of his other passenger.

'Blainey. Tim Blainey.'

'This is Golders Green station, Mr Blainey. You'll be back at your office in no time while I take Mr Muawiya on to Hampstead.'

'But we're going there together. He's coming to my mother's place for dinner.'

'In that case,' said Napier Hillingdon, obviously disappointed, 'we'd better go and inspect the various brands of Scotch whisky. It would never do for Mr Muawiya to be associated with anything inferior.'

Hillingdon drew up before a pub in the North End Road and led the way through a door marked LOUNGE. It was a room of

Windsor chairs, Latex cushions and an apparently glowing fire which turned out to be an electric-light bulb under a crumpled red skin. Over the counter they could see into the saloon where there were plenty of customers, but Hillingdon and his party had the lounge to themselves, and after he had ostentatiously wiped a table with his red handkerchief he called out for three double whiskies, a Johnny Walker, a Black and White and a Dewar's.

'Now, it's a very funny thing you should mention whisky,' he said when the drinks arrived, 'but I have many connections in the commercial world. I daresay if I were to look into the matter I should discover I had shares in a distillery. Nothing is more likely. I may be of some use to you, Mr Muawiya. Say when! You don't want to drown this stuff. When? Now I want you to smell the bouquet of each of them. To tell you the truth there's a better whisky than any of these, but you have to get it wholesale — not to be bought in a pub, my boy — and that's what I mean by being useful to you. I understand you once tried to murder Perry. Is that so?'

'Did Professor Perry tell you?'

'That's just the point! Can't get a word out of him, nor anybody else. Of course, I don't let on that I'm really interested.'

'Why are you interested?'

Hillingdon hesitated. 'Well, I *am* interested, you see.'

The Egyptian insisted on buying his round. This time it was his turn to drink the Black and White. After the third round they would each have sampled the three brands and so prepared themselves for a discussion of their commercial merits. Hillingdon said this whisky tasting was purely educational; one could be pretty sure these well-known brands would have their Middle East importers already.

'But about this murder,' he said. 'I don't want you to think my interest is merely vulgar. Met a chap back from Egypt who said it wasn't attempted murder. Perry tried to kill himself. Now if that's so it's a matter of commercial importance to me, apart from anything else. You may not know it but I own Helvetia. Perry rents it for a derisory sum because he knows I've an interest in fostering international goodwill. Besides, I *like* foreigners. I'm no bloody chauvinist. Reckon a landlord, though, has a right to know whether his tenant's a suicide type. You see what I'm getting at, Mr Muawiya?'

Hillingdon was physically the biggest Englishman Muawiya had ever talked to — certainly bigger than anyone he had met since landing at London Airport a couple of days ago — and in spite of a natural suspicion about what the fellow was up to he could not restrain some stirring of pride. One could respect such a man — and here he was, talking like an equal. You could not call him fat. The flesh was plentiful but hard — like a well-pumped-up tyre. From the Egyptian point of view the general effect of paleness was a little horrifying: the well-brushed lemony hair, the marmoreal cheeks and the blue, wishy-washy eyes. But make no mistake about it: a real jab from one of those fingers and *your* eye would be out.

'How nice it would be,' Muawiya said to Tim Blainey, 'if Mr Hillingdon could come with us as a guest to your mother's house. As it is, our conversation will be too short.'

Tim Blainey had just returned from the bar with his round of drinks and, after some discussion about whose turn it was to drink which, he drew a great deal of air into his lungs and said: 'I wish I knew what you two were talking about. What is all this about murder and suicide?'

'Exactly what I'd like to know myself,' said Hillingdon. 'Perry left Egypt under a cloud, don't you know. But perhaps we'd better be getting on, because we don't want to keep your mother waiting, do we? Have you ever been to Egypt, Mr Blainey? I haven't, but it's the dream of my life. In fact, I *was* an Egyptian in an earlier incarnation.'

So long as Hillingdon and Muawiya were talking Tim found it hard to think. He went to the lavatory, assuming that there at least he would be able to meditate on his mother's undoubted displeasure if he brought an uninvited guest, but as bad luck would have it a flabby, hard-breathing man arrived at the stand the same time as Tim did, saying he'd noticed the company in the lounge that evening and it was quite shocking the way coloured people were to be found everywhere these days; mark my words, a few years' time and there'll be a real problem on our hands.

'I think you're quite wrong,' said Tim shortly.

He found a telephone.

'Darling, I am so terribly sorry,' he said, after he had explained the predicament.

'Is he nice, this Mr Hillingdon?'

Tim hesitated. 'Frankly, no.'

'Then ditch him. He'll understand you can't gate-crash a dinner party like this.'

'But it's not so easy, darling. I think the Egyptian will think it a bit odd. They're such a hospitable people themselves.'

'Rubbish, Tim! Look at the wickedly ungrateful way they've behaved over the Suez Canal.'

'He's a journalist and if we cold-shoulder Hillingdon when he's just said he wanted the fellow to stay with us for dinner you've no idea the sort of implications he'll see and the sort of article he'll write.'

'Oh, damn all journalists and politicians. Look, Tim, if it's all as complicated as that then bring him along and we'll have to put up with it.'

Tim returned to the lounge to find Muawiya urging Hillingdon to let him drive the car, but Hillingdon was chuckling, raising his hands in mock horror, and saying: 'Oh no, my dear friend, not at this time of day. Have you got a driving-licence? No, well I'm sorry but it just can't be done.'

'Nobody could possibly know. I am an excellent driver, I can assure you. Do you know that I drive an Oldsmobile in Cairo? Cairo traffic is *much* more dangerous than London traffic.'

'Very tricky legal position, unlicensed driver involved in accident. No, Mr Muawiya, I'm sorry. You get a provisional licence and I'll *lend* you the car. Hoo — o — o — oh! look at that rain, just *coming* down! The road'll be like lard!'

They lifted their collars and darted across the wide pavement to the car. The buses swam through the murk, illuminated fish that paused now and again to pick up queues like so much ground bait. The interior of the little car reeked of damp clothes and whisky. The windscreen wiper cleared a fan of glass and Hillingdon set the overloaded Morris at the hill with a frown that seemed to indicate he was counting on buoyancy rather than horsepower to take them to the top.

'I love cars,' said Muawiya. 'Even old cars, like this one. I just love them, sir.'

'It isn't as old as all that,' said Hillingdon in a bit of a huff.

Now that the three whiskies had had time to slip into the blood-stream there was, however, the promise of a more genial atmosphere, and Tim said that in addition to themselves there would be two other guests at his mother's house — an Egyptian and his English wife. That meant there would be three and a half Egyptians present as against two English people.

'The Englishwoman is an Egyptian citizen by virtue of her marriage and I calculate that Mr Hillingdon is half an Egyptian by virtue of his previous incarnation.'

'You've got to remember,' said Hillingdon, 'that I was eighteenth dynasty. That ought to make me one and a half Egyptians, really, because we were, compared with the modern Egyptian, racially pure.'

'He's Captain Yehia, assistant military attaché at the Embassy,' said Tim in reply to Muawiya's question. 'D'you know him? He's the man who led the attack on Ras el-Tin Palace in 1952.'

'I do not know him. You say he has an English wife?'

'Elaine's an old friend of mine. The trouble is she won't go and live in Egypt and poor Mahmoud will probably shoot himself when he's recalled, as he's bound to be sooner or later.'

'Egyptians do not shoot themselves,' said Muawiya.

'Just a manner of speaking.' Tim looked into the back seat where Muawiya lay in an abandoned, oriental sprawl. 'Mahmoud's a level-headed fellow. But you'll see for yourself.'

At Whitestone Pond Muawiya asked once more if he could be allowed to drive. Tim said it was not worth it. His mother lived just off Heath Street — 'Next turning on the right!' he said to Hillingdon — but if Muawiya was as keen as all that to drive a car in London they could make application for a special licence straight away. Tomorrow morning, that was to say! If Muawiya held an Egyptian licence and had it with him!

'I am against bureaucracy of all kinds,' said Muawiya.

Mrs Blainey's house was one of three in a row, overlooking a courtyard, one-time labourers' cottages which had been gutted to make way for larger rooms with mock-Adam fireplaces, expensive sanitation and spiral, neo-Baroque, cherrywood staircases. It was the one in the middle, immediately opposite the door in the houseleek and valerian-encrusted wall, through which Tim led the way as soon as Hillingdon had tucked his Morris behind the grey Rover — Yehia's car. The wistaria held fat, serpentine coils to the pink-washed façade and the black leaves hung over the illuminated windows with a fine glitter of water drops.

For the first time Hillingdon showed doubts about the propriety of his joining the party.

'Mother just loves the unexpected guest.' Tim meant to speak reassuringly, but he detected the irony in his voice and lifted the knocker with the intention of arresting further conversation with a loud rat-tat. As always, the knocker stuck half way and had to be forced home, but noiselessly. As always, Tim shouted through the letter-box.

The widowed Mrs Blainey held the view that if only the rest of the world were like herself there would be no wars, not even any international bad feeling. She always got on very well with foreigners. She had spent March at a hotel in Malaga and the staff could not possibly have been more obliging. This was not the experience of everyone who travelled abroad; but she herself believed so much in seeing the other person's point of view, was such a good listener, complained so little and tipped so well that the Spaniards had simply loved her. It was the same in France and Italy. Just because she was English she did not think she was superior to any other middle-class, middle-aged woman of modest means who happened to live on the other side of the Channel. Only once had she told a story against a woman who was not English, and that was about the American she met in Venice who boasted about being such an expert traveller; she met this same woman again in Florence and learned with barely qualified pleasure that she had lost all her luggage. But, as she pointed out, it was not the fact of the woman's being American that bothered her: it was the boastfulness and, of course, you met it in English people too. No, she just loved foreigners. She drew the line at Germans because of what they did in the War, but the Spanish, the French, the Italians — oh, everybody, she liked them all and she did not care how badly they all seemed to speak English!

Captain Yehia was quite her favourite foreigner. He was *very* foreign, not even a Christian, not European; yet the ruddiness of his skin, the gold and grey in his tufted brown hair, the width of his face from cheekbone to cheekbone, would have allowed him to pass. He might even have been a Scotsman. Yehia came as near to sternness with her as he thought permissible whenever she spoke in this way. His unfortunate appearance was due to his Turkish-Circassian descent, but he considered himself an Egyptian of the Egyptians, a patriot, a devout Moslem, and as much a hater of imperialism as Arabi or Zaghlul or Gandhi. Coming from such a well-behaved and good-looking man this was perfectly acceptable to Mrs Blainey, who said it was just one of those issues on which they must agree to disagree and thought privately that Yehia would have to speak like that, holding the official position he did.

'Stop that, you two!' she said when she discovered Yehia and Muawiya talking to each other in Arabic, and she carried Muawiya off to a settee, feeling the fairness of her skin in contrast to his swarthiness. Here was a real foreigner and no mistake, with his crinkly black hair, his blue chin and perpetual smile.

'It is very kind of you to invite me into your home in this way, Mrs Blainey. I am nervous in case I make mistakes. I am quite certain to drink too much. Please be a good friend to me and say at once when I do anything wrong.'

'I'm quite sure you won't do anything wrong, as you call it, Mr M. Do you mind if I call you Mr M.? I've tried to say your name and it's out of the question. You didn't meet my son when he was in Egypt? He was there in 1952 for three months, so I'm sure you must have a great deal in common. Then there's his half-brother — not my son — who's in business in Alexandria. Eric. Now there's someone I'd like you to meet. He thinks there's no future for foreign businessmen in Egypt.'

'What is his business, may I ask?'

'Importing coffee and sugar mainly, I think.'

'Not whisky, not even gin,' said Tim from behind.

Muawiya glanced up. 'Oh no, I wasn't thinking of that at all, sir. But if you ask me how I think I can become a whisky importer when all the brands must have their agencies already, then I can only say there are too many Jewish business people in my country. When you think we are at war with Israel that is not correct. It is not international law.'

'Let's go in to dinner,' said Mrs Blainey. 'Tim, will you take Mrs Yehia?'

'Now, Alice,' she said to the housekeeper, drawing her to one side and waiting until the others were out of earshot, 'I want you to watch particularly the amount that young Egyptian has to drink. He reeks of whisky already — and there he was, drinking sherry. It's in his favour that he warned me. But you're to keep the wine on the side-table, pour it out yourself, don't let Milly touch it, and ration him very carefully.'

But it was Napier Hillingdon, not Muawiya, who to Mrs Blainey's astonishment provided the first embarrassment of the evening. Muawiya sat at Mrs Blainey's right hand, looking about with perfect self-possession and taking particular stock of Mrs Yehia who was opposite at the other end of the table, a pretty woman in her mid-thirties with blue eyes and a sharp nose. Hillingdon, however, this two-hundred-and-fifty-pound mass, poised on a specially strong chair which had been brought in from the kitchen, had developed a curious pinkness under the eyes and was drinking his soup with an intent sobriety which made Mrs Blainey think he didn't like it.

'Delicious!' he murmured, lifting his eyes and daring to look into hers.

Good heavens! she thought. He's shy!

Determined to put him at ease, she said: 'I know very little about you, Mr Hillingdon.'

'Believe me, Mrs Blainey — ' poor fellow, he was colouring like a sunrise ' — I'm only just beginning to realize I more or less forced my way into this party. Put it down to eagerness. You see, I've a great interest in everything to do with ancient Egypt— '

'You're a historian?'

'I'm nothing, Mrs Blainey.' Hillingdon put his spoon down and spoke explosively. 'I've wasted my life and now I'm a fat old rentier.'

'So am I, but it doesn't really worry me. This guilt-complex is out, so far as I'm concerned. Now, Alice,' she said to the housekeeper, 'shall I carve, or will you?' — which was her way of telling Alice to hurry up. 'And see that everyone gets a fair share of the trimmings.'

'I hope you like duck,' she said to Hillingdon, who was wiping his face with a handkerchief.

'I'm a gate-crasher, that's what I am.'

'You're becoming a bore into the bargain, too, Mr. Hillingdon. Let's change the subject. You tell me about your rentes and I'll tell you about mine. That reminds me, my oil shares. Mahmoud, your Colonel Nasser has already taken a couple of thousand off me.'

'You'll get it back, I'm sure, Mrs Blainey.'

'Thank God I've no Suez Canal shares.'

As the conversation turned to politics she found she could think of little but the oppressive bulk of this man at her left hand. Why was he so unhappy? On the telephone Tim had said he was not a nice man. She did not agree about this. Once he behaved normally he might display jovial and interesting facets to his character, he might even seem physically smaller — because he seemed to be inflated by some anxiety. If only she could lay her tongue to the right needling word he might subside with gasps of relief. For she was pretty sure that his embarrassment had something to do with her personally. She even examined herself surreptitiously to see whether anywhere she gaped immodestly.

'You've chosen an unhappy time to come to England, Mr M.,' she said, trying to catch Alice's eye as the woman filled his glass, 'and what the end of it all will be I just can't imagine.'

'Forgive me!' Muawiya leaned forward, smiling. His glass was uplifted in his right hand. 'It is not an unhappy time. It is a happy time. Let us drink to good friendship between England and Egypt.'

'Hear, hear!' said Tim.

'Anglo-Egyptian friendship!'

'All right.' Mrs. Blainey sipped her wine. 'I don't know what you mean by a happy time but I'll drink to Anglo-Egyptian friendship. Did you have a pleasant meeting with your old teacher?'

'Professor Perry? He was not glad to see me. No, no!' Muawiya raised his voice above the protests from Tim. 'He was very cold to me. Mrs Perry pretended not to remember me.'

'Oh come, I just can't believe — '

'He was polite, of course, but he was not glad to see me.'

Yehia studied his wineglass as though it were a crystal ball. 'You know you must not expect English people to be demonstrative. I am sure Mr Perry was very pleased to see you.'

'Forgive me, I understand English people. Mr Perry was not

pleased to see me. Mr Hillingdon will tell you that it was not a warm welcome. He was there. Well, I do not mind. I am not sensitive about these matters. But I was asked a question and I must reply honestly. I am a foreigner in this country and I expected more kindness from Professor Perry. Does he forget that I save his life? Not once but many times!'

'You saved his life?'

'Many many times.'

'Now, Mr M., you asked me to tell you if ever you did anything wrong. So I tell you now. It is better not to talk of such things.'

'But it is the truth!' Muawiya laid his hands flat on the table. 'Do you not speak the truth in England?'

By the time the lemon soufflé arrived they had discussed the effect of climate on national character, they had discussed (on a point raised by Hillingdon) the extent to which the Egyptian climate had changed since Pharaonic times, they had speculated why Egyptians were such good swimmers and squash players, there had been mention of the British Secret Service ('Their men are everywhere,' said Muawiya. 'Nobody knows who they are. I myself might be an agent! How would you know?') and Tim told a story against himself, a complicated story about his being mistaken for a policeman in plain clothes.

'The police,' said Muawiya. 'Can they really be incorruptible?'

Mrs Blainey saw, with satisfaction, that Elaine was taking more of a part in the conversation. Poor girl! She did look off-colour tonight. Only to be expected under the circumstances, no doubt — she an Egyptian national and quite possibly an enemy alien in a few weeks' time when we had to protect our interests in the Middle East. As a good liberal, though, Mrs Blainey did not in her heart think that the worst would happen. There were times when this kind of optimism was the very essence of her liberalism; it was quite impossible for the *really* disagreeable to come about. Nasser was bound to give way.

'Let's take coffee in the other room,' she said. 'Elaine, dear, it's so lovely to see you. Such a long time. But then, I'm an old woman. You won't want to — '

'When Mahmoud's recalled I suppose I'll have more time for visiting.'

The words struck everyone silent. Mrs Blainey was at the door, about to take Elaine's arm; but the sudden vehemence with which Elaine spoke made her pause. Her hand was arrested in mid-air. Muawiya looked from Elaine to her husband and back again. A vertical wrinkle appeared between Yehia's eyebrows. He caught up his wife's left hand, folding it and mumbling some near-incoherence about being sensible.

'I'm sorry, Mrs Blainey.' Elaine smiled, colouring like a child. 'I didn't meant to say that. I was rude.'

'Damn international relations, I say.' The rest of the party followed Mrs Blainey into her sitting-room. 'Damn them, damn them, damn them! But I'm quite sure everything will be clearer when Sir Anthony has made his statement. Now there's a man everyone respects.'

'I am quite sure,' said Muawiya, taking a place on the settee next to Elaine, 'that everything will be settled peacefully and happily. But it is not very nice of you not to wish to come to Egypt. We should be so honoured to have you.'

'Oh, please don't be nice to me, because I couldn't stand it.' Elaine jumped up. She refused coffee. 'I want to become a — a — oh, I don't know! A citizen of some country that has no dealings with any other country — an island where they live on vegetables and the fish they catch from the sea.'

'Sounds an excellent spot for an H-bomb test, if you ask me,' said Tim.

'Darling,' she said to Mrs Blainey, 'would you ever forgive me if we went home? I'm just ready to fall to pieces.'

This was not the question to be answered or even discussed in public, and Mrs Blainey, putting an arm round Elaine, whisked her out of the room. Alice went on pouring coffee as though nothing had happened and the men sat in silence until the vibrations of tearfulness, despair and isolationism had begun to subside.

'Has anything happened?' asked Tim. 'I mean, anything special this evening?'

'Eden has announced a military build-up in Cyprus. It was in the evening paper.' Yehia was standing to drink his coffee, feet planted wide apart. He stared across the room.

Now it was Muawiya's turn to be demonstrative. 'It'll all be England's fault. The fact that I am here in England — well, would Colonel Nasser have allowed me to come if he expected trouble? What does it mean, a build-up in Cyprus? I have never been in England before. Am I to go home? No! I shall stay the full month.'

'There's this whisky business to fix,' Hillingdon reminded him.

'There's that too.'

Mrs Blainey re-entered the room. 'You'd better take her home, Mahmoud. I'm sorry, but she's a bit under the weather, poor dear. There now! Give me a kiss on the cheek. She's waiting for you in the hall, and I told her I'd say good night to the rest of you on her behalf.'

'I would explain everything to her if only I had the chance,' said Muawiya.

So keen was Mrs Blainey for Elaine to leave without any more political talk that she even found herself pressing a liqueur on Muawiya. If it weren't for this Mr Napier Hillingdon she would have been in more of a tizzy than she actually was. How wrong Tim had been to speak of the man so disparagingly. He was gratifyingly attentive. As much as his bulk permitted he opened and closed doors for her, he fetched empty cups, he agreed with what she said. He alone was unmoved by all this political talk; the maturer mind, of course. Fifty? Fifty-five? Even sixty, perhaps! Yet coupled with an almost boyish sensitivity — witness the way those pink spots appeared in his cheeks.

'I'm terribly sorry.' Yehia appeared at the door. 'I can't get my car out until you move yours, sir.'

Hillingdon fought to rise.

'I'll move it.' Muawiya's arm went out like a lazytongs. 'Just give me the key.'

Hillingdon hesitated and, as though from ancient custom, looked at Mrs Blainey for guidance. He might have been in the habit of seeking her advice for years.

'He's younger than you to be dodging about,' was all Mrs Blainey said.

'Don't suppose it matters so much, just moving it without a licence, and I wouldn't mind betting it's a private road out there, anyway.' Hillingdon handed over the keys and returned to his brandy.

And once the keys had been passed, once Muawiya had taken them, grinned, tossed them in the air, caught them, they all knew the unexpected was about to happen. Even Elaine, waiting for Yehia in the Rover, must have detected the change; some vibration must surely have reached her. Hillingdon stared at Muawiya doubtfully. Mrs Blainey looked at her son. Tim wondered what would happen if he tried to take the keys from Muawiya, who was as sensitive to the new atmosphere as anyone and looked amused, challenging and outraged, all at the same time, rather like a politician denying a rumour. When no one spoke it was a minor triumph. He prolonged it by tossing the keys once more into the air.

'Don't worry, there probably won't even be the need to start the engine,' he said and hurried out of the room. Some moments later he could be heard in the yard, calling to Yehia in Arabic. Mrs Blainey, Hillingdon and Tim sat and waited. They were absurdly conscious of the speculation that was going on in each other's mind, but too uncertain of themselves to mention it. Muawiya had taken whisky, wine, brandy. Was he as sober as he looked?

'On second thoughts —' Hillingdon rocked backwards and forwards. When he had gained sufficient momentum he threw himself on to his feet and started for the door. Tim was at his heels.

'My god!' said Hillingdon once they were in the yard. 'My gears!' Neither he nor Tim doubted that the agonizing crashing came from the little Morris. The sounds were at once mechanical and zoological, the cries (as they might be) of a digital computer in labour. The rain had ceased, but in the headlights walls and pavements shone like sealskin. As Hillingdon emerged into the street the Morris, with presumably Muawiya at the wheel, turned its behind on him and shot down the lane.

'The silly fellow!' Yehia was standing with one foot on the running-board of his Rover.

'He's not *allowed* to drive it!' said Hillingdon. 'I mean, I don't mind being hospitable. But this! You'll be my witness that he took it without my permission.'

'You gave him the keys.'

The Morris had already turned into Heath Street.

'You'd better jump in, both of you,' said Yehia. 'We'll see if we can catch him.'

'What is it?' Mrs Blainey with a white wrap over her shoulders had come to investigate.

There was time only for Tim to say, instinctively, protecting her, as always, 'Nothing at all, darling! We'll be back in a few minutes' — before he and Hillingdon were thrown back in their seat by the violence of the acceleration. Elaine gave a short scream, and they also were in Heath Street bowling down to the traffic lights which Yehia crossed on the amber. He had spotted the Morris two hundred yards or so on its way to Fitzjohns Avenue.

As they plunged down the hill, caverns of clear sky holding a fragmentary moon in a remote recess with one or two thin stars, yawned before them. The clouds were massive, barred in black and pink like angel-fish. An avenue engulfed the cars and it was night again, the headlights playing down the green throat.

'The market value of that Morris of mine,' said Hillingdon, 'is a hundred and twenty-five pounds. It's insured for three hundred. The question is whether I get the three hundred or the market value.'

Tim was horrified. 'You think there's going to be an accident?'

'Anyway, I've no doubt at all he tried to kill Perry. He's as good as pinched my car. Capable of anything. Not drunk. It's just passion. You could see him just lusting to drive the car.'

Yehia's Rover was a good twenty miles an hour faster than the Morris, but it was difficult to know what to do with this extra speed when there was so much traffic about. If Yehia had drawn level he would have been in the oncoming stream and what purpose would it have served anyway? Hillingdon said he was not prepared to jump from one moving vehicle to another when they were both travelling at about fifty-five miles an hour. If they went on tailing Muawiya he was bound to pull up pretty soon. Young men would be young men and he did not think there was any real malice in the fellow. An appetite for life, yes. Impulsiveness, yes. Even ruthlessness; but no vice.

'I shall see to it,' said Yehia, 'that he's sent back to Egypt at once.'

Even Elaine protested against this, and they were so absorbed in their argument that they were into the Finchley Road with a police car between them and the Morris without a clear idea how it had happened. The black saloon must have come out of a side-street like a bullet. There was no doubt about its character.

The word POLICE glowed out of a little box on its roof and a siren wailed histrionically. It was only the oncoming flow of traffic that prevented Muawiya from being overtaken and forced into the gutter.

'If you *had* jumped aboard your car,' said Tim to Hillingdon, 'you'd have crushed it like a beetle.'

'Why doesn't the fool stop?'

'He's completely lost his head, if you ask me,' Hillingdon remarked diagnostically.

Traffic lights severed them from both Muawiya and the police car. By the time they were in pursuit once more the road had cleared right down to Clarence Gate. It was incredible that Muawiya had been able to travel so far. He could not possibly know where he was, and it was unlikely he even knew in which direction he was heading. The black glitter of the road, the buildings that reared in the darkness with a network of bright windows, the growing sense of immensity, diversity, complexity of streets and buildings which developed as they neared the Marylebone Road — all this must have been utterly bewildering for him. If he had panicked, the best to hope for was a harmless encounter with a brick wall before he killed himself.

*

Perry's establishment, the Helvetia School of English for Foreigners, had been running for two years before Waldo Grimbley arrived and was taken on as senior assistant. He made only one condition: that no Egyptian would ever be enrolled as a student. Grimbley had suffered at the hands of the Egyptians, certainly; he had lost his two thousand five hundred a year professorship overnight when the Wafd Government decided to sack all British officials without compensation; he even had to pay his passage home when the revolution came and the Embassy terminated his temporary employment in the Alexandrian Consulate. But other British officials had suffered as much — some, with families, a good deal more — and for the fundamental explanation of Grimbley's powerful hostility to Egypt and the Egyptians Perry thought one had to plunge pretty deep. There was no exaggerating this hostility. After being rebuked for mentioning the Pyramids Napier Hillingdon had even been forced to avoid all reference to his own occult interests. Grimbley hated the Egyptians, Perry thought, because he really loved them; indeed, wanted to *be* an Egyptian. In Cairo, as was well known, he had lived the part of an early nineteenth-century Egyptian bey, wearing the costume, eating the food, thinking the thoughts (all based on solid research in the University library) without going so far as to become a Moslem; and there were no women in Grimbley's life either — that was another difference.

Nothing angered Grimbley more than a reference to the way he once used to dress as an Egyptian. 'You know perfectly well that what I had in mind was the life of a Turkish-born official under Mohamed Ali. He was the last non-European really effective ruler of Egypt. Oh, I know he was an Albanian, but Albania isn't really Europe and in any case he was of Turkish descent. The oriental rulers of Egypt saw to a proper stratification of society and a man could be a gentleman without having to knock people down every ten minutes or so to prove it. The trouble with you, Perry, is that you never saw modern Egypt for what it is. You cleared out in 1950 before they took the lid off the cesspit. If you'd had my experiences you'd talk differently.'

Grimbley had been professor and Perry a mere lecturer in those Cairo days, so Perry did not care to argue too strongly for fear Grimbley should say he was exploiting the new situation to compensate for the sting of the old professorial whip. Grimbley had never taken this line, but there was in his bearing too much of the sergeant-major relaxing in the other ranks' canteen to persuade Perry the possibility was not frequently in his mind. And why not? Even Grimbley was human. He had suffered a real comedown in the world, and Perry tried to spare his feelings as much as possible by avoiding situations in which he might seem to be acting or speaking as the boss.

As over Egyptians, for example.

'*That* assassin!' said Grimbley when Perry had come to the conclusion he had better break the news about Muawiya's visit before Hillingdon returned and did it for him.

'I could scarcely refuse to see him.'

Still wearing his tweed hat and carrying the usual rucksack of books, Grimbley had been tramping up the stairs when Perry called after him. He turned and said, very seriously: 'You don't surprise me a bit. I don't claim to be psychic but the moment I came through the front door there was something in the air, you know. Not actually a smell.'

'He sent special greetings to you. We're all going to be invited to a party.'

'What sort of people does he think we are?'

'I think Mary and I will go.'

Grimbley slipped out of his rucksack and wedged it against

the banisters, preparatory to descending the stairs once more and following Perry into the office.

'Even I,' he said, 'didn't think you'd be so naively liberal as to accept an invitation from a fellow who tried to murder you. What's the matter with us all? Are all our guts rotted? I know you think I'm a frightful reactionary, but dammit there comes a time when liberalism looks like respect for everybody but yourself and people like you.'

'As you know, Muawiya didn't try to murder me.'

'He funked it at the last minute.'

'I wouldn't put it like that.'

'Shall I tell you how I'd put it? We're so corrupted by left-wing propaganda the possession of a coloured skin gives its owner a kind of divine right to blackmail and murder the rest of us. You know damn well that if this chap had been white you'd have kicked him off the premises. Well, anyway,' said Grimbley, remembering who he was talking to, 'you'd have shouted at him through the letter-box.'

'If Muawiya had a white skin, he and I would never have been in the particular relationship we were in Egypt.'

'Too bloody true you wouldn't. That's just what I'm trying to tell you.'

Perry was beginning to wish he had said nothing about Muawiya and had bribed Hillingdon to keep his mouth shut. Grimbley went on expressing annoyance with Egyptians, holding his head sideways rather as though his words were gaseous bubbles which would disappear up his large hairy nostrils if his nose were vertically placed above their point of origin. Perry saw the upward flow of bubbles burst on the ceiling and automatically pursed his lips to keep out the water. Imagination frequently had the better of him. He leaned forward, feeling the water take the weight off his heels, until he was balancing on the balls of his feet, his face no more than a foot from Grimbley's. It had not been shaved for at least two days and Perry wished the neglectfulness did not bother him so much. Surely he had not become so conventional! The Egyptians never made a fetish of daily shaving either! Grimbley's laxity was probably one more unconscious revelation that he really wanted to be Egyptian.

'Particularly at a time like the present,' said Grimbley.

'What?'

'I said, particularly at a time like the present. What did you think I said?'

Perry hurriedly went back over his thinking; daily shaving, underwater swimming, Grimbley's care not to breathe words up his nose, whether or not Muawiya had tried to murder him.

'Receiving Egyptians, accepting invitations from them — at a time like this,' said Grimbley, getting more and more angry. 'I'm not at all sure it isn't the worst kind of appeasement.'

'I don't look at the situation like that. I think Nasser's right and we're wrong.'

'You what?'

'I don't think we've got a leg to stand on. If Nasser decides to nationalize an Egyptian company I think he's perfectly entitled to.'

He'd done it now! Grimbley froze. Had he been standing on one leg he would have held the pose like a statue. Perry even thought that had Grimbley been caught, like Great Britain herself, with no leg at all to stand on (had he been jumping from his bicycle, for example) he would have hovered in space, sustained by the outraged incredulity brought on by the spectacle of a turning worm. How well Perry understood Grimbley's anger. One's fury is easily aroused by a show of independence and spirit from a quarter where resistance had not previously been encountered. Perry found himself sympathizing with

Grimbley. If he had been a militant communist Grimbley would have enjoyed crushing him. But he was just a sentimental liberal for whom Grimbley had little personal regard, and life really ought to have spared Grimbley the obligation of dealing with him.

'You know, Perry, if it's come to this the sooner you and I part company the better.'

'Oh, come off your high horse, for God's sake! Let's not talk about it, shall we? Agree to disagree. But I really can't see why I shouldn't see Muawiya if I want to.'

'Is it possible that I don't make myself clear? I said that if you're for appeasing Nasser I'm resigning.'

Just one more provocation and he would pick up his tweed hat and rucksack, swear, slam doors and be out of the house in a matter of minutes. Perry saw it clearly. The following day a taxi-driver would arrive with a note: 'See that this man has all my belongings. I have instructed him not to reveal the address to which he is delivering them. W. G.'

'Well?' Grimbley demanded. 'Are you going to appease Nasser or aren't you? Are you going to live the 'thirties all over again?'

'Not exactly.' Perry moved in the direction of the sideboard. 'But I'm going to have a whisky and soda and I suggest you join me.'

'Perry!' Grimbley caught him by the arm and swung him round. 'I'm serious.' Had it not been so impossible Perry would have said there were tears in his eyes; moisture, anyway, a damp gleam of anguish. Their faces were no more than a foot apart. Because of Grimbley's habitually loud manner of speaking Perry rarely approached within six feet of him, and to have the scored visage, the untrimmed moustache going grey at the roots and cinnamon at the tips, the nose like an upturned boat, and these swimming, blood-touched eyes, thrust so close as to be almost horrifically unhuman, was enough to make him reconsider the legality of Nasser's seizure of the Suez Canal. This enormous mask into which he gazed was that of an elderly man. Grimbley's hair was quite grey. His neck was beginning to look scraggy.

'I'm not going to let you resign. To hell with Nasser and the Egyptians.'

'Ha!' Grimbley's eyebrows shot towards the ceiling. His tone was condescendingly explanatory. It was almost a coo. 'Shall I tell you why you've changed your mind about Nasser so easily? You've no principles. You've nothing but a sense of guilt.'

'I don't see —'

'Suddenly you began to feel guilty about me. Now, didn't you? You began to think: what will the old fellow do if he leaves here? Didn't you? Answer me that! You think I'm utterly dependent on you and therefore you've got to agree with me.'

Perry had managed to reach the sideboard. He handed Grimbley his whisky and poised the soda siphon. 'You do put things in extreme terms, don't you?'

'It's true, isn't it?'

Perry could only probe the recesses of his guilt. He was making a commercial success out of teaching English to foreigners when, as he well knew, his own grasp of English grammar was shaky. At the very end of the summer term (to go back no farther) a Nepalese student had caught him saying 'Due to higher costs fees simply must go up.' A mild impostor, that was how Perry regarded himself in his sadder moments. This was one of them. Grimbley's charge that he was dominated by guilt made him think of English grammar, of his wife Mary whom he found it harder and harder to love in spite of the ever-repeated brave attempt; it made him think fleetingly of their son, Christopher, whom he had summoned into existence in the middle of the twentieth century; he even thought of minor unpaid debts and income-tax evasions. But Grimbley himself did not come naturally into the sequence.

'No,' he said, finally contriving to squirt soda into Grimbley's glass, 'I don't regard myself as having any special responsibility for you, if that's what you mean. Or do you?'

Grimbley drank his whisky and wiped his moustache with the enormous red handkerchief which, he had once said, was of the type used by nineteenth-century tramps to wrap up their victuals. He stood at the window, watching the rain slap the laurels in the lemony gloom. 'You think of me as a reactionary old fool, don't you — now, don't speak! — staggering on the edge of real trouble? Well, perhaps you're right! D'you think I'd stick here unless I had to? But whatever my own shortcomings let me tell you something about yourself. I understand you through and through. As I said before, what you lack are principles. It's only your sense of guilt that keeps you going. You're so busy understanding the other chap's point of view you haven't the time to develop a point of view of your own.' Grimbley was still watching the rain. 'But you've got it coming to you, you and people like you. And then, instead of guilt you'll be one big fatty mass of self-pity and the sun'll come out and reduce you to a tepid puddle.'

At this moment the telephone in the hall began ringing. As an economy Perry had asked the Post Office to install a telephone with a coin-box, and that is where they had placed it, in the hall. One of the pleasures of being out-of-term was the absence of a little queue of students waiting to call their girl friends.

'No, you must be wrong about that,' said Perry in reply to Grimbley's attack. 'You forget I'm an Anglican.'

When he returned from answering the telephone he found that Grimbley had helped himself to some more whisky.

'That was Hillingdon,' said Perry. 'He says that Muawiya has pinched his car, been chased by the police, smashed it up and taken refuge in the Egyptian Embassy where he's claiming diplomatic immunity.'

Grimbley stared, whisky dripping from his moustache. Perry was saddened by the northern bleakness of Grimbley's walrus-like appearance.

'It's just like that Russian woman athlete who went shoplifting,' Grimbley said. 'This is worse than any Suez Canal crisis in my view.'

CHAPTER TWO

THERE was never any real mystery about Muawiya's whereabouts. He was somewhere in the Egyptian Embassy buildings in South Audley Street. The taxi-driver said so. Knew at once, he said, something fishy was going on the moment this chap, a real *foreign*-looking foreigner, stopped him in Park Lane and asked to be taken to the Egyptian Embassy when, as everyone knew, this chap more than most (a real wog like he'd seen when he was in the Army), it was only just round the corner. And to be paid a quid, with no questions asked! He'd rung the bell and stood there on the Embassy steps with his forehead (it seemed) pressed against the door, so that he almost fell in when it opened. And they didn't let him in without an argument either, the cabby said. First of all there was a little man dressed like a waiter who tried to push him back down the steps, but he was not strong enough. Another man, very ordinary — might have been one of us — appeared. All the time they were talking Arabic, which put the cabby, so he claimed, at a bit of a disadvantage, no matter how far out of his driving-seat he leaned the better to hear. These Gyppos tumbled to it then that he had them under observation and they all went into the Embassy, closing the door. The cabby made for Park Lane and had not driven very far towards Marble Arch before he was held up.

The conductor of the bus in front said a private car was half way up a tree. As the rain had eased the cabby climbed down from his driving-seat. He said his instincts were aroused. Probably because of the sort of night there was not much of a crowd, and when he arrived at the site of the accident he found it was just as the conductor had said — an old Morris bust clean through the netting, just as though it was jet-propelled. You wouldn't believe it! Must have been some wicked driving. The bonnet of the Morris was squashed straight into this tree trunk. Policemen in wet capes were waving their arms. A police car was drawn up on the other side of the road. As soon as the cabby heard that no one had been hurt and that the driver had made off he went forward and said: 'That's my fare. I picked a bloke up at Stanhope Gate and he gave me a quid to take him round the corner.' When they said he was an Egyptian that, of course, clinched it.

Within a quarter of an hour of the crash, then, there was strong circumstantial evidence that Muawiya had taken refuge in the Egyptian Embassy. This was never proved. From first to last the Embassy spokesman lost very few tricks. The mistake was never made of denying that Muawiya Khaslat had been joy-riding with a criminal disregard of other people's safety; there was no attempt, either, to claim that he was being framed by the police, the British Secret Service, or any other patriotic body. Here again the Muawiya case differed from that of the Russian athlete, Nina Ponomareva, who lay possum in the Soviet Embassy after being accused of stealing half a dozen hats from an Oxford Street store. The Egyptian Press made no protestations of innocence. They claimed simply that in the present state of Anglo-Egyptian relations there was probably no limit to the savagery of British justice and that Muawiya, *wherever he was,* would be well advised to lie low.

'Is this the sort of man,' demanded an editorial in the *Evening*

Standard, 'the British taxpayer should be expected to spend his money on? The Muawiya Khaslat case is even worse than Nina's. At least we didn't have to pay the Russian lady's fare and maintain her in opulence during her stay in England. But that is precisely what the British Council has done for the Egyptian terror-driver!' The *Manchester Guardian* called on the Egyptian Embassy to disgorge Muawiya and show a little common sense. 'This London frolic by an Egyptian journalist should not be treated more seriously than it deserves. After all, he did not kill anyone.' *The Times* reported the incident under the words, 'Egyptian driver disappears: a possible question of extra-territoriality,' but made no immediate editorial comment. The *Daily Telegraph* remarked there were irresponsible elements in the country capable of arguing for a waiving of the charges against the Egyptian; fortunately British justice could not be manipulated in this way. 'Critic' in the *New Statesman* wrote a sharp paragraph about the difficulties experienced by visiting foreigners in obtaining British driving-licences.

'To make matters worse,' said Napier Hillingdon, 'the man is known to have been a terrorist.' At first Hillingdon was sustained by anger. He had been forced to witness his wrecked Morris lifted by a crane and dumped into a truck; the car was so smashed up it was not possible even to tow it away. The garage hands threw a number of fragments after the main body of wreckage and said that so far from repair being possible there would be a bill for disposing of all this junk; and Hillingdon, who had had the car for fourteen years and was genuinely fond of it, felt bereaved. To think that he had actually befriended this Egyptian! His behaviour had been worse than ingratitude! It was a kind of mad treachery!

By distending his imagination, like a man widening his eye to look for a piece of grit, Hillingdon could dimly perceive that there were men who lusted after motor-cars as others lusted after drink or sex. But it was all very queer! Surely, to return malice for friendship indicated real insanity? And wasn't there something uncanny about the accident itself? How could a creature of flesh and blood have survived it? The wheel was embedded in the back of the driving-seat. Unless Muawiya had flung himself out of the vehicle before the impact (very unlikely, Hillingdon thought) any explanation of his survival would have to border on the supernatural. Hillingdon's anger faded as his superstitiousness took hold. Was not Muawiya an Egyptian? Might not he have Powers? Hillingdon would willingly have taken back his remark about Muawiya being a terrorist, but unfortunately he made it to a bystander who thought it worth his while to telephone the *Daily Mirror*. A reporter arrived at Helvetia before nine o'clock the following morning. He succeeded in putting a few questions to Grimbley with the result that, much to Perry's annoyance, a story appeared in which he figured as a one-time professor in Egypt who was so beloved by his students that they protected him from patriotic terrorists. Grimbley was annoyed, too. This was not quite the story *he* had given to the reporter.

The telephone rang continuously, every shrub in the garden concealed a man in a raincoat, a film unit took a few shots of Mary walking with Christopher, and the police came repeatedly, both in uniform and out of it. Perry had to keep reminding himself that the cause of all this commotion was a young man who had smashed up a car that did not belong to him; all the questioning, speculation, denunciation, derived from a misdemeanour which at the worst probably merited three months' hard labour but which, because of the unhappy state of Anglo-Egyptian relations and because of the insult to British Common Law proffered by a country whose own legal system was grounded on the Code Napoléon, had created as great a sensation as scientific espionage. Airports were watched, docks patrolled, Pakistani and Malayan students removed from suburban trains for interrogation at the nearest police station. Perry thought that everyone he talked to seemed drunk and stupid, particularly Mary, who by this time had seen the film of Christopher and herself on television and talked of the splendid advertisement it all was for the Helvetia School of English.

'Matters have taken an ugly turn,' said Hillingdon, bursting in on Perry very dramatically one evening. 'I've been grilled.'

Perry had been preparing the fifty or so accounts of the students who had enrolled for the term due to begin in two weeks' time and wondering whether the Suez crisis would have any withering effect on numbers. It was some moments before he could adjust himself to Hillingdon's distress.

'They've only just gone. I've had a couple of policemen up in my room grilling me. They're trying to pin the whole thing on to me. *Of course* I gave the fellow the keys of the car. But that didn't authorize him to drive the car off and smash it up.'

'You gave Muawiya the keys?'

'He practically filched them from me. I tell you there's something evil and uncanny about him. No normal person would have persuaded me. But it was on the distinct understanding he was only going to move the car so that the others could get out. Well, that's reasonable, isn't it?'

'I hope your insurance company will think so.'

Hillingdon's mouth opened but no words were uttered.

'I mean,' said Perry who was desperately trying to cheer Hillingdon up, only to find the temptation to bait the great body almost irresistible. A body? Yes, it was hard to think of Hillingdon as a spirit. He was too heavy, too solid. 'I mean that if the insurance company discover you authorized Muawiya to drive your car and you knew all the time he hadn't got a licence they probably won't accept your claim.'

'What the hell!' Hillingdon trumpeted. 'They don't think I'll put up with that, do they?' and he rushed out into the hall to telephone the insurance company, only to find that as it was after office hours there was no reply. 'Well, I wouldn't have wanted to raise an issue with them they haven't raised themselves, would I?' Hillingdon replaced the receiver and prepared to demonstrate his acumen.

'Not yet, they haven't,' said Perry. 'But they will. It should make quite an interesting case. Everything will turn on whether your car was on a public highway or private ground.'

'How do you know so much about this?' said Hillingdon suspiciously.

'Well, I don't know very much really.' Perry said that he always made a point of reading the Law Reports in *The Times* and he seemed to remember a case very like Hillingdon's in which the owner of the car came in for a real lashing from the judge. Perry could not remember whether he was actually sent to prison.

'Prison?' Fortunately the telephone began ringing and Hillingdon, who was nearest, picked up the receiver to hear a woman's voice asking for him. Momentarily he was tempted to put the thing down again, saying nothing. He knew no women. This could only be some further development in the Muawiya business, almost certainly unpleasant, and he would have much preferred to go up to his room and think over Perry's remarks. But he took a grip of himself. His mouth became a firm line. The floorboard creaked as he shifted weight from one foot to the other.

'I'll take a message for him,' he said, his voice as dead as a slapped bolster. 'Who did you say? Mrs — oh!' He became three inches taller and his tone changed to a synthetic jollity. 'Well, of course, it's me speaking all the time. I just have to be careful when answering the telephone these days. What? Right away! Well, I don't know about that. I've just had the police here — ' He broke off and listened to the telephone as intently as though it were a stethoscope sounding his own heart. 'I'm entirely at your service, Mrs Blainey,' he said at last. 'I'll find a cab and come over as soon as I've changed.'

Hillingdon's behaviour had been so odd that Perry remained in the offing in case some kind of assistance were required; but Hillingdon was in no obvious need of support. He seemed bigger than ever, quite swelling under the restraint of his suit, excited, each feathery eyebrow with a twist in it over the wide, pale eyes. 'She wants to see me at once on a matter of confidence.' And before Perry could ask who *she* was he had gone to change into the clean shirt with the guaranteed non-creasable collar, the old Etonian tie (to which he had no right) and the lavender grey flannel suit which, by a happy chance, had been returned by the cleaners that very morning. He flicked the toes of his brown shoes with a silk handkerchief and then stood before the mirror for some moments trying to pull his eyebrows more to the side of his face; a vain gesture, he was perfectly well aware, but one he could never restrain whenever he saw his reflection. Bunched up on either side of his nose, they made his eyes seem too close; of that he was convinced.

Mrs Blainey asking to see him! And at once! What the devil did it mean? Perhaps she liked him, he thought. No, that was quite impossible. He dabbed his forehead with eau-de-Cologne and wondered if she wanted to borrow money. That was frequently the way with these women who lived on their own. Not Mrs Blainey, though. He told himself that whatever happened he must not behave like a fool. He would never take a step before she showed him the way. By God! he thought, as he ground the stair carpet beneath his feet, I'm actually excited.

It was not until he had found a cab that he realized he did not know Mrs Blainey's address. He told the driver to take him to Hampstead, to Heath Street, hoping that by the time they arrived he would remember whether the turning was to the right or the left. But he could not be sure. The rain, which had been a few drops on the windscreen when they started, was now bursting in gusts along the pavements, driving people into the doorways of shops. Hillingdon had not even an umbrella with him. There was a lot of traffic about. The cab-driver could scarcely explore all the byways of this part of Hampstead on the chance that Hillingdon would recognize some landmark. On the other hand the rain was so heavy that Hillingdon could not possibly explore on foot. The time was about seven, no later he supposed, but the evening had come prematurely and the reflected shop lighting spun in the gutter torrent. Hillingdon asked the driver to hang on a minute while he asked for information in one of the shops. Stepping out of the cab was rather like stepping under a shower-bath, and before Hillingdon had time to work his great bulk into shelter the back of his suit and shoulders went slate-coloured. Not until he was inside the shop did he realize it was a florist's.

Flowers! Hillingdon looked at the baskets of carnations, the roses, the clumps of poppies, the banks of erica — reefs and shoals of light, vibrating in a composite sweetness that momentarily dazed him. There were flowers he could have sworn he had never seen before. Certainly he did not know their names. Those in the window — they were orchids, of course. But these! And these! When the assistant asked if she could help him he knew perfectly well that he meant to say: 'Do you mind if I consult your telephone directory? I've stupidly forgotten the address of a friend. You don't know her by any chance? Mrs Blainey?'

Instead, he said, 'I'll take a dozen of those roses, please. No, those deep red ones,' and stood like a mouse, a monstrous mouse certainly, but a mouse in the calculated inoffensiveness which he suddenly assumed. What could be more innocent than flowers for a friend? It was years since had had bought flowers for a woman. Perhaps Mrs Blainey would think him presumptuous. Well, what if he was making a fool of himself? He could always say that once in the shop to make his inquiry he had to buy a few flowers. If she laughed at him, that is what he would tell her. He practically *had* to buy them!

'Mrs Blainey?' said the assistant. Yes, she knew the lady well because she was a customer. First on the left up Heath Street and then left again. Hillingdon lifted his shoulders towards his ears, clutched the roses in his right hand, and dashed for the cab. By the time the driver had found Mrs Blainey's house Hillingdon had discovered the roses were dripping water on to his knee. Perry's comment that the insurance company would be interested to know whether the road outside Mrs Blainey's house was public or private came back to him. Undeniably it was public, and as Hillingdon turned the point over in his mind he passed through the gateway into the little forecourt, feeling already an incipient melancholy.

'Good heavens! The man's quite wet.' Mrs Blainey, looking even younger than he remembered her in a brown knitted suit — Hillingdon had an eye for such details — appeared in a doorway at the end of the passage with the evening paper in one hand and a cat in the other. She put the cat down and shook the paper in its face to make it turn and go into a basket. 'Don't stand there, Alice. Can't you take those roses from him? Oh, aren't they lovely! Such a *smoky* red.' She was near enough for Alice, on the word of command, to lift the roses to her face. 'Of course they don't smell like the old roses do. But they *are* heavenly to look at. They *are* for us, aren't they, Mr Hillingdon? Yes? — well it's very very nice of you. Alice, just put them on the table in the kitchen. I shall see to them myself later on. Mr Hillingdon would like a glass of sherry, I'm sure.'

Napier Hillingdon became even sadder. Presumably men were always arriving at Mrs Blainey's door with bunches of roses. She had taken them quite as a matter of course. What if they had *not* been for her? he wondered. Would he have surrendered them, as he surrendered them now, before being led into the sitting-room where he was made to sit sideways on a chair, in front of an electric heater with a built-in fan which poured hot air over his wet shoulders? Would he have had the courage to say: 'I'm sorry, but there's been a mistake. I'm taking these flowers to — ' well, whoever it was? Probably not. The little room filled with the odour of wet clothes being dried.

'What is it you wanted to see me about?' If the question was blunt he could not help it. She did not seem to understand that a man of his age could get very bad fibrositis from a wet jacket.

'I don't quite know how to put it.' She perched on the edge of her chair watching him (rather narrowly) as he sipped his sherry and wriggled his shoulders. Her own glass was neglected. 'Thank you for coming over, particularly on a night like this. I'm worried about my son Timothy.'

Hillingdon drained the sherry and shifted the wet knee of his trousers. He did not think she was anything like as demonstrative as she should have been about the generous way he had responded to her call.

'Timothy is a good boy,' she went on, 'but I've had to be father and mother to him since his father died and my trouble is that I understand him too well. I understand him quite perfectly, and although he hasn't said anything to me I know he would be very glad and relieved if you would make a statement to the police that this business with the Egyptian journalist was really all your fault — you would know what to say — and then he could come out of hiding and go on with his British Council tour as arranged. I do feel,' said Mrs Blainey, pushing a faience cigarette box in Hillingdon's direction, 'that Timothy's career is at stake.'

Hillingdon did not want to understand. He would not smoke either. He knew that his shoulder-blades were creaking with rheumatism. Alice came in and, at a sign from Mrs Blainey, poured some more sherry into his glass. Corruption hung in the air.

'Poor Timothy! He hasn't been doing this job very long and when he's looking after somebody, like this Egyptian, he's not supposed to let them get into trouble.'

'But an old man like you,' she continued, 'with no ties as I understand it and nothing to do or worry about — '

'Oh but — '

'That's what you said, Mr Hillingdon. You said you were nothing but a fat old rentier, in this very house. But my Tim is only twenty-three and I just couldn't bear to have him discouraged. Just fancy if they dismissed him! You see, it's his psychology I have to think about.'

'I'm not old. I'm only fifty-five.'

'Are you? Oh, I do apologize. You looked so much older. But anyway, you're not young. Life can't hurt you.'

He almost believed her. She spoke so gently, smiling all the time. She anaesthetized each wound as she opened it. But no, he couldn't accept that life could no longer hurt him. It was hurting him at the moment, hurting like hell.

'I — I really don't know what you're suggesting, Mrs Blainey. I'm as vulnerable as any other man. Indeed, the longer I live the more vulnerable I feel. I'm sure that when I was younger I did not worry so much as I do now. I'm worried about my health. This Egyptian crisis upsets me, too. My life is a lonely one.'

If she had been near enough he would have caught one of her hands in spite of the way she had insulted him.

'Of course you're lonely. I'm lonely too,' she said. 'That proves we don't matter.'

'But this is absurd.' Hillingdon stood up and began to wave his right hand about. 'I feel as young, physically, as I ever did. I'm not going to sacrifice my legitimate interests for some young fool — '

'Yes, Tim is rather foolish,' she agreed.

'I don't necessarily mean your son. It's the principle of the thing. I'm fifty-five years of age and I have greater sensibility, greater imagination, greater energy, and a far, far greater capacity for suffering than I ever did. I'm a mass of sensitivity. But these young fools nowadays,' said Hillingdon, growing angry, 'they don't know the significance of things. How could they? The result is they can't feel.'

'I'm sure you've a great deal of sensibility. So have I. But that's not the point. We've neither of us careers to make.'

'We were talking about life in general. You said it couldn't hurt me.'

'Did I? Well, I didn't mean it. I'm afraid you'll think I'm a dreadful woman, sending for you like this and making you all these confidences.'

Hillingdon went and stood on one leg so that he could hold his wet knee before the electric heater. He no longer felt shy with her as he had on their first meeting, and that at least was a gain. She kept startling him, though, but — so far as he could see —

quite innocently. He even wondered whether she fully understood what she was saying now and again.

'Are you interested in the occult?' he demanded.

'Why do you ask?'

'Whenever I've met someone really out of the common I've found that they were interested in the occult. Now I myself am a dabbler. If one took reincarnation seriously, for example, one would say that in an earlier life you were in a position of great power. An empress.'

'Oh, Mr Hillingdon, I do think that's all a lot of childish nonsense.'

'Some very wise people have believed in it, and still do, millions of them. Especially in India.'

'No, it's all a lot of nonsense.' She folded her hands on her knees, a gesture of happiness. She smiled. 'Well, it *is* nice to know it's all decided. Tim would be very grateful if he ever knew. But of course he mustn't.'

'What's all decided?'

'Why, you're going to tell the police it was your fault giving this Egyptian the key, and then he can come out of hiding.'

'No, no.' Hillingdon dropped his right foot to the ground and winced as the rheumaticky pains shot across his shoulders. 'I never agreed. It is a complete misunderstanding. Besides, if I said that I mightn't get the insurance money on the car.'

'Money, money, money,' said Mrs Blainey, beginning to lose some of her social polish and exploding a match ferociously on to the end of her cigarette. She had waved Hillingdon back. She would not allow him to administer his lighter. 'Anybody would think that at a time when there is so little of it about people would be less obsessed with it. I'm sure I was never obsessed with money.'

From time to time Alice had looked in on them, and every

time she opened the door the aroma of cooking came in with her. If Mrs Blainey invited him to supper Hillingdon did not know what he would do. It was beyond his strength to refuse, and if he stayed he thought it very likely she would succeed in making him send this false statement to the police. He simultaneously longed for and dreaded the suggestion that he should stay. It did not come. When he left it was raining even more heavily than when he arrived and Mrs Blainey insisted on lending him an enormous golf umbrella, striped red and yellow.

How did he feel? Was he angry? He would have liked to remain calm and detached, but as he walked along in the shelter of the preposterous umbrella he knew perfectly well he would have to wait until his body told him how he had responded to Mrs Blainey's treatment. While he was waiting he thought he might as well have a drink. By the time he had ordered his double whisky in the lounge of The Cruel Sea his throat muscles were beginning to stiffen; he realized that his jaw must be jutting, his lower lip sneaking over the upper. Then the old flat board (that is what it felt like) was clapped to his stomach and he knew that he was so angry it was unwise to drink the whisky; it was bound to make him bilious. He drank it cautiously, hoping against hope that it would make him feel more relaxed. His head was aching.

'That's a pretty umbrella you got there. Serviceable, too.'

Hillingdon noticed for the first time that he was sharing the table; the fellow was only trying to be friendly, he knew. But he said nothing. He ignored him. He watched the wooden ferrule make a pool on the floor. Resentment, that is what he felt; resentment against life, against Mrs Blainey, against this fellow sitting opposite. Tomorrow morning he knew perfectly well that he would wake up with this resentment sitting on him like a toad. Mrs Blainey had been selfish and callous. He resented her more than he resented the way Muawiya had smashed his car. Well, so it seemed at the moment. *An old man!* That is what she had called him! He was going to brood over it for days.

'Brightens the place up, too,' said the man opposite who had not apparently noticed Hillingdon's lack of response.

The street door opened. Hillingdon heard a voice say the rain had stopped. He levered himself to his feet and went in search of a cab. That woman had made a real enemy! Well, perhaps she might have done if he'd been a younger man. One needed energy to keep the pot of enmity boiling. However, Hillingdon tried to think of himself as an enemy, and found after a while the occupation soothing.

At breakfast the following morning Mary Perry began teasing Hillingdon about the woman he had been to see. Why did he have to be so mysterious? Who was she? Why had they known nothing of her before?

Breakfasting together was quite an innovation. It was part of Hillingdon's agreement with the Perrys that his own top-floor flat was serviced, breakfast sent up on a tray, and lunch and dinner made available in their own dining-room whenever he wanted it. For a bachelor, he claimed, nothing could be more sensible. It meant, too, that before Muawiya made Helvetia a centre of public interest nothing was seen of Hillingdon before lunch-time. Muawiya changed all that. The need to see the morning papers as soon as possible brought Hillingdon downstairs in his dressing-gown, and he, the Perrys and Grimbley ate their cereals and bacon under the contemptuous eye of young Christopher, who sat occasionally lobbing porridge or some other pap in all directions.

'There's no mystery at all,' said Hillingdon with the *Daily Telegraph* propped up in front of him; and without mentioning the roses he described how Mrs Blainey had suggested he incriminated himself in order to save her son's skin. 'As if I could anyway. What does she think the law is?'

'Edgar said the moment she telephoned you rushed upstairs and put on your best clothes.'

'Oh, really, Mary —'

'But you did. Anyway, I don't see why Napier shouldn't have a woman as well as anybody else.' Mary was the only person who called Hillingdon by his Christian name and it ought to have made relations between them easier than in fact they were. Possibly he was old-fashioned. He was old enough to be her father, didn't really approve of Christian-name promiscuity between the generations, and never called her anything but Mrs Perry. For Mary it was a daily reminder how stuffy the old chap was.

'Did you say the name was Blainey?' Grimbley was wearing cord trousers and a beret, signs that he was going to spend the morning gardening. Well, digging a few potatoes, anyway. He frequently came to the breakfast table dressed for going out. Without actually preventing him from eating heartily of everything put in front of him, it served to underline his view that breakfast was a light meal, a snack, preferably taken on the feet. 'I knew some awful characters called Blainey when I was acting vice-consul at Alexandria.'

'Must be the same,' said Perry. 'It was a Blainey from the British Council who brought Muawiya here in the first place. Oh, and then ... I *see!* You went on to his mother's for supper, and it was from *there* —'

'You know, I've just realized something.' Grimbley dropped his butter-knife in the excitement. 'This other Egyptian —

what's his name? — the military attaché — well, he's got an English wife, hasn't he? A little pink and white woman with freckles. Knew her before they were married. She was a Miss Brent.'

'Can't imagine marrying an Egyptian!' Mary shuddered.

'Why didn't I think of it before? She escaped from Egypt on Farouk's yacht when he was kicked out. Did you know that now? I was acting vice-consul and I went on board to make sure she was going voluntarily. Her photograph was in the paper the other day. I *thought* I recognized it.'

'Mrs Yehia,' said Perry.

'That's it. Mrs Yehia. Well, her maiden name was Brent, and she was mixed up in some way or other with Farouk's abdication.'

'Perhaps they'd come in to supper one evening.' Mary's mind was not really on the subject — she was fighting to prise Christopher from his chair, the child screaming and refusing to go — or she would never have mentioned before Grimbley the possibility of inviting an Egyptian to the house; but all Grimbley said was that he too could not imagine why an Englishwoman should want to marry an Egyptian — he had no racial prejudice, mind — but their backgrounds were so different a marriage was bound to lead to trouble.

'When we go into Egypt, and I'm sure that's what it'll come to, what is going to be the position of an Englishwoman domiciled there even if she is married to an Egyptian? They'll just cut her throat.' Grimbley struck a humanitarian note. 'I hope she doesn't go off to Egypt with her husband, that's all. Maybe somebody ought to put the facts of the situation before her. She was quite a nice woman as I remember her.'

He had had to lift his voice over Christopher's screams. Having got him to the floor Mary was now dragging him by the right arm towards the door.

'I think Mrs Blainey is right,' she said to Hillingdon. 'If you can make things a bit easier for her son I think you ought to.'

Even now, at nine o'clock, Hillingdon's morning heaviness had not begun to lift, and as he had expected he was sour with resentment. He made no comment on Mary's irritating remark.

'After all,' said Mary — and as she spoke she gave Christopher a punitive shaking to stop his noise — 'all you need say is that you didn't know he hadn't got a driving-licence.'

'Your wife must think I'm a fool,' Hillingdon said to Perry as soon as Mary and Christopher had gone. 'Doesn't she understand that what makes this Egyptian's offence really serious is the way he drove and then smashed the car up! He'd be jailed even if he had a licence and was founder member of the Automobile Association into the bargain.'

'At least they couldn't say he stole the car.'

Hillingdon stared. 'You don't mean to say you're in favour of me perjuring myself, too?'

'Of course not. Anyway, let's be realistic. They'd never send Muawiya to jail. They'd give him a whacking fine — which the Egyptian Government would pay anyway — and pack him off out of the country.'

Grimbley lowered his newspaper. 'Why won't they jail him? I'm assuming, of course, that you think he deserves jail.'

'I expect the Afro-Asian block would raise it at the United Nations if we put Muawiya in jail. They'd say it was part of our general vindictiveness over Suez.'

'I'd like to see him come up at the Old Bailey,' said Grimbley fiercely, 'and make a real trial of it, by God, with evidence about the chap's character called for. Let all the world know the sort of young ruffian he is. Can't you just see yourself, Perry, stuck up in the witness-box answering questions about what happened at Sakkara?'

'Good heavens! You don't think it'll come to that?'

'Not if the bloody Gyppos can help it, it won't. They'll try to keep him under cover and smuggle him out in the diplomatic bag. Damn it, at this very minute they've got British subjects waiting trial in Cairo on rigged charges of espionage. Don't forget that, my liberal friend! I will see to it myself, *I promise you*, that once the police lay their hands on Muawiya I'll see to it that something more than a motoring offence is charged against him. I'll unmask him as a terrorist.'

'That's absolute rubbish, and you know it. No British Court is competent to try something that happened in Egypt five years ago.'

'I'd like to give him a real taste of British justice,' Grimbley shouted, the blood rushing up behind his whiskers. 'You don't seem to understand that a judge at the Old Bailey doesn't give a damn for the Afro-Asian block. All he's concerned with is justice, and I hope he lays it on thick and strong.' Grimbley had not heard Perry's remark that no British Court was competent to try an offence in Egypt, and he went on to threaten Perry with the various legal penalties he might undergo for withholding evidence about Muawiya's characteristically bungled attempt to assassinate him.

He was still talking when Ilse, the Austrian help, came in to clear the table and distribute some mail.

Hillingdon picked up a couple of envelopes and made for the door, saying he'd have to go into town that morning and talk with his insurance company before the police grilled him again. Since the story about Muawiya had broken no one at Helvetia took mail very seriously, for it seemed to consist mainly of letters from complete strangers — some of it eccentric, some abusive, some crazily xenophobic, and some pleading for various charitable causes. Ilse had a tidy mind. When nine o'clock came round she liked to see the hall table cleared of this mail and went round forcing the stuff on those to whom it happened to be addressed.

'What's this?' said Hillingdon stopping at the door with an opened letter in his hand. He turned, shuffled his hairy carpet slippers back into the room and waved a sheet of pale blue notepaper on which they could see writing in green ink. 'It's from Muawiya,' he said. 'What next, I'd like to know?'

The arrival of Muawiya's letter brought a new urgency to their thinking. Perry ran to the door and called for Mary so that she could hear of this new development without delay. Grimbley breathed out noisily, as though to express the relaxed content of a man who sees pleasure at hand. Muawiya had, to be truthful, become a little unreal to them. The publicity had built him into such a personality that he was no more convincing than anyone else they read about in the newspapers. But here was paper on which Muawiya had actually written. It was rather like receiving a letter from Jack the Ripper.

'I suppose,' said Hillingdon, suddenly folding the letter to the stained breast of his dressing-gown, 'I could sell this to the Press.' A gleam of light appeared in his pale, flat eyes.

'You won't gain any more for not reading it to us,' said Grimbley, 'and as there's a warrant out for his arrest I daresay we'll see the police taking charge of it.'

'But I might get five hundred quid — '

'It's probably contempt of court or something. Here, let me see!' And Grimbley tried to snatch the paper from Hillingdon's hand.

'No, this is my letter. I'm under no obligation to read it to anyone.'

'For God's sake — '

'It may contain something private,' said Hillingdon, and he

read the note quietly to himself while the others watched his face; it lengthened slightly and was stiffened to suppress signs of emotion. But his eyes gave him away. The eyebrows strained apart and the eyes themselves blossomed to twice their normal size. Without a word he handed the letter to Perry and stood with this expression of wide-eyed, arrested astonishment upon his face, the look of a tempest-washed ship's figurehead, incredulous that life should expose him to so much.

Perry began reading aloud:

as from c/o British Council,
London.
August 28th.

Dear Mr Hillingdon,
    You must be thinking very, very badly of me and I do not know how to say excuse. But all will be well, sir, never doubt. It was not at all my fault. This other car came out very suddenly, too fast, in the middle of the road and I turn right, like I would do in Cairo, Egypt, but I forget in that one moment only you drive on left side of road. He must be made to pay, this other driver. You must prosecute him, sir.

You will be thanking God for my safety. I am sincerely sorry that this driver caused your car to be damaged while it was in my care.

When shall we meet again, you and Professor Perry and his wife and Mr Blainey and Mrs Blainey? I will tell you. My party will be next Thursday evening at half past six. My invitation cards will be arriving shortly. You will not tell anyone about my party, certainly not the police or the Government.

I am sincerely sorry for the trouble I cause you and when we meet I will explain how I can repay you. Please burn this letter.

> Yours sincerely,
> MUAWIYA KHASLAT
> (*journalist*)

'A party!' Grimbley was the first to break the silence which followed the reading of this letter. 'Notice he doesn't mention me. Knew better. What's this about a party? He can't give a party.'

Hillingdon took the letter from Perry and read it with a determination that fixed his eyes in their sockets so that he had to turn his head from side to side in order to follow the lines. A little concentration, he seemed to be saying, and we shall understand it. He spoke the words to himself, softly, testing each one for a hidden significance. Coming to an end of the search, he looked up. His eyes met Perry's. 'I don't think he's a bit sorry. What a piece of effrontery.'

'You've got to make allowances for his bad English,' said Perry. 'I'm sure he's very sorry indeed. Where was the letter posted?'

The envelope was postmarked W.1 at six-fifteen the previous evening, so gave nothing away. No doubt the Egyptian Embassy would have strongly disapproved of Muawiya writing any letter, but if it was assumed this one had been smuggled out by an Embassy servant and posted in the nearest letter-box a W.1 postmark is what it would have received.

'I'm not a bit surprised, really,' said Mary. 'He's got enough cheek for a dozen. He's quite capable of walking into this room with a great grin on his face.'

'What would you do?' said Grimbley to Perry.

'What should I do?'

'Yes, what would you do if he walked in this very minute?'

Mary and Hillingdon both began speaking but Grimbley was pointing the stem of his pipe at Perry. 'No, you tell me what *you* would do?'

'We've enough to worry about without any hypothetical —'

'I'll tell you what you'd do! You'd ask him to sit down, you'd offer him a drink, you'd discuss ways and means of getting him out of the mess he's landed himself in, you'd make a rare fuss of the fellow.'

'I should certainly tell him to give himself up to the authorities.'

'But what if he wouldn't listen?'

'You wouldn't expect me to handcuff him, would you?'

'... imagining that other people are like you!' Grimbley had been trying to talk Perry down. 'The liberal fallacy of examining your own psyche through rose-tinted spectacles and then thinking you've got a bit of evidence about existence at large, that's what sticks in my throat. The bloody vanity of it! People are different from you, don't you understand?' Grimbley paused for a moment. 'And so are you, if it comes to that!'

'You're accomplices, that's what you are,' said Grimbley, triumphant that he had silenced everyone, 'in Khaslat's crime — emotional accomplices.'

'I don't see how you can include me in this.' Hillingdon was stuffing the letter into his wallet.

'Are you or are you not,' Grimbley demanded, 'going to hand that letter over to the police?'

'If we *did* go to this party,' Hillingdon said, picking his way, 'do you think Muawiya could be persuaded to sign a paper saying he took the car without my permission?'

The question was directed at Perry.

'Why don't you go out and flog the letter to the *Express*? That's what you're interested in, isn't it? Money?'

'The *Express* would still buy it after next Thursday.'

Sarcasm was wasted on Hillingdon, he clearly regarded both Grimbley's and Perry's attitude to Anglo-Egyptian relations as being much too theoretical. 'How on earth could he give a party, though? That's what puzzles me. I don't get it.'

Mary had left the room as soon as Waldo began shouting but now she returned, rubbing the pages of her diary over with her thumb. 'We're quite free next Thursday evening, Edgar dear.'

'There will *be* no party.' Perry wondered if Mary's particular kind of irresponsibility would have developed if she had married someone less of a prig than himself. If she had married Grimbley, for example, wouldn't she have been forced to acquire a few principles to compensate? Perry hated to put it this way, even to himself, but hadn't he rather spoiled her? 'There will be no party because Muawiya hasn't the slightest intention of arranging one. Surely you know Egyptians well enough by now to see that? That letter is only politeness. He wanted to say he was sorry for what he'd done, and oriental courtesy did the rest.'

Mary's disappointment was obvious.

'I'm glad you haven't entirely lost your wits, Perry,' said Grimbley; and he sighed deeply, communicating a sense of crisis passed, of steadiness and resolution having triumphed, and wisdom — *his* wisdom — belatedly recognized.

'Your Egyptian,' he said, classifying the breed for all time, 'is just not reliable.'

Hillingdon was frowning and studying Perry's face with a care that revealed he was impressed by Perry's assessment of the letter. 'I'd be glad if none of you would say anything about what's happened. There's no knowing what the implications are. I think I shall have to show the letter to my solicitor.'

The events of the day were not what they seemed. Of this Hillingdon was convinced. The Iron Curtain, the Cold War, the Berlin Blockade, the Korean War, and now Nasser's nationalization of the Suez Canal — all these phenomena could be explained more profoundly than with the help of any of those terms, communism, colonialism, national self-determination and the like, you saw in the papers. Just what this profound explanation would be he was not *absolutely* sure. But somewhere, someone knew! Hillingdon had a disposition to believe in the existence of sages, beings who looked at the world from some extra-human position and saw the springs of society laid bare and their manipulator exposed. For that there was a manipulator or manipulators Hillingdon had a confident expectation. He might even turn out to be the Devil. Hillingdon was not a Christian but he saw no reason for not using a Christian hypothesis.

He spent ten minutes in a parked taxi opposite Lancaster House watching some of the delegates arrive at the conference which was still sitting, and with an increasing sense of irrelevance, to decide the future management and control of the Suez Canal. He caught a glimpse of Mr Menon in the back of one of the limousines, but Hillingdon was too badly placed to identify anyone less striking in appearance. The cars drove up to the striped awning, anonymous figures were momentarily seen against a sunlit pillar only to disappear abruptly into the vestibule that was all the darker for the brightness of the day. The crowd was silent. Police strolled across the road to wave back a car or the occasional man or woman who tried to cross the road. Hillingdon was disappointed he had been unable to scrutinize the delegates from closer quarters; although he did not imagine he would spot a cloven hoof or tail there ought to be some discernible quality imprinted on the countenances of these men to reveal that they were unconsciously subject to a Hidden Power. A glazed eye, perhaps! Something mechanical in the gait! An unnatural smile!

Hillingdon asked the driver to take him to his insurance company in St James's Street, but half way up Whitehall he changed his mind and said he wanted to go to the London Library. He could not, that morning, face another argument over his policy, even though his solicitor would be there to back him up. Instead, he would telephone and make an excuse; say he was unwell.

According to the morning paper Mr Dulles had said the United States was prepared to concede 'liberty of action for the signatories if Egypt refuses' — refuses, presumably, international control of the Canal. As Colonel Nasser had simultaneously announced that Egypt would never accept international control Hillingdon foresaw violence. He sat in a leather chair, looking through the windows at the plane trees of St James's Square, wondering how the Egyptian Embassy would smuggle Khaslat out of the country when the rest of their staff was forced to leave. Perhaps there would be some absurd and undignified scuffle at the airport. What did it all mean? Why was there so much anger? Wasn't there too much anger in the air to permit politicians to be rational? Hillingdon's mind turned, once again, to the Devil.

The most common explanation for Muawiya Khaslat's behaviour — the theft of the car, the mad driving, the accident — was that he had taken too much to drink; a Moslem could scarcely be expected to hold his liquor. But this theory did not satisfy Hillingdon, who was under the impression that Khaslat had not drunk so very much, even for a Moslem, and he certainly seemed quite sober when he tossed the car keys in the air and went off to move the Morris. Hillingdon allowed his mind to play around this concept of the Devil. Of course, one did not apply it too literally, in the old medieval way, but surely it was not too absurd to say that the Egyptian had behaved like a man possessed? He had driven like a maniac. And then his escape! Hillingdon sat up in his chair as he remembered the driving-wheel thrust back into the seat. Surely the fellow had the luck of the Devil too! Hillingdon thought of his personal appearance. That crinkled black hair! Those bright dark eyes! And wasn't there something goatlike in his manner, a way of looking back at you with a sneering grin when you least expected it? Hillingdon reminded himself that this was the man who but for some providential accident would have murdered Perry (so the story went) those years ago in Egypt. It was an event which, at one time, it would have been impossible to relate without talk of a miraculous intervention. Perhaps the most rewarding way of thinking about Khaslat was as the Devil himself!

Hillingdon looked about him. The reading-room atmosphere had become oppressive. Well, it was a warm morning, and about time too, at this time of year, after so much rain. Hillingdon could feel sweat on his body. His underclothes were sticking to him in inconvenient places and when he lifted his hands from the leather arms of the chair they left moist patches. Anyone would think he'd been running about instead of sitting here quietly, thinking. He wondered whether any of the other people in the reading-room recognized him from the newspaper photographs. He wondered where Khaslat was at that very moment. The worst of a man's disappearing so abruptly was that it gave some promise of his reappearing with equal suddenness. If he were to walk out from behind that bookcase, now, what would one do? Khaslat would be certain to smile and hold out his hand.

As soon as Hillingdon was in motion once more he felt calmer. He walked out of the library into the square and wondered whether a haircut would quieten this peculiar fluttering in the breast; a barber's shop — a really expensive barber's shop, such as the one Hillingdon patronized — was the only respectable establishment left to Western man for the indulgence of modest sensuality; the London Turkish baths were much too rough an ordeal, quite unlike the baths of the Orient where Hillingdon imagined soothing orgies of massage and depilation; he would, in particular, have liked to lie on his back and have the soles of his feet gently rubbed. But he could tell by the loose way his trilby was riding that his hair had been cut within the last two or three days and even the delights of an occidental barber were to be denied him.

Hillingdon turned into Jermyn Street thinking what a nightmare experience it would be to discover, the next time he went to the barber's, that waiting for him in the cubicle, with comb and scissors, was Muawiya Khaslat!

In Piccadilly the crowds and the traffic, all the animation of a summer morning, cheered Hillingdon up enormously and he walked slowly through the Ritz arches, setting one well-polished brown shoe firmly in front of the other, throwing them well forward so that he caught glimpses of them, winking remotely, over the horizon of his dove-grey waistcoat. Holiday-makers up from the provinces were sitting on the deck-chairs in Green Park, and as Hillingdon sauntered along, trying to imagine himself into the skin of a Welsh tin-plate worker with fifteen quid to spend before Saturday night, he even became a little dreamy. In half an hour the pubs would open and he would have — no, not a whisky, he had gone off whisky — he would have a gin, because that was a light healthy drink with a beneficial effect (so he had been told) on the liver. There were plenty of pubs in this area. He crossed Piccadilly and walked up Half Moon Street into Curzon Street. Five minutes later he was in South Audley Street looking up, in shocked dismay, at the green flag and blazon on the building opposite, which told him that it was the Egyptian Embassy! Why had he come? Who had led him there? He had been told the supernatural was signalled by a drop in temperature and here he was, feeling cold fingers in his stomach on a hot morning.

And what a conventional building it was to be housing such a creature. The large windows of the neo-classical façade argued a kind of frankness in the people who lived there; but the diabolical frequently dwelt behind the most innocent exteriors, and in any case — Hillingdon reminded himself — he should not be thinking of appearances. Muawiya might, at that moment, be observing him from the dark window on the top floor. For what other reason had Hillingdon been drawn to South Audley Street? An inspection by the Satanic! The dryness of Hillingdon's mouth made him think of gin again — no, no, it would have to be whisky in the extremity he now found himself, and to hell with his liver! He corrected himself. Not to hell! Let him not so much as think of hell! What would he do, Hillingdon thought, if that brown door opened, a man appeared, walked down the steps and past the policeman, crossed the road and singled him out from the rest of the little crowd of idlers, saying: 'Would you please come inside?'

Hillingdon collided with a pipe-smoker in his eagerness to be off; the pipe was knocked sideways, scattering ash over a stained cardigan, and Hillingdon turned into South Street, hurrying, too fluttered to apologize, with the man's shout ringing after him. I'm fifty-five, Hillingdon was saying to himself, and much too old — in theory — to be shaken by experiences like this. But he was shaken. He had to be honest with himself. He was more than shaken, he was frightened!

The woman came round the corner so suddenly Hillingdon had to lift his hands to protect his stomach; and they stood there, the pair of them, momentarily looking into each other's eyes. Blue eyes, beautiful but unhappy. Where had he seen them before?

'Well!' she said, and drew to one side. She was carrying a basketwork contrivance which at first glance Hillingdon took to be for some animal: a snake, he found himself thinking. How extraordinary that a woman should be carrying a snake in a basket. And then he saw it was no more than a shopping-basket with a lid. He looked into the blue eyes again.

'What are you doing here?' she said.

It was Mrs Yehia, the Englishwoman married to the Egyptian military attaché. If it had not been for the way she had demanded to be taken home from Mrs Blainey's, Hillingdon would never have handed over his car keys to Khaslat, there would have been no joyride, and at this moment he would not be thinking of snakes and devils. Hillingdon was tempted to hurry on, pretending he had not recognized her.

'Well, I was just round at the Embassy, seeing if there was any sign of that blackguard.' This woman must know where Khaslat was, Hillingdon thought. Her husband worked in the Embassy. Perhaps she was on her way to see Khaslat now. 'Did you know he'd written a letter to me saying he was giving a party? A party, I ask you! It's just insincerity, of course. I wonder your husband doesn't use his influence to put a stop to whatever it is that's going on. Because I don't know what it is. I can't believe it's simply that Khaslat is afraid he'll be jailed.'

'I can't talk with you here,' she said. 'Let's go into the park.'

'I'm sorry, but I'm late for an appointment already.'
'Please.'
'You must know what they're thinking in the Embassy — '
'No, no.' She spoke so vehemently that Hillingdon was more apprehensive than ever. 'I know nothing at all. I scarcely know where my own husband is.'
'He's disappeared?'
The moment he saw that she too was suffering he no longer thought she was leading him into a trap. 'Your husband disappeared! How terrible!'
'I know where he is. He's in the Embassy and we can speak to each other on the telephone, but he can't come out.'
'That telephone is tapped, you can be sure.'
They stared at each other.
'Do you mean,' he said, 'that your husband is living in the Embassy and you're living outside, and you can't see each other?'
'I'm so terrified there's going to be a war.'
They walked solemnly towards Park Lane. The traffic was so heavy it was impossible to talk. They had crossed the road, entered the park, and were walking under the trees before Hillingdon so much as opened his mouth. The summery park was in such contrast to the streets it was too good to be true. The feathery trees and grazing sheep were a vision kindly interposed by some beneficent power at a time of special stress and — sure enough — when Hillingdon looked back he saw a flickering red among the greenery: on one plane London Transport buses; but on the deeper and truer plane, reminders of the flames of torment.

CHAPTER THREE

PERRY noticed Mary's disappointment when he had dashed the hopes of a party raised by Muawiya's letter; so, if she wanted a party — well, why couldn't they have a party, and on Thursday evening too? Perry's detestation of parties was well known but because he liked holidays even less than parties no one was at all suspicious of his proposal, not even Mary. That year he had persuaded her they simply could not afford to go to the seaside (he still winced at the thought of the previous season when a child screamed 'Daddy' on the beach at Boscombe and three or four hundred fathers rose from their deck-chairs) and as the holiday season drew to its close Mary judged that his feeling of guilt was growing stronger. She enjoyed seaside holidays so much it simply would not have been fair if Edgar had not felt guilty. So she wasn't surprised when he suggested a party, and the others — Grimbley and Hillingdon — were so incurious in their different ways about Perry's character they did not give the party much thought. That it was fixed for Thursday night might have made them suspicious, but it didn't.

Grimbley remarked: 'I don't know why you're looking so blasted gay.'

Perry considered this carefully. 'This time of the lunar month I'm in my manic phase,' he said. 'If you cut the party I shall be very offended. Would you like me to ask Miss Gunter?'

Miss Gunter had once taught part-time at the school. Her

contract came to an end shortly after she discovered Grimbley's birthday and presented him with a model Japanese garden in a cement trough. Grimbley insisted that she went. Unfortunately she travelled no farther than a secretarial college in Golders Green and from time to time she appeared at Helvetia, her gold-framed spectacles winking this way and that in search of Grimbley.

'You know very well you're not to invite Miss Gunter,' said Grimbley.

'Must say I've always liked her — '

'I will *not* meet Miss Gunter!'

'At least you'll come to the party?'

'Unless I've got anything better to do.'

Hillingdon was coming. It was at his suggestion that Mrs Blainey was invited — he even offered to contribute to the cost of the party if this were done — and, of course, that would mean inviting Elaine Yehia; she was quite a friend of his. Perry said Mary would be delighted to invite anyone Hillingdon cared to name, but wasn't it a bit odd asking Mrs Blainey when she had treated him so inconsiderately? And who was Elaine Yehia?

Hillingdon described his chance meeting with Elaine and her personal distress, married to an Egyptian diplomat and he unable to leave the Embassy, over the Suez crisis. She had no relations nearer than Birmingham and was living alone in a flat off Charles Street. Hillingdon had taken it into his head to telephone Mrs Blainey and ask whether she knew how worried Elaine was. The upshot, he was glad to say, was that Mrs Blainey had invited the girl to stay. Wasn't it wonderfully generous of her and just what you would expect? Hillingdon said he had been very wrong to quarrel with Mrs Blainey; he ought to have seen that she was only considering her son's interests, and that was natural enough, wasn't it?

'Mrs Blainey is a remarkable woman,' said Hillingdon. 'Very feminine, not at all the spiritual type, but quick as a mouse.'

'Why can't this Egyptian leave the Embassy? What does his wife say?'

'He says he's too busy to come home, but of course he can't give the truth. The Egyptians are bound to be a bit careful with a man married to an Englishwoman.'

Even when Perry tried to limit the size of the party to a half a dozen or so Mary merely thought he was being mean; it did not enter her head he was planning something not quite so innocent as the usual cocktails. She said it would not be a party at all unless at least a dozen people turned up. The Stringers would certainly expect to come. Then there was Mabel. She must invite Mabel. She mentioned a lot more names and Perry began to feel confused; but all he said was, 'Certainly dear, invite them all,' and instead of the melancholy she expected he was so cheerful she thought he could not possibly have understood. She drew up a list and showed it to him. He said: 'We've forgotten young Blainey — you know, the fellow who brought Muawiya to see us. Better put him down.' And he laughed delightedly.

'You're absolutely right, Mary,' he said. 'Let's have as large a party as possible. I ought to have thought of it myself.'

And what's more they would have champagne. Mary found his gaiety infectious and said she was quite sure the pub down on the main road would let them have a few crates on credit or return; but Perry would have none of this. He said that what they ordered they ordered and no one was to leave until it had all been drunk. It wasn't every year he felt like throwing a party. On this occasion he would not mind if a journalist or two turned up to see how Hillingdon was supporting the loss of his car and the confusion over his insurance claim; ring up the *Daily Express* and ask if they'd like to send someone!

'You certainly have got the bit between your teeth,' she said.

Perry thought the remark over quietly to himself and decided that although it was a terrible cliché it expressed his state of mind with accuracy. Without knowing his destination he was in full gallop, almost dotty with determination; good advice would be swept aside — even if anyone was in a position to offer it him, which they were not. The morning papers and the radio news bulletins gave the impression that international affairs had ceased to be two vague words; they had evolved a personality and logic of their own, and placed the Suez affair in a predetermined groove. He could not believe that the different countries concerned could individually be so idiotic. 'International Affairs' had them in thrall; they were behaving with a purblind rationalism that was worse than eccentricity. Perry was quite sure that Nasser would have responded to an eccentric handling of the crisis. In the first place, Mr Dulles should not have refused to finance the building of the High Dam at Aswan. This refusal was what all the trouble started with. The correct procedure would have been to promise the money and then fail to keep the promise.

No matter what Perry said or thought the Suez affair would spin along its groove to some disastrous conclusion, and perhaps champagne and as much of the dionysiac as the chaste spirit of Helvetia permitted were a suitable protest for the immediate present; political action, letters to his M.P., a speech in Trafalgar Square, could wait until Muawiya had shown just how dionysiac he could become.

Muawiya had telephoned in the middle of Monday morning when by a great stroke of luck Perry answered himself. Mary had gone out shopping with Christopher and Ilse could be heard banging about upstairs. Hillingdon and Grimbley had disappeared immediately after breakfast. Once Perry had recovered from his surprise he saw no reason why Muawiya and he should not have a normal conversation.

'You bloody fool,' he said, 'you bloody, bloody fool! Where are you speaking from?'

'Sir, I am in great trouble.'

'I'm furious with you. D'you understand? I suppose you've given yourself up to the police.'

'No, sir.'

'Then why are you telephoning me? It's very compromising. Is anybody listening to this conversation at your end? I can't promise my line isn't being tapped, you know.'

'I am telephoning from a call-box.'

'Where?'

'Does it matter, this detail? Sir, I telephone your number because I want to speak to Mr Hillingdon. He is not there? You know I wrote a letter to him? You are aware then that I told him of a party I was going to arrange. But unfortunately I discover I am not allowed to have this party. It seems very extraordinary, but I am not allowed. So I want *you* to give the party.'

'Me?'

'Yes, you and Mrs Perry. Please arrange everything as nice as you would like it. I will pay, of course. All the bills must be sent to me and I will pay them in full. But you see my predicament, sir. I cannot arrange this party myself. And if I have no party my word will be broken. No one will trust me again. You and Mr Hillingdon will not trust me.'

'But the police will arrest you as soon as they clap eyes on you. Frankly, neither Mr Hillingdon nor I really thought you'd be able to throw a party. After the war perhaps.'

'Let us not talk of such things.'

'How d'you know I shan't tip off the police?'

'Tip off?'

'How d'you know I shan't tell the police that you'll be in my house on Thursday evening?'

'Your character would not permit you.'

'Well — Mr Grimbley, then?'

'He would be my guest. Mr Grimbley knows very well that according to our religion there is a special relationship between a man and his guests. Besides, I have been given a gun.'

'You've been given what?'

'Not a gun, really. A very nice little revolver.'

'Listen!' Perry thought of the last time he had taken a revolver from Muawiya. 'You're *not* to bring weapons with you, understand?'

Muawiya chuckled. 'Spend as much money as you like on my party. I have plenty of it. Chicken sandwiches would be excellent. But whatever you like. Potted shrimps, for example.'

And he rang off.

The thought of Muawiya bringing a revolver worried Perry a great deal until he decided he would insist on frisking him the moment he arrived; and by taking such a decision he experienced a great sense of relief because he knew he had also decided to arrange Muawiya's party for him. After years of running Helvetia it was good to be acting like an irresponsible idiot once more.

Perry walked back into his office, closed the door and began taking deep, exciting breaths. His cocoon of Englishness slackened. Over the fireplace was a David Roberts print showing medieval Cairo a little more dramatically than the original probably justified; a pale mass of buildings, with mushrabiya windows and screens propped up on the roofs to protect the sleepers, standing in front of a murk of rubbish, tombs and minarets. Beyond the

Citadel the desert of Suez lay like a lake. Throw up a few blocks of Frenchified flats and put open tramcars, buses and policemen in the streets and the Roberts print would have looked reasonably like the city Perry remembered. Well, he would never see it again! The occasional wave of longing had grown weaker as the years passed. The faded ammoniacal goat-smell in the sun, the resinous reek of Khan el-Khalili, newly tanned camel leather, freshly cut water-melon filling a room with its perfume, sesame-seed sauce, their memory had faded. All, all gone! He would never know them again.

Or would he? Champagne and chicken might help a little. Muawiya would certainly help. When everybody had arrived and the champagne corks were popping Muawiya would throw up the sash window and hop into the room, the genuine Cairene odour about him, the Egyptian extravagance in his eye. His presence would be absurd; but then, the Egyptians were absurd. Perry would take the revolver from him, and that would be absurd and Egyptian too. What would happen then? Would Grimbley send for the police? It was silly to anticipate. Perhaps everyone would get tight. Perhaps it would be like one of those weird Egyptian parties at which everyone was genial and alcoholic, talking away with an exhausting exuberance about any subject but the one that was uppermost in their minds. Perry remembered a party like this when the British had just forced Nahas Pasha on the King as Prime Minister. Would Muawiya's party be the same? Would they talk about André Gide and Charles Morgan? Would it be deliciously Egypt all over again?

Well, probably not Gide and Charles Morgan. The Cairo that had talked of them had gone for ever. Even champagne and the calculated idiocy of Muawiya's party could not evoke it. Perry thought of the friends he had known before the revolution. The Princess was dead, lucky for her, because otherwise the revolution would have killed her. Only one letter had come from the Pasha since 1952; he was confined to a small house on what had once been his country estate, but he still went duck shooting; he had also become interested in capturing solar energy and – so far as Perry could make out – had developed some kind of metal suntrap which boiled water and drove a little steam engine. His wealth and power had gone. And who else was there? Boghos was killed in the Palestine war. The Dean of the Faculty had lost his job for political reasons – he was a keen Wafdist – and was now teaching in a school at Assiut.

Perry thought of them lovingly. History had done them down. They had scarcely known what had hit them. A corrupt and inefficient regime? Perhaps it was. But none of these people had invented it, and now they were dead or cut down twenty-five sizes. He hoped time would show the revolution was worth it.

Muawiya had not given the impression, the afternoon he turned up for tea, that the revolution had wrought any change in human nature. His talk of bringing a revolver to the party – well, Perry belatedly realized, that was a joke; and it showed how Muawiya had decided to treat the past. Do not let us forget it entirely; let us think of Sakkara from time to time and thank God that we are both still alive.

Let us have a good laugh, sir! I nearly killed you that time in the mummy pit and you know, in your heart, that I could have killed you if I had really wanted. Perhaps I am not a good shot, but I was so near to you that I could not miss. Frankly, sir, I did not try to kill you. How could I kill anyone for whom I had so much love?

'I have been given a gun!' Perry muttered Muawiya's words to himself and surrendered to a spasm of gaiety. 'A very nice little revolver.' That is what the silly ass had said! Perry thought of Thursday night. Just imagine Grimbley's face when Muawiya flung up that window and climbed over the sill! And Mary's face! And Hillingdon!

Perry lay flat on the couch, feeling his belly twitch with laughter.

'One minute!' said Hillingdon. He was wearing a linen jacket, a pink bow and white tennis shoes. Perry, whom he had stopped outside the Crematorium, thought he looked like somebody out of the beach pavilion concert party. 'One minute! I simply must tell you. Mrs Blainey and Mrs Yehia will not be able to come to the party tomorrow evening.'

'I'm sorry —'

'Yes, but you don't know why.'

'I suppose this means you're not going to pay your whack?'

'Don't let's worry about money. There are more important things. I really believe those women are in danger and I have given strict instructions they're not to leave the house. Unfortunately, Mrs Blainey won't let me inform the police. But I've a good mind to, behind her back.'

Hillingdon glanced up and down the road. He dropped his voice. 'I think the Egyptians are trying to capture Mrs Yehia.'

'Capture her!'

'The housekeeper saw a dark-skinned chap peering in through the outer door. You know Mrs Blainey's house is in a courtyard, and this chap didn't actually come into the courtyard, but he looked. He was hanging about the next day, too, she said.'

'But why should the Egyptians want to capture this — what's her name?'

'Mrs Yehia. Because her husband is an Egyptian diplomat. They've got him confined to the Embassy and they want her now.'

'Why?'

'I don't understand their psychology, do I? Mrs Yehia says she's not going to Egypt, whatever happens. They may have decided she's got to.'

Perry looked up into Hillingdon's face. It was a good nine inches higher than his own; and the body was bulky in proportion. It was like being in the presence of a different subspecies. If ever breeders got to work on human beings as they had on dogs there was no limit to the strains they could produce. Perry allowed his mind to dwell upon a breed of Hillingdons, human boxers, with reinforced floors, beds and staircases in their monster houses. He himself came into the fox terrier class.

'If this is all you've got to go on I think you've been frightening them unnecessarily.'

'Me frightening them!' Hillingdon was furious. 'Dammit, if it weren't for me they'd be hysterical.'

'I'm sorry they're not coming to the party.'

Hillingdon wagged a finger as large as a bridge-roll.

'I'm beginning to think I'm a fool to subsidize your school in the way I do. I'm beginning not to trust any of these foreigners. Of course, I know the rates are lower if the place is registered as a school. But there can be too much of a good thing. All these Asiatics learning English! It's beginning to make me uneasy, somehow.'

Hillingdon knew that at heart he was a very modest, almost a humble man and he wanted to say to the two women: 'I've been an instrument. I'm really very honoured to be of some use. After Mrs Yehia and I met it seemed natural to try and be helpful, so I telephoned. There was nothing remarkable about it.' The sight of Elaine in Mrs Blainey's sitting-room gave Hillingdon a sense of power; but for him she would not have been there. 'Please say no more about it.'

He was never given much of an opening for remarks of this kind. Mrs Blainey had forgiven him for his incomprehensible refusal to help Tim's career along; but it was a forgiveness she made plain not in words or smiles but in the granting of a few privileges; carrying coke up from the cellar, cleaning a drain, arranging with a builder to have a panel of glass bricks put into the wall of a dark passage, disputing the telephone account with the Postmaster General — Mrs Blainey criticized Hillingdon for his failure to speak to the Minister himself — taking shoes to be repaired and, the biggest prize of the lot, lugging a surprisingly heavy divan out of the box-room. Mrs Blainey helped him with the divan. He crawled along the passage on his hands and knees balancing the divan on his back and Mrs Blainey held it steady.

'Before taking it out of the box-room you ought to have run over the upholstery with the Hoover, Mr Hillingdon.' She gave the divan a slap. 'I never thought you'd have to get on the floor like that, dirtying your suit, or I'd never have asked you. Elaine probably won't use it, anyway. It's just that I thought of it lying there, doing nothing. If you want a rest you can lie flat and let the legs take the weight for a bit.'

Hillingdon thought it surprising that Mrs Blainey had been able to manage for so long without a man about the house. The problems were not only physical, lugging coke about and the like, but intellectual; how could women possibly grapple with such difficulties as noisy neighbours and rating appeals? One woman alone might not fare too badly, but women had a cumulatively incapacitating effect upon one another; now that there were not two — Mrs Blainey and Alice — in the house together, but three, Hillingdon could see perfectly well that they stood in need of all the advice he could give them and he did not shirk — no, he joyfully welcomed — the responsibility. He saw all the dangers. By examining Alice very carefully he was able to establish that the dark-faced man she had seen looking through the doorway was no Indian hawker. In spite of Alice's doubts he was able to prove that the fellow she had seen the next day was one and the same. He was well-dressed, wasn't he, and he wore no earrings or turban? It was Hillingdon who recommended they cut the Helvetia party.

Elaine looked surprised.

'There's no need to carry caution to extremes,' said Hillingdon, 'but I'd leave the house as little as possible, if I were you, for the next few days — that is, until you've seen how things turn out.'

'The Egyptians aren't interested in *me*.'

'No knowing what piece of valuable information you might have.'

'Not me, I haven't. These past few years I've seen enough of Egyptians to know they're not the sort of people to try and kidnap me in Heath Street. Besides, Mahmoud wouldn't let them.'

'You don't imagine he'd have much say in the matter.'

'No, it's nonsense. I don't believe that man Alice saw was an Egyptian. The situation is bad enough without allowing our imaginations to run away. Mahmoud can't come out because there's something frightfully secret going on. Either there's going to be a war, in which case he goes back to Egypt and I stay here; or there's not going to be a war and we shall go on living as we did before. That is, if they let Mahmoud stay here.'

'Elaine, darling,' said Mrs Blainey, not looking up from the letter she was writing. 'Would you be prepared to go and live in Egypt with Mahmoud? I mean, if there's no war.'

'If he has to leave London I don't see why he can't be transferred to somewhere in Europe.'

'No, I'm sorry. I think it's very wrong of you and it's terribly unfair to Mahmoud.' Mrs Blainey consulted her dictionary and went on writing. 'What you've got against Egypt I really can't understand — I mean, apart from the people. When Teddy was alive we had the most marvellous February at the Winter Palace in Luxor. It was absolute heaven.'

'I like it better in England, that's all.'

'Shouldn't think you feel like going to parties.' Mrs Blainey blotted her letter and sighed. 'Well, that's your letter finished and done with, Mabel Strong, and why you don't poison that husband of yours I can't imagine.'

'No, I don't feel like parties.'

'Then we'd better take Mr Hillingdon's advice, the both of us, and stay indoors. Personally I think there's more in what he says than you grant. I expect you've had a lot of experience of foreigners, haven't you, Mr Hillingdon?'

He thought of the Asiatic and African students who would shortly be coming back to Helvetia for the new term, and said yes, he supposed he did know a lot about foreigners but it was not because of *that* he was warning them to be careful. He had a feeling. It would be too much to say he was psychic; he was not at all gifted that way, at least not *very* gifted. Danger signals had gone up, that's all, and he had seen them.

'Your husband's asking for you on the telephone.' Alice's head appeared round the door and Elaine put her hand to her throat. 'I expect you'll want to take it in here, though if you want none of these others to hear I can take the hall telephone and plug it in your bedroom.'

'These others will go out and leave you to it.' Mrs Blainey picked up her cigarette case in token of her readiness to go.

'No, please stay, there's no need. Both of you.' She picked up the telephone and waited for Alice to switch the call through. 'Hallo, darling. I was expecting you.'

Hillingdon knew he was being rude, but as Elaine spoke to her husband on the telephone he could not take his eyes off her. She was actually speaking to someone inside the Egyptian Embassy! No doubt Yehia himself was a good chap (this nice girl would not have married him otherwise) but out of what atmospheric malevolence was he speaking! Perhaps Muawiya was in the next room! Hillingdon watched the colour gathering under Elaine's eyes. He saw the nostrils quivering – oh, it was barely perceptible, but he was not going to miss a flicker of an eyelash! The tip of the tongue appeared, then fine white teeth pressed on the lower lip. Why on earth didn't she say anything?

'You can always tell when anyone's tapping the line,' Mrs Blainey hissed in his ear, 'by the acoustic. I was reading about it in this spy book.'

'Where are you all eating?' Elaine began to pour out questions about her husband's living conditions. She ended up: 'Don't you think you're all behaving like a lot of children? Oh, I know you're not supposed to say anything of any consequence, but I might tell you I've just had about enough of it!'

And she would have dropped the receiver on to its cradle but Mrs Blainey sprang to her side and took it from her.

'Now listen to me, Mahmoud. You know who this is. Elaine is quite all right with me here and Mr Hillingdon is befriending us. There's somebody on the line listening to our conversation, isn't there? I can hear my own voice echoing, and this spy book I've been reading says that means my voice is being recorded. Elaine is quite all right, my dear, and that's all I wanted to say to you. It's my birthday next Thursday week and if you're not here for that I'll never forgive you.'

'Why did you mention my name?' As soon as she replaced the receiver Hillingdon was on his feet. 'That was most unwise.'

'In what way?'

'I'm not prepared to say in what exactly, but it was unwise.'

Mrs Blainey looked surprised by the vigorous way he had spoken, and when he saw, further, that she was a little pink about the face too there was no denying the quiet thrill he experienced.

'I'm sorry,' she said, and the thrill coursed in his belly.

'Well, you couldn't be expected to see all the implications of mentioning my name.' He sighed at the strain of reassuring her. 'Please don't give it another thought.'

Any time not spent in Mrs Blainey's house — or in the neighbourhood with an eye open for Egyptian kidnappers — seemed to Hillingdon a waste and he used up a lot of nervous energy convincing himself that the danger was as great as he pretended and that he was not calling too often. He stayed to supper on Wednesday and found himself helping Alice to wash up afterwards; he had no objection to washing up, mind, though he was naturally disappointed that it prevented him from sitting down with Mrs Blainey and Elaine to drink a cup of coffee; Alice said he would have to dry the dishes the moment they came out of the hot water, if he really wanted to make himself useful, and he could drink his coffee before cleaning the silver.

Thursday morning he happened to be passing (he had given no promise to call) when he saw Mrs Blainey come into the street with a shopping-basket on wheels. She immediately asked him if he would push it for her, and for a very happy half an hour they went round the shops together. Flowers, a box of crystallized ginger, a special wooden nutcracker which instead of breaking nuts *screwed* them into fragments (Mrs Blainey said it was much superior to the usual sort), Seccotine, ant-destroying powder, Japanese paper flowers for dropping into water, a miniature cactus, an eighteenth-century silver wine label, *Buddenbrooks* in a cheap paper-back — Hillingdon could see perfectly well that this was not real shopping; she was playing at shopping and he was charmed by it. She made him feel gay.

'I don't even know what to call you?'

'Call me, Mr Hillingdon? What should you call me?'

'My friends call me Napier,' he lied.

'*What* an unusual name!' she remarked, intent on bundles of asparagus.

'Well —' He breathed out enormously. 'You might like Archie better. That's my second name, though I don't use it much. Call me Archie, if you think it's better.'

'It doesn't suit you.'

'Then what does suit me?'

She looked him over. 'Roland.'

'Call me Roland if you like. What made you pick on Roland?'

'Can't think. Oh, but Roland has always seemed the name of a big man to me. But I really can't give you a special name like that and call you by it.'

'Yes, you can. I should be delighted.'

'I've remembered now. There was a man called Roland somebody who played full-back for Blackheath when Teddy used to take me to football matches. Roland *what*? He had big white knees like a woman, and Teddy, who knew all these players, said he was an accountant. Fancy remembering those knees!'

'Do please call me Roland.'

'No, it makes me think of white knees now. We'd better go home. Alice always brings out the coffee at eleven and she'll be furious if I'm late. Well, Mr Hillingdon, it's been nice to have you come shopping with me —'

'But I can't let you push this basket back to the house.'

'Don't tip it into the gutter then. What a man! Anybody'd think you'd never done a hand's turn at anything practical all your life.'

Hillingdon was transferring the contents of the basket to the kitchen table when Mrs Blainey called through from the sitting-room. 'Oh, I knew there was something I had to tell you. Elaine and I have decided to go to that party after all.'

He at once made for the door, intent on persuading her to change her mind, but Alice called him back, saying that if he was going that way he could carry the coffee tray. When Hillingdon entered Mrs Blainey's presence he was carrying silver tray, the coffee pot, cups, sugar bowl and cream jug, all tinkling crazily, and Elaine sprang to her feet in alarm.

'Put it down there.' Mrs Blainey, still wearing a hat, was busily knitting, and she broke off to point with her needle. 'It's very nice of this Mr Perry to invite us. He doesn't know us, and one should always be careful to increase one's circle of friends. At my time of life I can't afford to miss an opportunity to make a friend. D'you know, Elaine, dear — ' and she prodded her gently with a needle — 'when I was young we had such an appetite for life. We prided ourselves on never refusing a challenge or a relationship, and in a way I've always tried to live up to it.'

'But my advice — ' Hillingdon was shaking his head.

'Tim's going. He rang up and said he was going. He said it was all nonsense for us not to go. I said you'd warned us but he said it was all nonsense; and I'm bound to say, now I reflect on it, that I agree with him. Don't you, Elaine? Besides, a party would cheer us all up.'

'I just feel it in my bones you shouldn't go, Mrs Yehia.'

'Tim said he'd pick us up about six. Isn't it extraordinary what tricks memory plays? There I was talking to Mr Hillingdon about names and who should I think of but a footballer with white knees I saw thirty years ago, and I hadn't thought of him since.' Mrs Blainey drank her coffee. 'Teddy just loved watching football in those days and of course it bored me, but then I loved *him*. All I can remember is that footballer with white knees called Roland somebody. But Roland *who?*'

Just before six Perry began to feel nervous about the party and took a stiff whisky. It was a bad preliminary to champagne, he knew, but to be candid he did not really like champagne; even the best made him feel bilious and he did not suppose that the two cases they had sent up from the off-licence would be anything remarkable. He did not believe this talk of the evils of mixing grape with grain; it never seemed to make him any drunker. From the point of view of economy, though, it was silly to begin the evening with five bob's worth of whisky when in half an hour's time there'd be all that fizz. He needed a preliminary drink, though. The trouble with champagne — quite apart from its being filthy stuff to drink, so indigestible — was that you couldn't just open a bottle and take a nip. That was the beauty of whisky. Whisky was more intoxicating, too. He went to have a word with Christopher who, for that evening, was in the charge of one of Ilse's friends. The boy said he wanted a rope ladder for his birthday so that he could climb out of his window in the middle of the night and go into the park when no one was there. Perry promised him a rope ladder, kissed him good night and went to the bedroom where Mary was still in her petticoat, rubbing white cream on her face.

Perry was wondering whether it was too late to cancel the party.

'If anything untoward happens it won't be my fault.'

'What on earth do you mean?' Mary stopped rubbing and looked at him.

'Well, I mean there's a limit to what one can do to ensure the success of a party.'

'This isn't a party.' Mary began dragging a pad of cotton wool over her face. 'This is just people coming in to drink.'

'You don't want to play games, do you?'

'Provided they're the right games, I don't see why not. People never know what to talk about, anyway. Go and see what Ilse's up to with the food. This is a fine time to be discussing the principles of parties. The Stringers said they might bring a friend, and was it all right.'

'I've done my best,' said Perry. 'I'm not responsible if anything goes wrong, that's all.'

He looked in on Ilse, ate a smoked salmon sandwich, and went out to buy an evening paper. The Suez Canal pilots were demanding repatriation and Nasser was asking for volunteers. There was no mention of the 'prisoner in the Embassy' as some of the papers had taken to calling Muawiya. He had dropped from the headlines. Well, that was a silence soon to be broken, and Perry stood with his back against the gatepost, allowing the warm evening sun to play upon his closed eyes, wondering how Muawiya's capture would involve the Helvetia School of English. If he was accused Perry decided that he would say yes, he certainly knew that Muawiya intended to put in an appearance, that the party was in fact Muawiya's. Perry thought that if the confesson made him an accessory to crime, or whatever the legal expression was, he could always claim it was a stunt to publicize Helvetia and so put down the cost of the party as a legitimate expense against income tax. Money again! Even at the most serious moments his thoughts turned to money. Had he become hopelessly commercial?

Standing as he was, sheltered by laurels and wattle fencing which trapped the heat of the afternoon, some of his anxiety about the party began to fade. It was too warm for worry. He kept his eyes firmly closed. The lids were brilliant, cherry-coloured.

The sun made them into glowing and consoling fires; and he thought, apropos of nothing at all, of Muawiya — oh, years and years ago, when he was still a student and before even Mary came out to Egypt — buying tickets at Cairo Station for both of them to go to Tanta. They were going to stay with Muawiya's married brother who was a kind of legal clerk in the police force. Perry could not remember the brother's name but it was understood they were actually going to sleep in his house. Perry remembered the argument about who should pay for the tickets; Muawiya said that Egyptian courtesy did not permit Professor Perry, who was the guest, to pay for his own fare. He remembered the conversation on the train. They talked of marriage. Why didn't Mrs Perry come out to Egypt now that the war was over? Muawiya asked. It was shameful for a man and his wife to be separated. He himself was thinking of marrying his sister-in-law's sister but she was only fourteen and they would wait until he graduated. Did Muawiya marry, Perry wondered? Extraordinary to think of a Mrs Khaslat, with children!

He remembered that Tanta visit in some detail. By the time they arrived it was dark. Instead of going straight to Muawiya's brother they walked rather vacantly around the streets until Muawiya suggested they went into a restaurant and had something to eat. Perry was so hungry he had not questioned this behaviour; but when they had eaten Muawiya picked up both their suitcases and said the hour was now too late for them to disturb his brother's family; much better to stay at an hotel and call in the morning.

That hotel! The latrines were awash, the beds were hung with mosquito netting which gave off a choking powder to the touch, bugs swarmed out of the cracked walls as soon as the light was extinguished, and arguments went on below the window all night. Perry did not really mind. He spent most of the night sitting in a chair (it was less infested than the bed) thinking from time to time of Muawiya's words to the hotel clerk as they came into the hall: 'I have booked two rooms.' He spoke in Arabic, assuming, no doubt, that Perry's ignorance of the language was complete. But Perry knew enough to realize there had never been any intention of sleeping in the house of Muawiya's brother, and when they went there the following morning he thought he understood why. He was not allowed to meet Muawiya's sister-in-law. She prepared the breakfast, but Perry and Muawiya did not enter the room until the dishes had been set out. She could be heard in the kitchen, clattering her pans and talking to some other woman, a servant probably. Muawiya's brother, a clean-shaved intelligent man of about thirty, made no reference to his wife, and they talked noisily of the amount of crime in the Egyptian countryside, drowning the female voices and the chink of crockery.

Not a satisfactory visit! After breakfast they had sat in a café overlooking the main square, talking a lot of rubbish about Muawiya's future career; in those days he wanted to be an actor. He gave a comical imitation of a Scots soldier haggling with a shopkeeper. Idlers from all over Tanta (so it seemed) crowded round the door of the café to see Muawiya perform. His real gifts lay in tragedy, he said. He declaimed 'To be or not to be' in Arabic, and then he, his brother and Perry bought bread, boiled eggs and dates, hired an open carriage pulled by two skeletal horses and drove through the flat delta countryside, eating until they were somnolent. When the heat was greatest and the horses were kicking up so much white dust it became difficult to breathe there was a sharp crack and a lurch. The driver climbed down from his seat of green fodder. Muawiya climbed out too, and together they went to the back of the arabiyeh. One of the wheels was damaged, he explained, and when Perry went round to investigate he saw that the hub had torn away from the spokes and the wheel had become wedged against the side of the carriage. There was a long walk to the station, by the side of a brown canal. He travelled to Cairo alone becuase Muawiya had, he explained, some business to do. Not a memorable visit and Perry had scarcely given it a thought until now. What a clot he had been to see no more in the plan to put him up at an hotel than the orthodox Moslem passion for keeping their women invisible!

He saw now that it was more properly an illustration of the Moslem passion for turning personal issues into the impersonal. If Muawiya had said: 'My brother will be delighted to welcome you to Tanta but you can't stay in his house because it is small and you would see his wife. You will have to stay at an hotel.' If Muawiya had said that, the failure to provide bed and board under his own roof could be squarely charged against the brother and his old-fashioned ideas. This (Perry could imagine Muawiya reasoning) may cause resentment against the brother. How much better to go to Tanta on the assumption the brother is an open-hearted, westernized sort of chap, with an emancipated wife, if you like, and then let circumstances — circumstances over which no one can be supposed to have control — prevent the embarrassment of having an Englishman in the house. It would be too late to rouse the brother and his family. A mistake had been made in the trains. They ought to have arrived hours ago but because of his, Muawiya's fault (Perry could remember more and more) they had taken this later train, and look! it was already night. There was no alternative. Fate had decided they must put up for the night at an hotel.

Perry wished that Mr Dulles could have known Muawiya and been invited to Tanta by him. Perhaps he would not then have refused so abruptly to pay for the High Dam. The gesture was too personal. Lack of money should have been pleaded. Robbers at Fort Knox. A succession of financial emissaries struck down by plague. Drought in Texas. The imminence of the International Geophysical Year. Anything but the blunt refusal, person to person. But all this was in the realm of international politics and Perry was more interested in the immediate question of Muawiya's party. With Tanta in mind he ought, perhaps, to be preparing to protect Muawiya against the shock of any real nastiness by some dodge that would show it to be nobody's fault; as Grimbley telephoned for the police Perry wanted Muawiya to think of him as impersonal necessity. Upon such foundations would future Anglo-Egyptian relations be built.

He opened his eyes to find Miss Gunter looking at him. He was so surprised that he almost blurted out 'Good God! I didn't invite you, did I?' when he remembered, yes, he certainly had invited her, just to annoy Grimbley, and at the thought of his former gaiety some of Perry's spring came back to him. He lifted himself off the gatepost and smiled into those twinkling lenses. Hell! They were having a party, weren't they, a champagne party? and he began to speak to Miss Gunter with a great deal of liveliness, saying that Waldo was certain to be somewhere around, though he privately doubted whether Waldo would ever come to think of *her* as impersonal necessity.

'As what?' said Miss Gunter, twitching her buttocks so that the hem of her cotton dress swirled.

'I was thinking of something different,' Perry explained, 'and the words rather slipped out.'

'I know perfectly well I'm not welcome.'

'Not welcome?'

'I'm only here to make up a number. You don't really want me because of myself.'

Perry wondered what she looked like without her glasses. One twitch and they would be off. He subdued the temptation without too much difficulty and thought but for these large businesswoman's glasses she looked sexy. It had never struck him before. She had this neat little waist and bold bosom. Perhaps he noticed because for the first time in their acquaintanceship she was being rude. Well, not rude. Cheeky!

'I wouldn't have invited you if I didn't want you to come, I can assure you of that.'

'I'm not welcome. But I don't care. I'm here. I just wanted you to know I hadn't been taken in.'

Miss Gunter had never been as forthright as this while she had been at Helvetia. What was the secretarial college at Golders Green doing to her? Perry decided that he preferred Miss Gunter this way. He could see now that she was really quite angry with him. Her cheeks were pink — such smooth, lovely skin, too, he noticed — and her lips were set. He wanted to tease her and see whether she became even angrier.

'Let's go into the house and have a drink. Perhaps you'll feel better then.'

'Certainly I'll have a drink. I mean to enjoy myself.'

'I don't know why you should think you're not welcome.'

They walked to the front door, invisible rapiers flickering between them.

'As for drink,' she said, 'judging by appearances I'd say you'd started already.'

Miss Gunter needed little steering. She turned sharp right into the drawing-room and made for the buffet which had been set up under the window at the far end. Following at her heels, Perry saw a man in a light-coloured suit replace a bottle on the table and assumed he must be the waiter sent up from the pub.

It had been Mary's idea to hire a waiter. She said it would place too great a strain upon her, when drinking, to make sure that others were drinking too. But this waiter was dressed so oddly.

'This is all excellent, sir.' He turned towards them smiling. 'No prawns? Perhaps they are out of season. This champagne is excellent, sir, excellent. How many guests are coming? I was afraid I should be late.' He bowed towards Miss Gunter. 'It is very kind of you to come to my party.'

Perry murmured the introductions.

'I'm sorry I didn't catch the name,' said Miss Gunter.

'Muawiya Khaslat, miss.'

'How on earth did you get into the house?' Perry was at last getting him into focus. Muawiya was wearing a grey suit of peculiar brightness; it was as though metallic silver thread had been spun into the material. A stage conjuror might, conceivably, have worn such a suit. Perry could imagine him, saw in hand, his suit flashing like a semaphore, waiting to cut a woman in half. For private wear it was too distinctive, particularly in association with a bow tie, striped red and white, and yellowish suede shoes mounted on thick crepe soles. Muawiya's crisply curled hair shone with oil. He smiled around all his teeth.

'Well, you see I did not wish to attract attention, so I climbed over the wall.'

'Where?'

'People might see me coming through the gate, so I climbed over the wall. Oh, in the corner of your front garden. There are a lot of bushes. Nobody saw me, not even the taxi-driver. I waited until he had gone.'

'But I don't understand.' Miss Gunter had examined him carefully. 'Why shouldn't people see you coming through the gate?'

'You don't know?'

'Why should I?'

The smile slipped from Muawiya's face and he turned to Perry. 'Well, you see,' said Perry, 'Mr Khaslat is here incognito, so to speak —'

'Good heavens! You don't mean he's the Egyptian the police are looking for?'

'Exactly so,' said Muawiya, happy once more, and at that moment the waiter — the real waiter this time — a little man in tails came trotting into the room, followed by Mary who looked very lovely (Perry thought) in her white summery dress and old gold silk scarf draped over her shoulders. Discreetly, the waiter opened a bottle in a corner and began filling glasses.

'Mrs Perry,' said Muawiya, snatching one up as though to propose a toast. 'You are my guest! It is wonderful for me! Let us all drink to our happiness.

'Fancy seeing you!' She sounded much less surprised than Perry had expected. He even wondered whether she realized who she was speaking to.

'I don't understand.' Miss Gunter had taken her glass of champagne at a single draught. She was speaking to Mary. 'If this is the man all that fuss is about what is he doing here?'

'He's the most frightful character, Ellie —' Ellie was Miss Gunter — 'and I don't wonder at him turning up anywhere.' Mary spoke so loudly that Muawiya could not fail to hear and he turned with a look of exaggerated pain on his face.

'It's isn't polite to say things like that about your host.'

Perry had overlooked the strength of Mary's dislike for Muawiya and he would have liked to stand back and see how the quarrel developed. But that would never do. Mary was bound to make a fool of herself. She was hopeless at quarrelling. She could never think quickly enough and as a result stammered, went red and produced insults that were so obviously off-target, her opponent could greet them with a smile. It was not like her to be rude, even to Muawiya, and Perry ascribed her behaviour to shock. Coming on the fellow suddenly had unsettled her. Prepared for one kind of party, she saw in the blink of an eye that she had to put up with another. Come to that, Perry had been given something of a shock himself. How had Muawiya managed to enter the house without being seen? It was uncanny.

'I'm afraid my wife has never forgiven you for what happened at Sakkara.'

'At Sakkara?' Muawiya looked at Mary incredulously.

Mary cut in. 'What did you mean by saying you were my host?'

'This is my party, Mrs Perry. You see, I had promised you all a party and then found that in the Embassy they would not let me give it. So I telephoned Professor Perry —'

'Edgar, this really is too bad.'

The expression on Mary's face gave Perry his first hint that the party would go off the rails. Why did women lose their sense of humour so young?

'I seem to do nothing but accept hospitality in some form or other from this Muawiya of yours. We go for a picnic in the desert and he pops up with refreshment there. He tries to murder you into the bargain, but we'll say no more of that. We jump on a train in order to get out of his country and, save us, there he is again with a hamper. You'd think we'd be safe in our own house. But no! Champagne and smoked salmon —'

'Forgive me, I must correct this story about Sakkara.' Muawiya had looked increasingly shocked as Mary's speech continued. 'I did not try to murder Professor Perry. I saved his life. But look, Mrs Perry.' Muawiya took the dish out of the waiter's hands. 'Do please have one of these delicious asparagus rolls. For God's sake, let us be friends!'

He thrust the plate at her so fiercely, raising his voice, that

Mary was taken aback. She looked from the asparagus rolls to Muawiya's face and back again.

'You are a fanatic and a would-be murderer,' she said, 'and I don't know why somebody doesn't telephone the police to say you're here.'

She picked up a sandwich and a glass of champagne. Catching sight of Grimbley as he entered the room she walked towards him, crying excitedly: 'I just want you to look who's here! Can you imagine it, and it's all Edgar's fault too!'

Waldo was wearing his tropical suit. He brought it out once or twice every summer just *after* the hot days usually because of the time taken to pluck up courage. It was cut in the style of 1910, out of straw-coloured linen — six brown buttons up the front and a neck scarcely large enough to reveal the full splendour of a loosely knotted Liberty kerchief. It always looked sadly crumpled; this had the odd effect of accentuating all the lines and cracks on Waldo's worn face. He looked, in fact, as though he had been hastily strapped down in a large basket somewhere south of Khartoum and released in the hall. He even gave off a tropical smell, something like scorched blotting-paper, and he moved stiffly, showing a great deal of hairy wrist.

He looked past Mary and saw Muawiya in his shining suit.

'God!' he said. 'An Egyptian!'

'Professor Grimbley, sir, how are you? You are my guest, sir. Let me bring you champagne. It is five years since I see you!'

'Edgar's been behaving like a lunatic as usual.'

Judging by his insouciance the waiter had been to a lot of parties like this in Hampstead Garden Suburb, because he stood in front of Grimbley, food on one tray, champagne on the other, with his lids half way down his eyes. Grimbley accepted a glass and drank deeply. He sucked his lips and looked about him.

'Where's your huband, my dear? Perry, there you are! For

God's sake what's this fellow doing here? I suppose you realize this is very tricky.'

'I don't see why it should be.'

'Perhaps something's happened I don't know about. Have the police withdrawn the charges?'

'Waldo, I know your attitude towards Egyptians —'

'This isn't a question of attitudes. It's a question of law. Dammit, if a policeman were to walk in this minute he could arrest this chap, cart him off, and I wouldn't wonder he could cart you off too. In the present state of Anglo-Egyptian relations I'm not sure that a most serious charge couldn't be made. What's he mean, anyway, saying I'm his guest?'

'I'm paying for all this food and drink,' said Muawiya, sobered by Waldo's outburst.

'His guest! Well, it takes more than the ability to pay for food and drink to make a host. You've got to know how to behave, for one thing, Khaslat.' He took a couple of egg sandwiches and stuffed them into his mouth. 'It passes my comprehension how a fellow like you becomes the guest of the British Council. You took a damn poor degree as I remember it.'

'I have always been a friend of the English people and of English culture.' Muawiya's face brightened when he saw how Grimbley was knocking into the champagne. 'My degree was not of the best, perhaps. But I am not a scholar. I am too imaginative. If Professor Perry had stayed in Egypt I should have taken a better degree. He understood my temperament. It was a great blow to me when he left. He was driven from the country by bureaucrats.'

'Rubbish! He was driven from the country by you, principally, trying to kill him and then funking it, as I understand the story, at the last moment. That's why Professor Perry left the country and well you know it. If he'd stayed it would have been quite impossible to hush the story up and you'd have been jailed for ten years. Professor Perry sacrificed himself for your welfare.'

'Well, well,' said Perry. 'Any more champagne for anyone? Miss Gunter, I can see your glass is empty. Hallo, here are some more guests. Let's have another window open, shall we? It's getting a bit stuffy in here. Mary, you're not eating anything.'

'Have some of this delicious smoked salmon,' said Muawiya. 'It is most excellent, I can assure you.'

As Waldo had been speaking there was the sound of a car drawing up on the gravel outside. Shoes clattered in the hall and Ilse, putting in her first appearance of the evening, walked into the drawing-room announcing the guests in the manner that Mary had carefully coached her.

'Mrs Blainey, Mr Blainey, Mrs Ye ... Ye — '

'Yehia,' said Elaine.

'Oh, and it's you, is it?' said Ilse to Napier Hillingdon.

'Welcome, welcome, all of you!' Muawiya danced forward. 'I know I'm in disgrace, but welcome. You must forgive me, Mrs Blainey. And Mr Hillingdon! I expose my neck to your knife.'

'Take no notice of him,' Waldo was shouting. 'It's the most impertinent thing you could ever imagine.'

The calmest person in the room (apart from the waiter) was now Mrs Blainey, who advanced with regal poise, a gentle smile on her face, to allow Muawiya to seize her hand and press it to his forehead. She was wearing long white gloves and a wide-brimmed straw hat and was obviously resolute for gaiety.

'This *is* a surprise,' she said to Muawiya. 'What a naughty boy you've been. Your name's been in all the papers, I suppose you know that?'

'It is so wonderful that you are my guest. And you, Mrs Yehia. I could not let your husband know about the party. He does not know where I am. He would be very angry. Isn't everything crazy? The Egyptian Embassy is not supposed to know where I am. And now that they really *don't* know where I am they would be so angry.'

If there had been an instrument in the room, other than Perry, for measuring astonishment it would have registered a marked rise with the entry of the Blainey party. Pressure had, in fact, been rising for some time. As Miss Gunter and Mary increasingly realized the implications of Muawiya's presence, as Waldo Grimbley added his powerful shot of amazement, so the emotion soared. Quite a lot of champagne had been drunk too. With the entry of Hillingdon the tension reached such a pitch Perry felt that if anyone brushed against him he would crackle like a cat in a thunderstorm.

Hillingdon was staring at Muawiya and muttering to himself, it might have been in incredulity, it might have been, as a precaution, a spell. He wiped his face and turned to Mrs Blainey.

'You see, Margaret?' he said.

'See what?'

'I advised you not to come.'

'If I'd missed Mr Khaslat's party I should never have forgiven myself.'

Hillingdon stepped between her and Muawiya. 'No, I can't allow you to speak to him. He's — oh, he's not at all the sort of person you want to know. Let me take you home.'

Mrs Blainey had to move back in order to look up into Hillingdon's flushed face. 'But you mustn't talk to me like that!'

'This is not a time for politenesses. I beg you to let me take you home.'

'Certainly not. Don't get so excited. No, Tim, shut up.' Her son had begun to speak to Hillingdon but she cut him short. 'I can manage perfectly well, thank you. What on earth do you mean,' she said to Hillingdon, 'he's not the sort of person I want to know? How do you know the sort of person I want to know?'

'Forgive me — '

'Just because he happened to smash your old car up!'

'It isn't that at all. He's — oh, I can't possibly explain here with everybody listening. At least let's go out of this room.'

'Thank you.' Mrs Blainey took the glass of champagne from the tray on which Muawiya himself had proferred it, and drank it steadily, smoothly, as though it were milk, staring at Hillingdon all the time with a sobriety that, under normal circumstances, would have checked him like a halter. He was so shaken to discover himself in such proximity to Muawiya that he put out a hand and it seemed, momentarily, as though he was going to take Mrs Blainey's glass from her. He did not see how angry he was making her.

'Please, Mr Hillingdon.' Muawiya pushed the tray towards him and Hillingdon looked down, like a guest of the Borgias, his eyes wide with speculation at the little buttered rolls, the pink wisps of salmon, the puffs of cottage cheese.

'No, no.'

'Don't you understand that you are my chief guest — '

'For God's sake — '

'I have done you a great injury.'

'I must get out of this room.' The temperature was not really very high but Hillingdon's face was shining with sweat. He moved towards the door, loosening his tie; but then, when he was eight or nine feet from Muawiya, he returned. 'In my own house! This is my house. I own it. You are giving a party in *my* house. It is like being possessed. How can you stand there, Margaret, drinking his champagne in my house? Can't you see there's more in this than meets the eye? How did he get here? What does he want? You see, it's not natural.'

Muawiya gave the tray back to the waiter who took not the slightest notice of the row that was going on, and circulated decorously among the guests; but for Hillingdon, they were all drinking.

'Strictly speaking,' said Perry, 'you're only the landlord, so I don't see why you should raise this point about the party being in your house. It isn't as though we don't pay the rent.'

'I shall telephone the police.'

Surprisingly, it was Waldo Grimbley who stopped him. He popped between Hillingdon and the door, and said: 'This is a situation in which you've got to be clever.'

'Let me pass!'

'It's very tricky.'

'He's wanted by the police, isn't he?'

'Yes and no.'

'What d'you mean, yes and no?'

Grimbley dropped his voice and steered Hillingdon into the corner that was farthest away from the rest of the party. When Grimbley dropped his voice its volume was the same as that of anybody else's. He knew that Muawiya, Perry, Mrs Blainey — the lot — were listening, but he did not care.

'I'm just as horrified as you are by this chap turning up like this. But he's not a fool. There must be some reason. Perhaps he *wants* us to call the police.'

Grimbley persuaded Hillingdon to sit down, saying he looked flustered and needed a cool drink. This time when the waiter came up with the champagne Hillingdon took a glass and as he listened to Grimbley drank thirstily. Grimbley was a fellow whose judgment he had always respected. A very shrewd, soldierly man of the world.

'I don't know that we can *afford* to have him arrested and jailed at a time like this,' Grimbley was saying. 'He might get a couple of years. Wonderful propaganda for Nasser. Everybody in Asia and Africa would believe it was a frame-up. Well, I think we must beat these chaps at their own game.'

'The clue to my character,' Muawiya was saying to Elaine, 'is that I am so lazy.'

'It's probably the clue to mine too.'

'No, but I am serious. You think I am always gay, like I am this evening, giving parties, joking. Not so. I am a sad person really. You should ask Professor Perry. He knows me better than anyone else. We have known each other intimately for fouteen years. He would tell you that although I appear very gay I am tragic. When I intended to be an actor it was always the tragic parts that attracted me. Like Hamlet, or like Falstaff. Don't you think Falstaff is a very tragic character? Nobody understood him. I think that is the worst thing, not to be understood.'

'Giving this party and actually coming to it, that doesn't seem to me the act of a lazy man.'

'D'you know why I know I am sad and lazy really, in spite of appearances; and in spite of my own feelings, sometimes? Yes, I am very active and laughing much of the time, but I know that my inner heart is sad because when I think of what would make me really happy I think of sleep and quietness.'

Muawiya had drawn Elaine into the window, behind the buffet. Like everyone else she had been amazed to find him at the party. How would it affect Mahmoud if he was taken by the police? If it was really true that Mahmoud would be angry to learn that Muawiya was at Helvetia then wasn't it her duty to see that he returned as quickly as possible to the Embassy? She could not collect her thoughts sufficiently to understand the implications of Muawiya's presence and just prayed, rather numbly, she was not going to be called upon to act in one way as Mahmoud's wife and in another as an Englishwoman. Surely Muawiya and his silly prank were too insignificant to present her with that kind of choice?

'I don't associate you with quietness, I must say,' she said.

'Yes.' Very seriously. 'My happiness is quietness and sleep. A hot night, for example, and a new moon. I am sleeping on my veranda in the country. Oh, the country in Egypt is so quiet. You lie there, hearing only your own heart. You are not really asleep, and you are not really awake. That is when I am happy.'

He thought for some moments. More guests had arrived, a couple in evening dress who apologized loudly and said it was only because they were 'going on'. For Muawiya they did not exist. He had switched suddenly from an ostentatious noisiness to brooding, holding the bowl of his champagne glass on his upturned hand, the stem trailing between his fingers.

'Or perhaps you can hear a pump going,' he said, 'miles away, perhaps, pop! pop! pop! like that, very gentle. You can hear nothing but this pump popping. You go to sleep. You wake up, and it's still popping.'

For the first time Elaine realized that it was possible to like Muawiya. She had been too upset to take much notice of him at Mrs Blaineys supper-party; and subsequently, by reading so much about him in the newspapers, she had formed the view that he had all the Egyptian qualities she particularly disliked: unreliability, too much gush, plain dishonesty. And his appearance this evening had confirmed what a perfect horror he was. That suit! That tie! Mahmoud said she was unredeemably English. Perhaps she was. And why not? Better, surely, than being unredeemably Egyptian like Muawiya? The very short time Elaine had spent in Egypt — it was at the time of Farouk's abdication — she had been repelled and frightened by the violence.

Muawiya was violent. She believed this story about his being involved in some attempt to assassinate Mr Perry. But the moment he began talking about quietness and happiness she forgot that he was an Egyptian and wondered what it would be like, really like, in the remote Egyptian countryside. Perhaps even she would sleep soundly at nights there.

The party ceremonial continued. Perry brought the couple in evening dress up to Muawiya and introduced them as Mr and Mrs Stringer. They apologized for their clothes, but they were clearly delighted to pretend they were living in a social whirl. They were so taken up with the impression they were making, he very stiff and creaking, she never looking at anything or anyone for more than two seconds at a time, that they never realized who their host was. Grimbley and Hillingdon sat in a corner, looking straight into each other's eyes, talking and drinking. Mrs Blainey was chatting with Mary.

Poor Tim, looking quite alarmed, had now worked himself sufficiently close to Muawiya for conversation.

'What has happened? Has everything been settled?' He could not believe that Muawiya was present without police permission.

'Ah!' Muawiya snapped out of his nostalgia and thrust forward a hand. 'Mr Blainey, why doesn't your British Council tell the police that I am innocent? Or, if I am not innocent, well — my crime is trivial. If you were the guest of the Egyptian Government this would be arranged.'

'No, no, I'm sorry — '

'If you committed a crime in Egypt our Government would naturally protect you.'

'The law — '

'The law is for man, not man for the law,' said Muawiya smartly, 'as you English know very well, or you wouldn't be denying President Nasser's right to nationalize the Suez

Canal. He has *every* legal right. He is the greatest man in the world.'

Perry examined young Tim thoughtfully: a fresh-faced, blue-eyed, official with a conscience. He was not at all surprised when Tim came up and suggested it would be much the best for everyone concerned if Mr Khaslat were smuggled back to the Egyptian Embassy where he belonged.

'I suppose it really is the case that he's here unofficially?'

'Absolutely. Both the police and the Egyptian Embassy would be furious.'

'We must get him back before he's missed.'

'Now look.' Perry gave Tim a half-full bottle of champagne and told him to help himself. 'I don't understand. I thought you were on the side of law and order.'

No mistake about it, young Tim was thoroughly upset. He spilt a lot of champagne, trying to pour it into his glass.

'Under ordinary circumstances, yes. But these are not ordinary circumstances. I mean, the fact that he's an *Egyptian* —'

'Coloured,' said Perry.

'Well, he's not European.

'Completely Afro-Asian.'

'You see what I'm getting at. Much better for everyone concerned if the police *didn't* pick him up.'

Perry considered this seriously. 'I don't see how you're going to get him back to the Embassy without attracting a lot of notice. He'd have to break in when it's dark. But even when he's there the problem remains. Do you know what I think you ought to do? I think you ought to smuggle him out of the country.'

'Me?'

Perry nodded. 'I don't know how you'd do it. Perhaps you could get him across to France in a fishing-boat. What are the rules about going to Northern Ireland? Once he was there he could slip over the frontier into the Free State. Or you could fly him out secretly. Do you think the British Council would run to a charter plane?'

'Good God, no! You're not serious?'

'I must say I think you've a special responsibility. You British Council chaps invited him here, he was in your personal care. Well, if I was in your shoes I wouldn't want him to be run in. Perhaps it's all gone too far now.'

'But *smuggling* him out of the country — '

'These are very serious times.' Perry had now drunk enough champagne not to care what it tasted like. 'I'm sure the Kremlin is watching the case very closely.'

He introduced Tim to Miss Gunter and went over to rescue Muawiya from old Stringer who was talking of the need for better school cricket pitches if the standard of the game was to be raised.

'Did you marry your brother's sister-in-law?' he asked, without worrying too much about the way he was interrupting Stringer in mid-sentence. 'I remember you once told me you were going to marry your brother's sister-in-law.'

'How wonderful that you remember such things, sir! It is most kind. No, I married my cousin, and that is really better from the family point of view. My father and my uncle are very happy. We have two little sons.'

'Two boys, eh?'

'One is four and the other is two. If only you would come back to Egypt, even if it is only for a visit. Is it not possible?'

'I don't think Englishmen are very welcome visitors in Egypt.'

'But I assure you, sir — '

'And where did you get this nice suit from?'

'Real Egyptian cloth, cut in Cairo. It is my own. Owing to the present misunderstanding the Embassy had to send round to my hotel and collect my bags. Oh, this police business! When I am arrested I know the judge will be vindictive.'

'Then why did you come to this house?'

'Sir, I do not understand.'

'You didn't think you'd manage to get back to the Embassy without being caught?'

Muawiya lowered his glass and looked around him. A natural pause in the general conversation happened to come at just this moment and Muawiya's movement attracted attention, even Hillingdon's, who with a hand on each knee was levering himself to his feet with Grimbley standing over him. Grimbley surveyed Hillingdon's efforts with the interest of one watching the working of an elaborate mechanical toy; and then he, too, looked at Muawiya, his jaw hardening.

'You can't mean that there is a trap?' Muawiya looked into as many faces as time and distance permitted.

'Why shouldn't there be?'

'But you are Professor Perry. You are English. You would not do it. You would not arrange this party for me — my party! — and then fix up a trap. We are brothers.'

'Hillingdon doesn't regard himself as your brother. Neither does Professor Grimbley, for that matter.'

'But they are my friends,' said Muawiya dramatically. 'They are my guests. They would not betray me.'

And rather to everybody's astonishment it immediately became apparent that Muawiya was right. Grimbley tried to bury his chin in his neck, a sure sign that he was embarrassed; and Hillingdon, under control once more, was peering down his nose at the brass buttons of his fancy waistcoat. They looked like two men discovered in a subterfuge. Enough of Grimbley's conversation had been heard to reveal he thought calling in the police a bad idea; his air of irritated rectitude and Hillingdon's quivering self-control could be due only to Muawiya's assumption that they were loyal friends and their knowing they had already decided to act in a way that might make them really seem friends. Of the two faces, Grimbley's was the more sensitive register. Irritated rectitude was replaced by an injured expression. I may behave like a magnanimous Englishman, he seemed to be saying, but if you really think I'm magnanimous, God help you! I'm really a snake!

'After the perfectly disgraceful way I was treated by the Egyptian Government,' he said, pointing his empty pipe like a pistol, 'I don't regard myself as having any particular loyalty to Egyptians. Quite the contrary in fact. I don't hold it against Nasser. It was before his time. But somebody' got to pay the compensation for wrongful dismissal, and it can only be Nasser.'

'I've always wanted the English teachers to be compensated.'

'Shut up! You want us to call the police, don't you? Yes, you do. You see yourself as a political martyr.'

Mrs Blainey spoke up. Her voice was gentle but firm. There is no doubt that she thought to introduce a note of reasonableness into the evening. The words were nodded out. 'Of course we won't betray you, Mr Khaslat. We are all English people here and we all know what the honourable thing is to do, particularly as you've given us such a nice party, and we are your guests and everything. Mind you, if you were a Russian it would be different. I shouldn't hesitate. But when you come to know more about the English you will know that they are specially considerate and courteous to the underprivileged and backward, like yourself, for example.'

She was opening her mouth to continue but Ilse appeared in the doorway, saying: 'There's another gentleman come, and he won't give his name.'

A square-shouldered figure in a grey suit marched into the room and looked about angrily.

'Mahmoud!' Elaine cried.

'This *is* a pleasant surprise, Captain Yehia,' said Mrs Blainey.

'I called at the house and Alice told me where you were.'

He looked at Muawiya and spoke to him sharply in Arabic.

'Your conduct is disgraceful. There is no alternative but for you to surrender to the authorities at once.'

Muawiya smiled broadly and told the waiter to take the captain some champagne. Although Yehia's appearance had been quite unexpected he had not permitted himself even the widening of his eyes. In answer to the various questions he explained that Captain Yehia had said he must go to the police.

'Oh no,' said Miss Gunter. 'I thought it had all been decided differently.'

'Excuse me,' said Stringer to the waiter, he being the nearest person, 'what *is* going on! I'd like to know?'

The waiter spoke for the only time that evening. 'As far as I can make out it's a matter of a foreign gentleman,' he said.

He placed the brimming glass on the tray and walked over to Yehia, who ignored him and stared at Muawiya.

'We leave immediately,' he said. 'I'll hand you over to the British police myself.'

Like everyone else in the room except Perry, Yehia had been quite unprepared for the sight of Muawiya but he had an advantage over the others in that he was already angry about something else. It would be too much to say he took Muawiya in his stride; but he was not at a loss; he knew immediately what to do. He moved his anger up a couple of gears.

His manner was so forbidding that for some moments no one spoke or moved. It would not have impinged on Yehia, the storm he was in, if any one of them had started to make a speech —

anyone, that is, except Muawiya. But for the two Egyptians the room was empty. In a way of speaking, the room itself did not exist. The house was not there. All London, all England, was irrelevant. Yehia was confronting his fellow-countryman on some primal plateau of feeling. The great wind rose, the clouds flew, and the disproportionately enormous storm burst silently into the room. Yehia stood there with his fists clenched, suffering it all. His eyes were large, horselike; his nostrils were distended. The way the head was forced back on the neck had a sculptural arrogance. Even Muawiya was impressed.

Whoever spoke first, no matter what was said, risked an almighty snub. Yehia would not have answered them. He would neither have answered nor moved, not even turned his head, if warned that a fiery pit had opened at his heels.

The waiter decided that this new gentleman wanted no champagne and retired to his side-table for potato crisps.

Yehia began to shout. 'You think you are an Egyptian, but I tell you you are not a true Egyptian because you do not understand what the needs of Egypt are and you do not behave like a patriot. You have no dignity. You are a fool. Don't you know how everyone despises Egyptians and spits on us because we are people without dignity? You break out and come here this evening! It is mad and irresponsible. If the police come now and find us both here, what will everyone say? They will say we were *caught*! I tell you we shall be a laughing-stock.'

Muawiya raised his shoulders and thrust his head forward with an exaggeratedly mild expression on his face, not unlike a tortoise. He opened his hands beseechingly. '*How* can it be undignified to be caught?'

'I tell you it is undignified to be caught. If there is to be an arrest at all the correct procedure is to give up oneself.'

'In any case I shall not be caught.' Muawiya looked for

Hillingdon and once he had spotted him called out: 'You are the guest of honour at my party, sir, and I must apologize for this interruption. It loses me a lot of dignity. Yes, that is right,' he said, turning back to Yehia, 'you lose me a lot of dignity by coming to my party and making a scene like this. How did you know I was giving a party? Who invited you? Why don't you have more consideration for my feelings in front of all these people?'

'Where's the telephone?' Yehia looked about him.

Champagne gives impetus to a party almost without it mattering what kind of interruption takes place, particularly if the waiter, through disdain or sheer professionalism, ignores everything but his job. The waiter at this party might even have been genuinely stupid. He had no difficulty in pressing more drink on the Stringers; for some time Mr Stringer had been asking Perry who the devil these foreigners were and Perry had frowned at him, putting a finger to his lips, quite enough to give the Stringers offence, and they drank fiercely with splayed out upper lips. Mary ate smoked salmon and even exchanged small talk with Mrs Blainey before Mrs Blainey smiled and turned her attention once more to the two Egyptians, her glass at her lips. Miss Gunter presented her back to the argument. She had penned Waldo in a corner and he looked out over her shoulder, like the mask of Tragedy.

'You talk of dignity,' Muawiya was saying to Yehia. 'But is it dignified to behave in the way you do at a party?'

Yehia made for the door and Muawiya stuffed a few salted biscuits into his mouth before calling after him: 'Very well, telephone the police, but remember there'll be some questions asked when you return to Cairo next week.'

Yehia turned sharply. 'How did you know I'd been recalled?'

'There'll be a lot more questions asked too, let me tell you.' Muawiya was waving an empty glass. Now that victory was in sight his exuberance was touched with hysteria. 'Everyone knows you are not loyal to the regime.'

Yehia tugged the door open and marched into the hall, closely followed by Perry, who said: 'I'm not quite sure who you are. So many new faces this evening. But my name's Perry. I used to teach at the University in Cairo and that's where I met Muawiya, of course. He's a bit of a roughneck.'

'Roughneck?'

They were alone only sufficiently long for Perry to discover that the fellow was almost numb with anger. He plainly meant what he said about telephoning the police, but he was in such a state that he looked at the instrument for some moments without realizing what it was. Before he could lift a hand, though, the fair-haired woman had scurried through the doorway and flung herself into his arms.

'It isn't true that you've been recalled, Mahmoud?'

'What do you mean, he's a roughneck?' Yehia held his wife tightly in his arms but looked over her head at Perry, as angry as ever and grimly determined to do his duty.

'Mahmoud!'

Yehia gripped her only the more tightly, and she stood quietly with her face resting against his shirt front, her eyes closed. Suddenly he dropped his head agonizingly and kissed her on the crown. Perry walked off, meaning to rejoin the rest of the party, but Yehia called him back and when Perry turned he saw that the embrace had been broken and the girl was patting her hair.

'Mr Perry, I must apologize for the way I came into your house this evening.'

'Go ahead if you want to call the police.' Perry nodded at the telephone. 'I suppose you dial 999?'

'No,' said Elaine, 'no, no, no, no. You mustn't, Mahmoud.

You heard what that man said. He's a government spy, I know he is. You heard what he said about the regime.'

'Do I care what he is or what he says?' Yehia picked up the receiver and realized for the first time that it had a coin-box. He felt in his pocket for the money only to find he had nothing but silver. 'Has anyone four pennies, please? I must telephone the Egyptian Embassy.'

'We find that a telephone with a call-box is more practicable in a school,' Perry explained. But he had no pennies either. Elaine said she had left her handbag on one of the chairs, and Perry was about to go and fetch it when the door opened and Waldo emerged with eyebrows bunched together over the bridge of his nose.

'Has he done it?' he asked Perry. 'Phoned the police? I couldn't get away from Miss Gunter. I tell you I'm through with this school. Bloody Egyptians about the place, and that woman! You knew my views and yet you deliberately invited her.' He stopped and looked at Yehia. 'Have you telephoned the police?'

'I want to telephone the Egyptian Embassy. Have you got change for sixpence?'

'No, I haven't, and if I had I wouldn't give it to you. Perry, we must get all these Egyptians off the premises at once, or Khaslat will be arrested here and you know what that'll mean. There won't be an Afro-Asian alive who doesn't think we were responsible, and where'll Helvetia be then?'

'Not,' he went on, 'that the future of Helvetia is any concern of mine. I'm quite definitely resigning. But the larger issue concerns me. It is not, in my considered opinion, in this country's interest to have this Khaslat chap arrested at all.'

It is quite absurd that the course of events should now be determined by whether or not four pennies could be found. Perry foresaw that this Egyptian diplomat would have to challenge everyone in the house in turn, ending up with Muawiya himself, before obtaining them. It would be quite like Muawiya, learning that Yehia proposed telephoning the Egyptian Embassy and not the police, to produce the coins with a flourish and refuse to accept Yehia's sixpence in return. They would stand round Yehia while he telephoned. The number would be engaged. And then what would they talk about?

'Are you quite sure you've got no coppers at all?' Perry asked Grimbley.

Yehia walked impatiently back to the dining-room with a sixpence between thumb and forefinger. He was followed closely by his wife, by Waldo and by Perry who were immediately aware, on entering the room, of a subtle change of atmosphere. There was a general ease and affability. Even Hillingdon was talking pleasantly and urging more champagne on Miss Gunter. Mrs Blainey was sitting with her back to an open window, listening with mildly patronizing interest to the two Stringers who were taking it in turns to retail some adventure in a holiday hotel.

'Where is he?' Yehia asked.

Faces turned inquiringly in his direction.

'Where's Khaslat?' Yehia strode to the window and looked out. 'Where's Khaslat? He was here a moment ago.'

Hillingdon could be heard breathing deeply and painfully. These sudden appearances and disappearances stirred him deeply. Delighted as he should have been that Muawiya had gone, he showed, nevertheless, signs of weariness and apprehension. He raised eyebrows and hands in a melancholy way and then walked over to Mrs Blainey saying he hoped she was none the worse for these experiences; as for himself, he knew he was witnessing phenomena.

The open window was the only possible means of escape. There was an easy drop of about five feet to the ribbon of coarse grasses that wound itself all round the house; and then to the gravel. Muawiya would walk round to the front of the house and hail the first taxi to come along.

To judge by the fierce way he took control of himself Yehia had decided he was now faced with a problem of great seriousness. He put on a stony face and asked Perry whether there would be any objection to his climbing out of the window too.

'I'll come with you,' said Perry.

They dropped to the grass and hurried round to the front where Grimbley appeared on the steps, saying that they would be well advised to search the shrubbery before looking any farther afield. But Yehia jumped into his grey Rover and was moving the car down the drive before Perry could drag open a door and join him. For ten minutes they explored the streets in the neighbourhood without any success. Yehia would not allow Perry to ask any of the passers-by whether they had seen Muawiya, and after some hesitation he parked the car at a point commanding not only the front of Helvetia but the length of the road running down past the Crematorium to Golders Green. Yehia produced a pack of American cigarettes and they smoked in silence, waiting presumably for Muawiya to pop up out of somebody's front garden.

The sun was far enough down the sky for the light to be thinning, falling glassy and superficial on sooty leaf and brick. A finger of smoke rose from the Crematorium chimney and premature leaves drifted from the avenue trees. Slaty clouds, full of rain, stretched over Hertfordshire, to the north. Sudden bursts of wind came from nowhere and a woman pushing a pram on the other side of the street had to grab at her skirts. A cat poked a face through the valerian on top of a wall, a feline cherub in a pink cloud. The wind rocked the car slightly. The two men said nothing. They sat smoking and looking at the passers-by. It was hot with all the windows shut. Perry had the impression that the captain had more than Muawiya on his mind.

Tim Blainey appeared at the gateway of Helvetia and looked up and down the road without noticing the Rover. The wind lifted his yellow hair into a crest. Blue-eyed and trim, he was the schoolboy's hero coming out to bat, pulling his gloves on carefully as he walked down the pavilion steps. Modest, uncomplicated, conventional — that is what he would be! How could so English a young man make anything of an Egyptian like Muawiya? How would he explain *superbia*? Young Blainey looked so complacently English that Perry could imagine him classifying Muawiya's flamboyance as 'foreign'. Perhaps such unimaginativeness was healthy. Perhaps one got on all the better with foreigners by remaining quietly inside one's own national skin instead of allowing so much empathy to flow that one almost lost one's identity. After all, why did one yearn so much to see the world from the foreigner's point of view? Uncertainty, Perry thought. Failure of nerve. Very well, then, he was uncertain, and his nerve had completely failed. He was a write-off so far as the Waldo Grimbleys of this world were concerned. Even now, as he sat there in this overheated car, smoking cigarettes that were too strong for him and feeling the champagne working like yeast, he did not know whether he approved of Muawiya's escapade or deplored it.

Tim Blainey went back into the house and Yehia said: 'That is a very nice young man. He is my greatest friend.'

'Really?' Perry was surprised.

'Ah, if all Englishmen were like Tim and all Egyptians were like me. But Mr Perry, I have not sufficiently asked your pardon for what has happened this evening. Really, I am filled with shame. My behaviour should have been better.'

'I can assure you — '

'No, no, I was impossible. I should have handled things better.'

'I hope your being recalled to Cairo doesn't mean bad news politically.'

'Ah, this Suez business.' Yehia smacked his hand down on the steering-wheel. 'It is quite awful.'

Perry wound down a window and put his head out to smell the evening. The hum of distant traffic vibrated up the avenues and a couple of girls walking down the opposite pavement set up tiny echoes with their tapping feet.

'I must be getting back into town,' said Yehia, 'so do you mind if I drop you here?'

Perry looked into his face. It did not surprise him that he had given up the pursuit of Muawiya as a bad job. But what of his wife?

'No, I really must go, I am late already.'

Perry could see that he was trying to sound businesslike, but it was a poor act. There was nothing he wanted more than to rush back to his wife and to hell with Muawiyas and Suez crises! He wanted to get out of the car and go legging it across the road to Helvetia probably more than he had wanted anything for a long time; but he was wearing this stiff, tortured expression which meant 'Listen to my words and not to what I say', and Perry thought it best to do exactly as the captain had requested.

'What shall I say to your wife?'

Yehia raised a hand and even managed to smile. He pretended not to have heard this last question and had wound the car round the corner before Perry could say another word.

Perry looked about him, expecting Muawiya to emerge.

CHAPTER FOUR

PERVERSELY, this was the beginning of one of those short periods of passion. Perry thought that at forty-five he ought to be growing out of them; but, on the contrary, the libidinous fits came as hotly as ever and seemed to last longer. Perry thought their duration had something to do with his no longer feeling ashamed. At his age a man began to wonder when signs of physical decay would begin to set in and the recurrent evidence of vigour came to be welcomed as evidence of perpetual (or at least protracted) youth. He had never *really* felt ashamed. But questioning, perhaps? A little critical? A bit miserly? At forty-five it was much too late for a lot of prissy self-discipline and Perry was only sorry that his moments of ardour did not coincide better with Mary's. He wondered sometimes if she tortured him deliberately. 'Oh God!' she would say in a big sleepy voice. 'Do stop it! I'm so tired.' And then, before he was awake in the morning, she would be downstairs cooking the breakfast or playing with Christopher in the nursery; and when Perry opened his sad eyes he saw the bedclothes neatly folded back and a waste of sheet like the white Antarctic.

Perhaps, this time, it was the drink that had started him off. He could trace the first stirrings back to the moment when he had walked up the drive with Miss Gunter, noticing her figure and wondering what she looked like without her glasses. She had been a bit cheeky, too. He liked that. He liked spirit. One teasing twitch of her buttocks (quite unconscious, no doubt) and Perry felt the descent of the goat. The result was that during the next few days, when everyone was scanning the newspapers and listening to the radio bulletins in vain for some mention of Muawiya's appearance in Hampstead Garden Suburb, Perry could not keep the problem at the front of his mind. No newspaper seemed to have got wind of the party. Presumably Muawiya had regained the security of the Egyptian Embassy. Perry, though, was slipping an arm round Mary's waist and agreeing with her — yes, it had been damn silly to encourage Muawiya in the way he had!

Everyone except Mrs Blainey seemed to think him very much to blame. It was only to be expected that Waldo would become hysterical at the sight of Muawiya in Helvetia (the pleasurable expectation of Waldo's response had been in Perry's mind ever since Muawiya telephoned), and Hillingdon, too, had thrown off so many dark accusations he might have been nursing a real shock. Young Tim Blainey was too green to voice any criticism, though it was clear from his manner — he shook hands with the tips of his fingers and they were very cold — that he thought there had been an indiscretion. Mary, of course, was just angry. Only Mrs Blainey behaved like a human being, and Perry, who was quite taken by her smile, readily saw the power by which poor Hillingdon was held in thrall.

She had held Perry's hand after shaking it. 'I'd like to be sure of seeing you again, Mr Perry. You and your wife must come to supper. I'll telephone. Of course, I'm only an old woman, I know.'

The thought of Mrs Blainey fishing for compliments reminded Perry of this Elaine who just could not believe that her husband, Captain Yehia, should clear off again without so much as saying goodbye. It was not quite true, then, to say that everyone except Mrs Blainey seemed to blame him for Muawiya's appearance at the party. Elaine Brent did not appear to blame him for *that* surprise, but she did seem to hold him responsible in some degree for her husband's abrupt departure. At first she was incredulous. But didn't he say anything? Didn't he leave a message? Which direction did he go? Questions like that came after intervals of doubtful wondering, and Perry tried to reassure her by saying the captain would want to return to the Embassy before Muawiya; but he was not convinced, himself, that the captain was thinking of Muawiya so much as his own recall to Egypt. It was not pleasant having this very attractive woman hating him, even moderately, for not bringing her husband back, and he took refuge in wondering whether she was a better wife to the captain than Mary was to him. She was fair, blue-eyed and sunburnt, like a late-Victorian picture of an intrepid lady missionary. Did she take fire? Had she any children? — and, if not, why not? Perry's guess was that any Englishwoman, even if she were a bit evangelical in appearance, who married an Egyptian would be less inhibited than one who thought in terms of, say, chartered accountants or teachers like himself. Mrs Yehia was clearly a nice woman, though, and Perry was ashamed of having so many sex-thoughts when he was ostensibly trying to explain her husband's disappearance. He blamed Miss Gunter more and more.

No doubt she had started one of his glands leaking some secretion into the bloodstream, exciting and fortifying him. He was more optimistic about the outcome of the Suez crisis. Although *The Times* reported that Russians were volunteering as Canal pilots, the Lancaster House Conference had talked itself to the point of sending Mr Menzies to Cairo with a plan for international management of the Canal and Nasser had said he would meet him. The most likely outcome of the scare was some face-saving accommodation in which both Egypt on the one hand and Britain and France on the other each thought they had secured the advantage. In the glow of international accord the Egyptian Embassy would release Muawiya for trial and an impartial court of law would fine him handsomely. That, Perry thought, was the most likely course of events, and even Waldo Grimbley could not shake his confidence.

'I think you're very hard on Miss Gunter,' he said to Waldo in the passage, and Waldo had made no answer to this at all except to request, coldly, an interview at eleven o'clock that morning. Whenever Waldo had a really serious point to make he always did it by appointment. The considered opinion tossed off at the casual meeting lacked force. Waldo set the scene for his more important speeches with the cunning of a dramatist. He had been known to make an appointment with Perry for five minutes later and spend the interim in the lavatory. He loved to arouse expectation and, if possible, anxiety.

Ilse brought the coffee and Waldo produced an envelope from his wallet and extracted a saccharine tablet.

'Now look, Perry, you know me.' He waved the biscuits aside. 'You know my history and you know my views. The appearance of those Egyptians in this house the other evening was a serious matter. It was serious for me personally. Now, was everything as it seemed?'

'I don't know what you mean.'

'That Khaslat fellow. Was there anything more in his turning up than met the eye?'

Perry thought that Waldo would be shocked that it was neither caffeine nor nicotine that was responsible for the glassy fortitude with which his presence was being endured. But then, he would not have believed it if Perry had told him. Waldo distrusted science completely and was probably sceptical even of the circulation of the blood.

'I still don't know what you mean.'

'Hasn't it struck you what an extraordinary coincidence it was that you should be giving a party and this fellow turns up?'

'Frankly, it has.'

'Such a coincidence he was so delighted he actually got up and claimed he was giving the party himself. You see what I mean? Was there anything more than met the eye?'

Waldo was giving one of those performances in which ponderous stupidity and low cunning struggled for dominance. He watched Perry as he spoke, the cup at his lips.

'It *was* his party. I thought everybody understood that. He rang up and asked me to arrange it for him.'

'And you did?'

'I did!'

'You actually did.'

Perry nodded. 'That's it.'

Waldo drank his coffee, dropped it noisily on to the tray, and barked: 'That's exactly what I suspected! I knew it! You must be mad! I suppose you're only sorry Khaslat didn't smash *your* car up?'

'As you know, I don't possess a car.'

'And doesn't it sicken you,' said Waldo, 'that you hadn't got a car so that Khaslat could have smashed *that* up and you could have suffered even more? That's your trouble, and by God it's taken me a long time to spot it. You want to suffer. You're like some religious martyr, or one of those Russians with their Slav souls. I'd be ashamed of myself! You were damn sorry, in a way, that Khaslat didn't shoot you at Sakkara. You would have liked to be horribly wounded. Don't ask me why! Do I read all this psychological stuff? You want to be hurt and humiliated, and there's nothing that would give you greater satisfaction, is there, than being run in for harbouring a known criminal? You'd like to take your stand in the dock on a charge of comforting the Queen's enemies. I'll tell you what — ' Waldo looked particularly grave as he prepared to deliver this final charge — 'I wouldn't mind betting you're hoping I'll keep my word and resign. Nothing could be more inconvenient from your point of view — the beginning of term, and so on. You're a self-pitying lunatic. You'd like to go bankrupt and you'd like your wife to leave you, so that everybody would be sorry for you.'

'You mean I'm a masochist?'

Waldo winced at the word. 'If you like to put it that way.'

'Well, maybe you're right, for all I know.'

'I think all liberals are masochists,' said Waldo.

Coming from Waldo this was extraordinary language and Perry wondered whether it would be in order for him to reveal the psycho-physical state into which Miss Gunter had thrown him; if, indeed, it had been Miss Gunter.

'Is this what you wanted to see me about?' Perry asked.

'It would do you a lot of harm if I were to walk out of Helvetia. I don't believe you even realize the harm it would do you. If it weren't for me you'd have these Asiatics and Africans running the place. *You* think you'd be upset because I went because *you* think I'm an old fool who has to be looked after, and as I've said before that is precisely what you want, to be upset and unhappy. I tell you, Perry, I'm not going to play this game. I'm standing firm, not so much in my own interests as in yours. *I'm not leaving!*'

He looked at Perry, his eyes narrowed, obviously wondering whether he had been talking over Perry's head.

'I shall carry on here,' he said, 'until my going causes you no inconvenience and until I have an obviously better job to go to.'

That was all. Waldo went after this speech and Perry was left to reflect on the falsity of his theory. It was quite untrue that he wanted to be unhappy. He was much, much too selfish. What mental discipline he possessed was directed towards the evoking of pleasant thoughts, more especially as a means of inducing sleep at night, but also during spells of boredom; he thought of himself, recumbent on a sunwashed marble balcony with umbrella pines and remote blue mountains fringing his area of mesmerized vision; or lying on his belly among water-reeds listening to a river. He was afraid of unhappiness. He ran from it. He funked funerals. The incurably sick frightened him. He would do a great deal to help someone who had a reasonable chance of surviving a bad run of luck; but if there was really no hope Perry did not know but that he would want to keep out of the way. Misfortune was contagious.

It no longer even bothered him a great deal that he was so selfish. What was wrong with the desire to be surrounded by healthy, happy and wealthy people? He liked his friends to be wealthy and untroubled. Life seemed sensible when one could count a lot of obviously fortunate people among one's friends, and Perry was heartily glad to be old enough to have these thoughts without feeling guilty about them.

Waldo was not like this. Mary was not like this. All right, they were better than he was! But that did not entitle either of them to try and teach him a lesson.

For Perry was quite sure that Mary's frigidity was assumed in order to discipline him and make him feel ashamed. The evenings following Muawiya's party Perry followed Mary up to bed, trying to temper eagerness with conciliation, and refusing until the last to believe that she could be so single-minded. He always bathed in the morning so the evening washing and tooth-cleaning only took a few minutes, by which time Mary was wearing her yellow silk dressing-gown. He lay in bed, pretending to read, but noticing for the umpteenth time that she took longer strides in a dressing-gown and the light worked on her thighs like oil.

Mary always bathed at night, and she did it rather noisily, splashing and gasping on the other side of the door as though she had had to break the ice. Perry could not read. He put his book down and listened. High up at the window there was a triangular gap between the curtains through which he could see a black shivering twig and faint stars. There was an odour of lilies of the valley from Mary's dressing-table. This is happiness, he thought, to be seeing a star through the window, smelling lilies of the valley, to be lying here relaxed between the sheets and thinking of my wife, naked and soaping her breasts in the next room.

He read two pages of his detective story while she sat at her dressing-table, putting cream on her face and brushing her hair. She did not speak. Whether or not she intended to read was never known until she had settled herself in bed and taken the twenty-five deep breaths, raising her arms vertically, which she believed to be a necessary preparation for sleep. She had a Boots library book on her bedside table, *The Sun is My Undoing*. Sometimes she propped this book on her stomach and read grimly; but tonight she immediately lay back, sighing deeply to convey her exhaustion, and put her arms firmly over the covers as though to prevent their being disturbed. Perry, with his book six inches from his face, tried to look at her without turning his head. He could see the pink frill of her nightgown delicately laid against her throat. Her countenance shone from the anointing she had given it. Her eyelashes did not so much as quiver, even when he put out his left foot and touched her right.

He switched off the bedside lamp and lay there wondering what to do. She had not even said good night. A moist, bath-salts impregnated warmth seeped through the bedclothes.

'Are you awake, Mary?' he whispered.

No answer.

He moved his left hand and laid it on her thigh.

'Mary!' he said.

No reply or movement. She was breathing very steadily.

Suddenly he turned to take her in his arms and she gave a snort, as though awakened out of deep sleep. She contrived to get an elbow into his stomach.

'Now I shall never get to sleep,' she said. 'I was just dozing off. Why can't you keep still?'

'Mary, for God's sake —'

'I shall have to take a pill.'

He gave up and retired to his own side of the bed. It would have appeared silly to switch on the light once more and continue reading his detective story; but that is what he would have liked to do. After Mary had groped in her drawer and found the pill, Perry thought he would do a little groping himself. His hand came back with a packet of cigarettes and some matches. Mary hated him to smoke in bed, so he lit up and puffed away with a deal of unnecessary noise. He wondered whether he should go downstairs and get a drink.

'Dammit all,' he suddenly shouted, 'I can't help it if the fellow insisted on turning up here, can I?'

'There now, you've wakened Christopher.'

Sighing heavily Mary rolled out of bed and hunted around for her dressing-gown.

To be candid he had not really wanted to switch on the light and go on reading his detective story. He had wanted to rape her, and when she returned to bed after visiting Christopher — he had never stirred, Perry was sure of that — the accidental contact of her thigh made him groan along his cigarette. They were too long married for a double bed; he would put it to her, as soon as he tactfully could, that they ought to buy single beds. Stimulus at night, if unappeased, was damaging to the nerves.

'Well, perhaps we'll be able to get some sleep now,' she said.

'Mary, darling.'

'Yes?'

'I'm sorry.' When there was no reply, he went on: 'You're quite right. I should never have encouraged Muawiya to have that party. It was very silly of me.' How much more abject, he wondered, could he possibly become?

'All right, darling,' she said unexpectedly and slipped a hand into his. The gentleness of her tone sent a shock of violent pleasure through him, converting him magically from one state to another. All the starch in his body turned to sugar, black became white, the darkness light; and, stupidly, all he wanted to do was cry. There were no tears and his face undoubtedly preserved the same expression as before, but he was crying inwardly. His lust disappeared. He could not have remembered what Miss Gunter looked like even if he had tried. He lifted Mary's hand to his lips and kissed it. 'I must go downstairs,' he whispered.

'For God's sake!' she said in a helpless tone.

'It's impossible,' he said, 'impossible!' and climbed out of bed, still holding the cigarette in his right hand, and rushed out of the room in his pyjamas. She is quite right, he was thinking, I've been the clown again. All I think of is myself. It is wrong to be so obsessed with sex. I am in the wrong. I am usually in the wrong. I am always in the wrong.

Not until he felt cold linoleum under his feet did he begin to get a grip of himself once more. He wondered if he was going to have a nervous breakdown. All that groping about in bed, he thought, when poor Mary just wanted to go to sleep. I'm a lascivious beast and I really do feel thoroughly ashamed of myself! What a darling she had been to call him darling! He switched on the electric fire in the office and crouched in front of it until he felt as crisp as toast. When he woke at three o'clock he found that he was lying on the settee with a blanket over him.

Now who had walked in with a blanket? Someone must have found him asleep and covered him. Who? It could only have been Mary. The electric fire was still glowing. God! he was tired. He was exhausted to the point of desperation. He was still crying inside.

The *Express* carried the most extraordinary story that morning. Perry took his bath at six and was shaved, dressed and downstairs before the papers came, so he was the first person in the house to know about it. The headline was 'OUT AND ABOUT WITH KHASLAT' and Perry's first thought was that the story of the party had at last leaked. But even if the *Express* had known about the party they would have considered it trivial compared with the story they *had* secured. In Finchley a debating society met for the first time after the summer break to consider the motion 'That in the opinion of this House, all men are brothers', and none other than the prisoner in the Embassy, the Egyptian firebrand Muawiya Khaslat, had actually made an appearance. He had, in fact, spoken against the motion.

The Sidney Lodge Debating Society (that was its name) sounded an improbable survival of the Victorian past. The *Express* reporter was so taken up with the phenomenon of Muawiya's public appearance that he had no space to account for the existence of Sidney Lodge at all, and this was just the information Perry needed to convince him the story was true. A debating society outside a school or university was an absurd anachronism. However, here was the account, a circumstantial one with the secretary of the society named as a Mr Arthur Candle, schoolmaster and Unitarian.

According to Mr Candle, the first intimation of 'the Egyptian gentleman's appearance' had been a telephone call that afternoon from someone with a thick foreign voice, who said that he had seen the debate advertised in the *New Statesman*. Were visitors admitted? And if they were admitted were they allowed to speak? Mr Candle had said there was only one answer to these questions — yes; though as it was a subscription debating society he would be expected to make a donation to the funds. It was unusual for a complete stranger to telephone Mr Candle about the affairs of the debating society. The advertisement gave his name as honorary secretary but no telephone number. This foreigner, then, had gone to the trouble of looking him up in the telephone directory and Mr Candle said he didn't mind confessing it gave him a funny feeling, the thought of this foreigner looking up his name. He was sure to be a Russian.

Mr Candle said he did not realize who their guest was until near the end of the session. He had arrived at seven-thirty—ten minutes before the first item on the agenda, the election of officials — and Mr Candle was bound to say he looked very smart indeed in a nice grey suit, though he was obviously not a Russian, and more tropical to his way of thinking. Even then he would not give his name, though he did hand a large subscription—a whole pound, as a matter of fact — to the treasurer, before sitting in the middle of the front row. He could not make his speech, naturally, until the debate was thrown open to the floor. Mr Candle said he spoke most professionally, with gestures, saying that he opposed the motion that all men were brothers unless it had been proposed with the story of Cain and Abel in mind, which he took leave to doubt. He went on to say that the white races of the world were beginning to talk of the brotherhood of man nowadays because they knew that before very long the coloured people would have the upper hand and they wanted the coloured people to treat them decently, like brothers. But it would not work. The coloured people would repay exactly what they had received and it wasn't a bit of good whining. All this was rather terrifying, but it was delivered with such jollity the members laughed a great deal.

This foreigner was the only person present who was not a member of the Sidney Lodge Debating Society, which was an entirely British, Christian and non-political organization, Mr Candle said, so he had an advantage; nobody knew his background nor how seriously to take him. When the debate was over and they were standing round chatting, Mr Edwards, it was, who works on a local newspaper, who asked him flatly who he was and where he came from. When he said he was Egyptian and his name was what it was, Mr Edwards had said: 'Oh, you're the one supposed to be shut up in the Embassy for manslaughter, then?' Naturally the Egyptian had denied the manslaughter but he confessed his identity.

No, Mr Candle said, nobody had sent for the police.

In spite of the illiberal views he had expressed and the knowledge that he was wanted by the police not a single member of the Sidney Lodge Debating Society had wanted to hand him over to the law. Had it not been that Mr Edwards was a journalist the possibility is that the story of Muawiya's visit might never have been revealed; and even Edwards waited for half an hour after he had gone to make quite sure he had got clear.

'It didn't seem right,' Mr Candle was reported as saying, 'to tell the police. By coming to our meeting, speaking his mind, and then telling us who he was he showed that he trusted us.'

The possibility remained that the Sidney Lodge Debating Society had been hoaxed, but Perry did not think so; he could see the gleam of enthusiasm on Muawiya's face, hear his rabble-rousing rhetoric, and almost — but not quite — visualize the self-conscious solemnity of his audience melting into laughter. An eccentric West Indian might conceivably have taken it into his head to make the flesh of a white audience creep, and been seduced by the temptation to joke. That sounded very West

Indian. But no West Indian would then have tried to pass himself off as an Egyptian. He would have been too proud of his own identity. If life in the Embassy had become such an intolerable bore to Muawiya that he was capable of breaking out and addressing semi-public meetings like the Sidney Lodge Debating Society, the police would certainly catch him before long; at Speakers' Corner, probably, standing on a borrowed chair, with a Home Rule for Wales speaker on one side and the Rev. Donald Soper on the other. Nobody in the British Council would dare read the *Evening Standard* for weeks.

The Times made no reference to Muawiya and Perry expected Waldo to be sceptical about this supposed escapade; normally he believed nothing until it was reported in *The Times*. But the account of Muawiya's threat to the white races of the earth entirely won Waldo over; the report, he said, had all the marks of authenticity and the only comfort it gave him was that it showed Muawiya to be a bigger idiot than he had thought. The police were bound to pick him up in the next few days if he went on behaving like this, and these inflammatory speeches would provide valuable evidence at the trial.

Hillingdon was both angry and alarmed. He wanted to know why the police hadn't arrested Muawiya either when he left the Embassy or when he returned. Didn't they see what fools they looked? However, Hillingdon did not press his attack on the police too strongly. It was life itself he was angry with. If only Perry had not known Muawiya in the first place they would have been spared all this trouble. He would still have his Morris. All these arguments with the insurance company! And then, to be in relationship with a man who came and went as he pleased, in defiance of the police, laughing at them and threatening.

'You could have telephoned the police if you'd wanted to,' Perry said, 'when he was here.'

'I wouldn't like to be the man,' Hillingdon said solemnly, 'who is responsible for this Egyptian being caught and punished.'

Perry turned to Grimbley. 'Well, why didn't you turn him in?'

Grimbley looked sour at being taken up in this tactless way. 'Hillingdon and I had our reasons.'

They were in agreement on one point. During the morning there were telephone calls from various newspapers and to each of them the same answer was given: that they knew no more of Muawiya's supposed visit to the Sidney Lodge Debating Society than they had read in the *Express*. They had no comment. Mary went shopping with a meat-knife in her basket. If Muawiya suddenly appeared, as well he might, she would not have the slightest compunction in sticking it in him. In all probability she would have to act in self-defence, anyway. There was not a jury in the country that would find her guilty under such conditions, particularly when it was revealed that Muawiya had already attempted to murder her husband. She was not at all sure that Muawiya's threats about what would happen when all the wogs and niggers got on top didn't amount to an indictable offence.

'To think that he was actually here, in this house!'

'Mary, even assuming this newspaper report is right, can't you see he was only talking for effect?'

'That's what you think.'

Perry knew very well that she had been intending for some time to take this particular knife down to the ironmonger's for sharpening; so he was not over-impressed by her show of blood-thirstiness. The talk of 'wogs and niggers' upset him a great deal more, even though he knew she only used the words to annoy him. If only he had responded last night when she had softened and taken him by the hand. But like a fool he had come down-stairs. Well, she had hurt his pride and that was the truth of the matter. A pill! He had offered love and she had chosen a pill!

Even if, as seemed likely, she had put that blanket on him during the night, she had experienced no real change of heart, judging by this wog and nigger talk. One day she would probably be using that kitchen knife on him! The marriage service ought to be simpler. Instead of the optimistic words about honour, worldly goods, in sickness and in health, for richer and for poorer, how much more *honest* it would be if the couple promised not to torture, maim or murder each other!

The three men were still talking when Ilse came in, saying there was a young man in the hall who said he had an appointment with Dr Perry. They thought it was a journalist trying to bluff his way in until Perry remembered that Helvetia had still not succeeded in appointing someone to succeed Miss Gunter and only yesterday the scholastic agency had telephoned to say they were sending along a Mr — what was his name?

'He says his name is Todd.'

'That's right, Ilse. Show Mr Todd in. Don't go, you fellows. I'd be very glad of your opinion. Besides, it's a very nasty business interviewing anybody. Never know what to say.'

Mr Todd, when he entered, was impressive. He was about twenty-five, had a rugger full-back's chest, probably touched the scales at twelve stone and had grey eyes that matched exactly the beautifully cut suit he was wearing. His appearance was calculated. He knew precisely the effect he created, approved of it and was at ease.

'You must forgive me for being five minutes late.' He examined all three, one corner of his mouth twisted in what might have been a smile. 'Which is Dr Perry? The agency said my interview was with Dr Perry.'

'This is Mr Grimbley, my senior assistant,' said Perry. 'And this is Mr Hillingdon who owns the house. I am Perry, but I have no doctorate.'

With the exception of Miss Gunter, the staff of Helvetia had been recruited from the ranks of all those Englishmen who in recent years had been thrown out of jobs in India, Pakistan, Malaya, Burma, Palestine, Jordan, the Sudan, Egypt, wherever the imperial burden had been lowered on to other shoulders. They stayed briefly, only until they found better jobs, but few of them bore Perry any ill will over the miserable salary which was all he could afford to pay. Mr Todd looked quite different from the ex-imperialists. Quite apart from youth he had an undefeated air which meant, probably, that he had travelled little beyond the shores of Great Britain. What *could* the agency have told him about Helvetia? Perry asked him.

A normal candidate for a job would have been asked to sit and offered a cigarette. The room had too much the atmosphere of a tournament to justify concessions of this kind. All stood, and on guard.

'Why, the job's to teach English to foreigners, isn't it?' he said, surprised.

'But why should *you* want to do it?'

'Frankly, it's only a stop-gap. I'm trying to get a job abroad.'

Perry nodded. He was glad the fellow hadn't the idea of making a career at Helvetia. 'Do you think you could teach English?'

'I took a first at Cambridge, then came up to L.S.E. for phonetics. I did quite well. Then I did my National Service and now I'm writing a grammar of spoken English.'

'Are you against split infinitives?' Grimbley broke in.

'No.' Todd seemed perfectly well aware that Grimbley had hoped he would say yes, so that he could quote Jespersen and Fowler against him.

'I've put in for a job at the University of Benghazi,' Todd said, 'but even if I got it I shouldn't go until the new year.'

'You'd like to come here for one term?'

'Yes.'

He was a very strong candidate and he knew it. Having absorbed as much information as the appearances of Perry, Grimbley and Hillingdon could give him, he was now studying the detail of the room. A typed envelope lay on Perry's desk and Todd took in the address, upside down as it was, and stored it away in his memory. What made Perry all the more suspicious was his refusal to be puzzled by his cold reception. Even a journalist would have been asked to take a seat.

'We'll think about it,' said Perry. 'There's only the one job going and the agency will be sending a few more candidates along. Frankly, one term is a bit brief for us.'

'Was it your car that Egyptian smashed up?' Todd suddenly threw the question at Hillingdon. 'I read about it in the papers.'

'Perhaps you'd like to leave your telephone number.' Perry handed him a pencil and a jotting-pad. 'I could give you a ring.'

Todd nodded and wrote down his number. 'I'd no idea when I first read about that Egyptian I should be applying for a job here and meeting you. Is it really true, Dr Perry, that you narrowly escaped assassination at his hands? Well, it was very magnanimous of you even to see him again after that, I reckon.'

'The salary we offer is rather low.'

'Money doesn't bother me, provided the work is right. I have a small private income.'

'Food is a problem too. There are no restaurants near at hand and unless staff live in the neighbourhood they have to bring sandwiches. As I say, though, I'll give you a ring.'

Perry walked with the young man as far as the front door, and then returned to the study to stand with Grimbley and Hillingdon to watch him give the house a steady scrutiny before finally disappearing through the gate.

'The only unsuspicious thing about that character is his complete lack of charm. Exactly what you'd expect of a man who's writing a grammar of spoken English, whatever that means. But I don't believe he is writing a grammar of spoken English. Do you?' Perry asked Grimbley.

Grimbley lifted his chin and scratched his throat, making a surprisingly loud rasping noise.

'I thought he showed he knew a lot about it, personally.'

Hillingdon narrowed his eyes. 'It's no business of mine, but I can't say I took to him. It was very cool, saying he'd only come for a term.'

'I don't believe he's writing a grammar of spoken English,' said Perry, 'and I don't believe his name is Todd either. It would be interesting to know how the agency came across him.'

Hillingdon said he would like to see Perry on a matter of business and led the way up two flights of stairs, his new suede shoes creaking painfully, to the top floor flat. Clearly, Hillingdon was going to speak as the landlord. He had tucked his chin in, his voice had deepened, he took more weight on the balls of his feet; a more alert and calculating Hillingdon was to be seen. Perry knew the routine. As soon as they entered Hillingdon's rooms he would pick up some notebook, lick the tip of his index finger and turn the pages, peering at them short-sightedly and muttering. It would mean nothing. He would put the book aside.

Only very rarely did anyone but Hillingdon and his char see the inside of Hillingdon's rooms, but once seen they lingered in the memory. An Eskimo kayak was suspended diagonally across the ceiling; and in one corner, six feet high, was the vermilion and blue face of a creature which might have been beast, fowl or alligator, and was probably a combination of the three – it appeared to be swearing and was, Hillingdon claimed, the top of a Red Indian totem pole. Over the desk was a singularly hideous African mask, made of straw; the orange eyeballs stood out from the head on white stalks. In a glass case was a shrunken head. A mummified cat from Bubastis occupied a niche on one side of the fireplace; on the other, by way of counterpoise, was the upper jaw of a swordfish. Machetes, spears and blowpipes occupied the walls. A large scarab (obviously a forgery) served as a paperweight. From the head of Nefertiti rose a reading-lamp. Gibbon's *Decline and Fall*, Maspero's *Dawn of Civilization*, Breasted's *History of Egypt from the Earliest Times*, and various works on theosophy and primitive religion occupied a bookcase under the window. On the floor was a tiger-skin, the head still attached and watching with its glassy eyes a mousehole in the skirting-board.

Hillingdon licked a finger and leafed through a pocket diary.

'As you know, Perry, our agreement comes to an end at Michaelmas and I must tell you I don't want to renew it.'

'Michaelmas! But that's next month.'

'I blame myself for not raising the matter before. But it's only in the last few days that I've been able to see the situation in its true colours. I'm not blaming you. Don't mistake me. But I have been deceived and disappointed. What I had hoped for has not come to pass. You remember how we launched this experiment?'

Perry nodded. At the time he had thought the chance meeting with Hillingdon a wonderful stroke of luck, but as the years had passed custom and familiarity had persuaded him there might have been happier encounters, with other landlords who had property in a part of London better served by public transport than Hampstead Garden Suburb. They had met at a tea-party given at the Egyptian Institute of Education in Curzon Street shortly after Perry came home from Egypt. Hillingdon said he came to the Institute to borrow books from the library.

'Have you ever wondered,' said Hillingdon, 'what my *real* motives were in letting you this house for such a nominal rent?'

'Well, it's five hundred a year and you do get your board.'

'But *I* pay the rates.'

'Well, all right,' said Perry. 'I agree. You've been generous. But that doesn't justify turning us out at three weeks' notice.'

'Ah! Let's sit down.'

Perry sat on a carpet-topped elephant's foot. 'Do you want more rent, is that it?'

'You don't understand me, do you, Perry? You've never considered life from my point of view.' Hillingdon lay back in his chair, looking at Perry over the elongated prominence of his stomach. 'Otherwise you would never mention rent. No, I have no wish to increase your rent. What is more, I like and respect you. I even like your wife and little boy. It would give me no pleasure at all to harm your prospects. But there is my own interest to think of. After all, I'm fifty-five. I can't live for ever. I must do something in the next fifteen years. At the moment I'm getting nowhere. On the contrary, I'm being strangled by circumstances. That Egyptian turning up at the debating society is the last straw.'

'I don't understand.'

Without moving any of his bulk Hillingdon contrived to set up such a quivering agitation of hands and face that Perry could see the explanation was going to be difficult and, even, that Hillingdon himself was not the best person to give it. The wobbling of lips and cheeks, the fluttering of hands amounted to a disavowal. 'My dear chap, it's all so silly and contemptible, but I'm afraid I am what I am.' That was the sort of thing Hillingdon appeared to be hinting at. The museum pieces by which he was surrounded, the totem effigy, the long-dead cat, the primitive weapons and the rest, constituted something more than a hint.

It was impossible to see them without doing what Perry had already been accused of neglecting: looking at life from Hillingdon's point of view.

'I don't understand at all,' said Perry.

'I went out of my way to be courteous to him. You know perfectly well, Perry, that I was even going to help him become a whisky importer into Egypt, or whatever it was he wanted. We actually sampled whisky together. Nobody can accuse me of ill will. Then what does he do? He smashes my car up most recklessly! He actually gives a party in my own house. He defies the authorities by speaking in a debating society. The country has become a complete laughing-stock. What do you think the American newspapers are saying? But apart from considerations of national prestige I feel personally threatened. There is no knowing where he is going to turn up next. He might be outside in the road at this very moment. He might be in the hall. He might be coming up the stairs.'

Both men listened.

'Why do you think I let you have Helvetia so cheaply?'

'It isn't all *that* cheap, you know.'

'I will confess to you,' said Hillingdon solemnly, 'that it was a great disappointment to me that when you started your school here you did not call it the Hillingdon School of English. I know the house already had a name; but I should have liked it called the Hillingdon School. You should have thought of it. Not because I am vain. I am not at all vain, but I care a great deal for learning and knowledge and culture, all these things. One of these days I shall tell you about my life. I was *thwarted* of knowledge. My mother took me away from school when I was fifteen. Now, what I should have liked to do with my life is to have made a lot of money, like Lord Nuffield, and founded a college somewhere and have it called Hillingdon College. Of course, I never made enough money. I never did any work, for one thing. But if I couldn't have Hillingdon College at Oxford or Cambridge, at least I might have had Hillingdon School of English. You should have thought of it. You know very well you told me the need there was for a school where foreigners coming from overseas could perfect their English in a way that wasn't possible at their colleges and universities. Well, I saw it as a great ideal. You said such a school was unique. Well, it's too late to change the name now. Besides, I don't believe in the idea any more, I tell you. Foreigners learning English! What I'd like to do is offer the house to a learned society to have meetings in.'

'You never told me about all this before.'

Hillingdon was out of his chair and lumbering about the room. 'You're not a chap to inspire confidences, Perry. Has anyone told you that? I've come to a crisis in my life or I'd never be speaking to you with this kind of frankness. There has never before been the occasion. Always did keep things to myself. Now Grimbley, I could have confided in him. But not you. For one thing — I don't want to be offensive, old chap, but if I don't speak the truth now I never shall! — I never really knew what to make of you. Sometimes you seem quite intelligent, then you are so extraordinarily silly — like over this party, for example — and I just ask myself, I say: Well, even if I unburden will he understand?'

'I don't mind calling the school the Hillingdon School, if that's what you want.'

'No, no, no. It's too late for that tomfoolery. You see, I've come to the conclusion I don't really like foreigners. It wouldn't be honest to carry on, feeling the way I do. Perhaps I ought to have travelled more as a young man. These last few days I've had the feeling of dark men rising up all round me. There are too many of them. Walk about the streets of London and every other person you meet is coloured. I mean, I'm as large-minded as you like, but this situation perturbs me. You see, I look on things rather differently. I know that everything has a meaning. Well, what is the meaning of this? I ask.'

'I think you're a silly, bloody fool,' said Perry.

'What's that?'

'I said I think you're a silly bloody fool — '

'There's no need to lose your temper.'

' — trying to lay down the law about what kind of a school I run. There's an option clause in that lease, I'm sure there is, that entitles me to another twelve months — '

'There is no option clause.'

'Then why didn't you bring this question up before? Giving me a month's warning like this. I should have thought I deserved better than that! Well, I suppose I've got to bring a lawyer in.'

'I'm sorry, but my mind is quite made up.'

'I'm not interested in your mind. It's the law that matters. I shall fight you. Another thing — you disgust me! Take a look at yourself, sitting here among all this rubbish and saying you don't like foreigners — '

'Let's talk about it when you're calmer.'

'I don't want to be calm. I despise you, Hillingdon! I think you're a louse — '

'Get out of my room.'

'You fascist-minded, race-conscious neurotic!'

'Will you please get out of this room?'

Perry went, slamming the door behind him, and Hillingdon sat listening to him clump down the stairs. The interview had gone not at all as he had imagined. Perry had not even given him time to explain there was no intention of insisting the lease was terminated at Michaelmas; Hillingdon was quite prepared to consider granting a reasonable extension to permit Perry to find alternative accommodation, a whole year if need be. But on the main issue, Hillingdon's mind was made up. He was tired of patronizing a school for orientals and would like to look round for some dispossessed learned society to whom he could offer a home. The Warburg Institute — that would have been ideal, now, with its tens of thousands of books and its research workers all bringing out little works from time to time on astral demonism and Mithras-worship; but it would be known as the Hillingdon Institute and he would sit up here, in this very room, not doing much research himself but thinking deeply, and in so doing adding to the psychic force of the institute. The researchers would never know how he was helping them. Perhaps the Warburg was too large. He might have to be less ambitious. Now that Ogden was dead what would happen to his Orthological Institute? It sounded a bit too rational for Hillingdon's tastes. What about heraldry? Or psychic research? He remembered reading an article by Robert Graves on mushrooms and primitive religion. To have Graves back in London, presiding over an Institute of Religious Mycology, that would be just the thing. *Just* what these wealthy American foundations liked to put their money into.

But by flying into a temper Perry had prevented a sensible discussion of the possibilities. He would have liked Perry's advice because Perry was a scholarly sort of chap in his way. Rudeness like that was unforgivable, though. If he had refused to leave Hillingdon would certainly have struck him. He would have jumped up smartly and knocked the chap flat. Fascist-minded! Neurotic! Hillingdon sat quietly in his chair, reflecting on the words, and thinking: Well, it's all up with you now. I'll have you out of here by Michaelmas, by God. I'll have you out — lock, stock and barrel!

He went into the bathroom, soaked a flannel in hot water and pressed it to his face in order to soothe away (as he imagined) some of the wrinkles and worry lines. He dabbed a little cold cream under the eyes and massaged gently with the tips of his fingers. The encounter with Perry had been a thoroughly nasty experience, as shocking as it was unexpected. After all these years of friendship and patronage Hillingdon had been very nearly forced to knock the man down. No doubt he would be along to apologize for his filthy temper, but Hillingdon was not going to accept any apologies. The incident was too serious. Unforgivable words had been uttered. Hillingdon suddenly felt a tiny bubble of giddiness float up from the soles of his feet and take up position just behind his eyes. He had to lean against the wall for a few moments. Shock, he said to himself. Delayed shock! He could see perfectly well now that if he had not ordered Perry out of the room the fellow might have attacked him. His face had been crimson with anger. Real, foaming, anger! And the eyes! Hillingdon thought how they glittered. It was easier to imagine such a man assassinating this dreadful Egyptian than being assassinated by him. As the dizziness passed Hillingdon considered this new facet of the situation. If *Perry* had been the would-be assassin at Sakkara it might explain the curious hold the Egyptian seemed to have over him. *Arranging a party for the Egyptian.* Hillingdon shuddered and wiped the slight greasiness from his face with cotton wool. He examined his tie in the mirror and thought the knot looked rather dirty. He undid it and knotted it in a different place. As he was going to call on Mrs Blainey to ask her advice he wanted to look at his best.

His new shoes squeaked like a pen of pigs on the way downstairs and he half expected one of the doors to fly open and Perry emerge to renew the argument. It would have been no use. No apology would make the slightest difference. Out they went, the whole pack of them, on September the twenty-ninth, and it was not a bit of good fretting. Perry had thoroughly upset him. What would Mrs Blainey say? As soon as Hillingdon had read the newspaper report about Muawiya speaking at the Sidney Lodge Debating Society he had determined to go and discuss the matter with Mrs Blainey. She was always delighted when he dropped in with no warning or excuse. But it was better to have a reason. 'What do you think of this latest exploit?' he would say. He wanted to discuss with her, too, this plan to found a learned society at Helvetia with funds from the Ford Foundation.

As for the School of English — Hillingdon walked down towards the Crematorium wondering how he could best tell Mrs Blainey of his decision. 'I've turned 'em out.' Perhaps he would click his fingers. No, that would never do. He did not wish to appear ruthless.

Would it all constitute sufficient excuse for a call? Hillingdon stopped, suddenly alarmed that he might be giving Mrs Blainey cause for thinking him a nuisance. Was he calling too often? The last time was the day of the party and that was three days ago. Three whole days! Reassured, he walked on, severing the heads of invisible dandelions with his cane and marking the glint of the sun on his right cuff-link. There was a great deal to talk about. Too much! Perhaps he would not mention his decision to bring the School of English to a close until he had sounded her a little on the subject. With that son of hers in the British Council there was no knowing what views Mrs Blainey had on the teaching of English to foreigners. Perhaps, he thought with a new pang of dismay, she was in favour of it.

It worried him that he was not a widower or a divorcé. No knowing what a woman would think of a bachelor of fifty-five. She might even think he was an old pansy trying to reform. On the other hand she might think he was just a selfish brute. But which of these views Mrs Blainey adopted she was bound to think poorly of him, she a widow with a grown-up son. Hillingdon felt that he had to make his attitude to the other sex quite clear to Mrs Blainey before very long, and he could see no way of doing it with delicacy. He wouldn't tell any actual lies, but if she *did* ask him why he had never married he would have to answer creditably. If she were to say to him 'I can see you've had no time for women, Napier,' he probably had to reply: 'I made the mistake of having too many women.' Flatly untrue, of course. But what else could he say? Come to that, what was the truth? Why hadn't he had a lot of women! Was he undersexed? Hillingdon did not think so.

Sex was one of the few subjects on which his mother had not addressed him. There were times when he still seemed to hear her voice — 'Napier, I will dictate'(she dictated all her letters to him); or, 'Napier, I want you to read this book carefully so that we can discuss it seriously afterwards,' passing him the biography of a Victorian statesman — because he was over forty-six when she died and he had never left home. He had been born in Helvetia and hoped to die there. When he was fifteen his father died and she had taken him away from school to be more of a companion to her. For thirty years she had dictated her letters to him, discussed books, taken him on holidays to Bournemouth or Buxton, kept him in reasonable comfort and happiness, but although she had given him permission to marry when she was dead never at any time had she told him what to say if asked to explain his prolonged bachelorhood. Of course, she never realized how old he was getting. She always spelt out the more difficult words in her letters, even to the very end, and said 'Comma!' 'Full stop!' 'Colon!' to show how uncertain she was of his punctuation. There was no reason why she should not have written her own letters. She just said she was proud of his handwriting.

The walks they used to go together! The books they read! The plays they saw! She had much more energy than he; small, thin, hairs on her upper lip (in a foolish moment he had offered to shave them off), quick as a bird. Her love of walking was just about the only one he did not share; it used to exhaust him so. Frankly, he used to dread Sunday mornings when she would cut up sandwiches for the day and tell him they were going for a ramble. She always walked in front, her long spindly legs working away under her tweed skirt, Napier struggling to keep up in fear of missing anything she said. It was natural that even now, walking past the Crematorium where he had attended her for the last time, Hillingdon should fancy he could hear her voice.

What would she think of Mrs Blainey? It had never occurred to him before. What if they had met? Well, they would have got on well together, and no mistake. Women always had something to talk about, and his mother in particular was never at a loss for a subject. It was queer even fancying the pair of them together. He did not like it. It worried him. He was almost down to the main road before he caught a cab, and as he sank back in the seat, sighing and bringing his cane gently to rest between his outstretched feet, he tormented himself by imagining a scene in which he said: 'Mrs Blainey, I should like to introduce my mother.' No, that was wrong. 'Mother, I should like to introduce a friend, Mrs Blainey.' No, it was quite impossible! He almost stopped the taxi. As he realized he would never, never, never have to introduce Mrs Blainey to his mother his mind was irradiated by a naive wonder and he looked out of the window with rounded eyes at the people on the pavement, and the traffic and the shop fronts and pub signs. But he had not disposed of the real question, which was how to show Mrs Blainey that he was a perfectly normal man although he *had* remained a bachelor.

'I just happened to be — ' Hillingdon checked himself. Alice had opened the door and he reminded himself that he did not have to explain his presence to her. 'Is Mrs Blainey at home?'

The woman hesitated, looking at him in such a curious way that Hillingdon was nettled.

He could see her uncertainty. 'Is anything the matter?'

Mrs Blainey's voice could be heard calling from inside the house. 'Who? Who did you say? I can't hear? Oh, him, is it! Well, why don't you show him in?'

Hillingdon did not like being referred to as him but he followed Alice meekly into the drawing-room where he found Mrs Blainey standing with one foot on the brass surround to her fireplace, smoking a cigarette.

'Hallo, Napier,' she said. 'I thought you were a policeman. Well, this is a pretty kettle of fish, isn't it?'

'What is?'

'Haven't you read the paper?' Mrs Blainey tossed her half-smoked cigarette into the empty grate. 'I mean about our Egyptian friend appearing at a debating society.'

'Yes, I saw that.'

'Alice, take Mr Hillingdon to the spare room and then bring him back here, there's a love. He may not be able to see it.'

'See what?' Hillingdon had been growing increasingly jumpy.

'I don't want to influence you one way or the other,' said Mrs Blainey, and she lit another cigarette by way of indicating that the first part of his audience was at an end.

Hillingdon could now understand that expression on Alice's face when she had opened the door to him: it was the look of one who did not know whether to credit her senses. As he followed her up the stairs he experienced, very distinctly, the small hairs stirring at the back of his neck.

'Here we are,' said Alice with the false heartiness of a hospital sister, tapped on a door and then opened it to reveal a man's black and curly head pillowed on his folded arms. Hillingdon saw the head before he realized what it was. He took in, then, that the man was sitting at a bare table, facing the door. Hillingdon noted the silvery jacket and the crepe-soled shoes. The head lifted and Hillingdon looked into the dull eyes and expressionless face of a man who had abandoned all hope.

'Hallo, sir,' said a sad voice. 'I reckon I could take some food and drink now.'

Momentarily the face lightened. The corners of the lips rose, the lines about the eyes relaxed, and a remote gleam like midwinter sunshine looked out of the pupils.

'Cheese sandwiches,' he said. 'Chicken would be better.'

And he allowed his head once more to sink to his folded arms and Alice closed the door very softly, as though on a sick man.

'I'm not bringing him any food,' she hissed with unexpected ferocity.

Mrs Blainey was waiting for them downstairs, still with one foot on the brass rail, still smoking. 'Did you see it?'

'Of course I saw it.'

'Can you describe it?'

Hillingdon was so upset that he almost screamed at her. At Mrs Blainey! 'It's — it's — him!'

'He's been here about an hour,' said Mrs Blainey, beginning to enjoy Hillingdon's distress. 'He says that the people at the Egyptian Embassy are so angry with him over this debating society lark that they decided to hand him over to the police. So he decided to run for it. He says that once the police get hold of him he'll be jailed for years and years and years.'

'You mean he's run away from his own people?'
'He says I'm the only friend he has.'
'It's a plot,' said Hillingdon wildly. 'You can't believe a word he says.'

Mrs Blainey had quickly told Muawiya that he had far better give himself up to the police. But he would not listen to her. He said the British would punish him in revenge for President Nasser's taking over the Suez Canal. If she, his best friend, would only help him to cross the border into Wales! They had a long argument about whether or not Wales was a separate country. Mrs Blainey was quite sure he would not be safe in Wales. Scotland would be better. The law was different in Scotland. You could have verdicts of not proven brought against you if you committed a murder and it was well known that they married just anybody. She would have to ask Tim whether it was a good idea to make for Scotland. Herself, she would avoid the place. The Festival would be on at Edinburgh and it would be impossible to get a bed anywhere. Much better go straight to the police, serve the prison sentence and take up the British Council tour where he had left off. Muawiya was firm. He would not have run away from the Embassy if he'd been prepared to stand trial.

She was quite touched that he had come straight to her in his trouble, and in spite of Alice's protests (she wanted to show him the door) sent him up to the spare room to calm down while she herself considered the situation. She was on the point of telephoning Tim when Hillingdon arrived, and at the very sight of him Mrs Blainey found a new angle. She would have called it 'more adult'. Only the day of the party Elaine had accused her of exploiting poor Napier. He was for ever shopping, cutting dead wood out of the wistaria, polishing silver, moving furniture; but, as Mrs Blainey pointed out, it was embarrassing to have such a big man standing about and saying nothing; she suggested these little jobs as a form of amusement for him. And, of course, it certainly made his presence more attractive to her. Apart from his usefulness it was as though the atmospheric pressure was reduced when he was found a job to do. If it weren't for the jobs he would give her the most terrible, oppressive headache. Exploitation was a silly way to describe all the consideration Napier received in her house.

She was quite sure that dear Napier would take this young Egyptian off her hands.

She enjoyed, too, what she would have described as a good old British regard for reconciliation. She was not sentimental about it, but if ever she saw the chance of patching up broken friendships or even bringing together people who strongly disliked each other then it was delightedly snapped up. She enjoyed bringing them together without warning and under circumstances when they would have to endure each other's company for quite a while — a dinner-party, or, on one occasion, a visit to the pictures in Kenwood with a recently divorced couple. The alienation between Muawiya and Napier was not so deep-rooted that she despaired of achieving her first success; for, to be frank, she had never succeeded previously, although the encounters had given her a great deal to talk about.

Helvetia — a further consideration — was a much larger house than her own and if Muawiya insisted on hiding, it would be more suitable for him.

'I'm expecting Elaine in any minute for lunch and he must be out of the house before she comes. I can't have her being upset any more with these Egyptians. I told her it was her own fault for marrying an Egyptian in the first place. It would have been different, of course, if *he* had been English and she had been the Egyptian.'

'I shall telephone the police,' said Hillingdon.

'Alice, you can tell him to come down now. Mr Hillingdon will look after him.'

By now Muawiya had pulled himself together. He could do with a shave, and his slackly knotted tie, an affair of striped pyjama pinks and greens, hung like a halter around his neck; but there was spring in his step, a wide grin on his face and a determined cordiality in his handshake. He came into the room like a boxer from his corner, prancing (to Hillingdon's anxious eye) for the kill. 'You and I, sir, have become good friends. Whatever differences there are between England and Egypt, Mr Hillingdon and I will love one another. I am betrayed! Mrs Blainey will have told you that my own countrymen were preparing to give me to the police. They are not real Egyptians. Colonel Nasser does not know how he is represented in London. I shall tell him. They will be swept out. Perhaps he will make me Ambassador. Then you will have dinner with me regularly.'

'Well, goodbye, Mr Muawiya.' Mrs Blainey extended her hand.

'Goodbye? What do you mean, goodbye? I have thrown myself on your discretion.'

'No, no, Mr Hillingdon's discretion. I have never had any.'

'Your best plan is to go straight to the police.' Hillingdon had to use his left hand to disengage his right from Muawiya's clasp. 'You'll never get away with this.'

'It is cowardly to surrender to the enemy.'

'No, no,' Hillingdon was saying to Mrs Blainey, 'I really can't involve myself.'

'Are these two gentlemen staying for lunch, please?' Alice asked.

'No,' said Mrs Blainey. 'Alice, go and find a taxi.'

'I am not going away in a taxi!' Muawiya shouted. 'You cannot abandon me like this. I am helpless at the moment, but one day I shall have power and wealth to reward you all.'

'Napier, dear,' said Mrs Blainey, 'if you don't take him out of my house I shall be ill.'

'Is none of you personally friendly with Sir Anthony Eden?' Muawiya was now working himself into a passion. 'You have friends in Government who can intervene?'

'If Mrs Yehia comes in, as she's likely to at any moment, she's liable to telephone her husband, and then for all I know your own people will get in touch with the police.'

'Yes,' said Muawiya in sudden sorrow. 'Captain Yehia is my enemy. You are right. I should not have come here. I am a trusting fool. From English literature I learned about the honour of the English people. I believed it all. All! Well, I shall go now, without even tasting your food.'

'Dear Napier,' said Mrs Blainey, pressing his hand.

And so the two men, one who looked from side to side like an angry cat, and the other, separated from him by the width of the pavement, who took as many as six paces without opening his eyes (and then they were enormous), walked up the hill past Christ Church as the clock struck half past twelve. Before crossing Heath Street the stream of traffic had kept them so long on the pavement that Hillingdon began to hope someone would recognize Muawiya and denounce him. He looked appealingly into the faces of passers-by. Rescue me! For God's sake rescue me! His tongue stirred but his lips did not move, and no words came. When they had crossed the street Muawiya had demanded where they were going. He shook his head. The question was mockery. Muawiya was walking with all the certainty of a man who knew where he was going.

'It is quite possible to swim to France. I am an excellent swimmer. I could do such a swim well, sir. But I could not arrive naked in France! You could wait for me on the beach with my clothes. No, this is all madness. I cannot swim to France.'

They had reached the edge of the heath and Muawiya was glowering down at the houses in the Vale of Health. A couple of youths were locked in a mock wrestle on the slopes beneath the hospital, rolling over and over, croaking with laughter. Muawiya watched them with a hand resting gently on Hillingdon's sleeve. The sun stirred a faint cheesiness of smell from the wet, yellowing grasses. The trees passed patches of shadow from one to the other, like children playing a game.

'Let us continue our walk. It is sweet to walk with a friend.'

'No, I'm not going down there. It's too steep! I'm not going.'

'How beautiful England is, even London.' Muawiya was holding Hillingdon by the elbow, smiling now and urging him onward. 'Over there is a seat. Let us go and sit on it. There are these trees, and the grass, and the hills. As soon as I am in the open air I am calmer. Look at me! You can see that I am calmer. I could sit here all day looking at this scenery. It is like a painting.'

Perturbed though he was to be alone with Muawiya, Hillingdon was sufficiently a creature of habit to think it was time he had his lunch. If the morning had gone better, if there had not been this shocking bad luck of Muawiya turning up, he would have been sitting down to a grilled chop and green salad with Mrs Blainey at that very moment. Dammit, he was hungry! Hunger seemed to intensify the superstitious alarm that Muawiya aroused in him. It wasn't that he thought the fellow might attempt to do him some physical injury. Then what? Hillingdon was too troubled even to think. The very landscape seemed to be changing its characteristics. A descent through the trees, over packed earth slippery from rain, gave him the feeling of walking into an ambush. The trees took on a tropical enormity. The hill, when at length they set themselves to climb it, billowed away to a remote horizon crowned with feathery, un-English, glittering trees. Heat collected in the hollow where they paused to rest. Hillingdon's underclothes were gummed to him with sweat.

'No, I'm not going any farther. Mrs Blainey will be expecting me.'

'You cannot go.' Muawiya turned to him passionately. 'This may be the last time you see me and you must forgive me before I go.'

'Forgive you?'

Muawiya, surprisingly, produced a banana from his pocket, pulled down the skin delicately in four flaps which concealed his bunched fingers like the bloated and exhausted petals of a flower with a monstrous pistil. 'Do please accept this.'

'No, I don't want it. Where'd you get it?'

'There is only this one. Break off half and I will eat the rest.'

'No.'

Muawiya ate the banana slowly, watching Hillingdon intently out of eyes that protruded slightly from the effort of mastication. He threw the skin on to the grass and wiped his lips and fingers with a white silk handkerchief which he carefully drew from his sleeve and as carefully replaced. 'I have also some chocolate.'

'No thank you,' said Hillingdon.

'Why do you not look at me in the eyes when I speak to you? It is not polite to look away, as though I'm not worth anything. Why do you not look at my eyes?'

Hillingdon set himself to climb the hill, remembering that he had once seen a police car drive along the dirt track at the top. Muawiya panted at his side, occasionally catching at the grasses, rubbing them between his fingers and saying: 'Milk! You see, it is full of juice.'

He ran ahead and turned to offer Hillingdon a helping hand, but Hillingdon pretended not to notice and blundered past him to the seat where he collapsed and ran a handkerchief over his streaming face. The groan of traffic on Spaniards Road was reassuring; fellow-humans were at hand. But before him stretched a wild landscape of hanging forests, bold hills, chasms and forbidding valleys. A pale wash in the distance, the silhouette of a factory chimney and a tower, was London itself. Distances were vast. His own height was prodigious. To his distended imagination it seemed not impossible that he might glimpse beyond the remote Surrey hills the glimmering outline of the coast and, beyond the sea, dark Europe with its estuaries. To his immediate right and left were groves of trees. What did they conceal? If Muawiya said 'Look, there is a lion!' Hillingdon would certainly have seen one. If he had said 'There's Africa!' Hillingdon would have seen the palms. A scarlet band, about the size of a six-inch rule, hung in the trees somewhere between the buttons on Hillingdon's waistcoat and London. He shut his eyes, opened them once more, squinted, focused. MANN'S BROWN ALE, he read, and realized it was an advertisement on top of the Vale of Health Hotel.

'In Egypt,' Muawiya was saying, 'I have a political career in front of me, and it would be very bad for it if I was handed over to the British police. If my own countrymen did it, how could it be thought of as martyrdom? It is impossible to have a political career nowadays without being a martyr first of all.'

Hillingdon breathed through his mouth, looking straight ahead. He wondered if it would be any good offering the fellow money.

'When the British left Egypt there was not much chance of being a martyr, sir. It was very bad. That is one reason why I am in London. Imagine that the police catch me after great difficulty, and break my arm, perhaps. They injure me. They put me in prison. Well, if it is for three months, that is excellent. I could go back to Egypt as a hero.' Muawiya unwrapped the chocolate, snapped a piece off and offered it to Hillingdon between arched fingers. 'I am sorry you do not eat. But now, sir, tell me like a good friend that you forgive me for my bad behaviour.'

Hillingdon knew from his theosophical studies that the newly-dead found it hard to realize their condition. He wondered if the same was true of the newly-insane. Life seemed very much the same as it had been before his call on Mrs Blainey that morning; but it was exaggerated. The peaks were higher, the depths lower. The dramatic landscape held greater possibilities than the Hampstead Heath he remembered. Caverns could, and indeed *might*, open if he gave way to temptation.

No, he could never forgive Muawiya.

'D'you mean you deliberately smashed up my car to get notoriety and make yourself a martyr, or a hero, or something, and all for political reasons?'

'Oh no, sir. It was accidental. That is why I ask your forgiveness. But when I saw the smash I remembered that man was a political animal.'

But for themselves, there appeared to be no one on the heath. Hillingdon looked about cautiously. The slopes, the groves, the very pale, almost flesh-coloured paths, were deserted Nobody was about yet everything was under observation. That was where the uncanniness lay. Their situation was rather like that of two actors on a stage. From behind the trees, or clouds, an intense scrutiny was being brought to bear. Hillingdon wondered whether Perry had suffered in this way when on that ambiguous occasion at Sakkara he also had been quite alone with Muawiya and Muawiya had attempted, or threatened, to kill him: or Perry had been prevented from killing himself; or even that Perry had come near to killing Muawiya! For the first time Hillingdon began to sympathize with Perry. After an unusual experience in which the only other person concerned was this Egyptian it must be difficult to decide exactly what had taken place. Hillingdon did not know whether Muawiya was serious or mocking. What would he do if Hillingdon said: 'All right, I forgive you. There is really nothing to forgive.' He might well shriek with laughter. Hillingdon was certain of nothing except that he was in a situation where every word and gesture was important. He could well imagine that every twitch of his eyebrow was being noted down to be used as evidence on some future occasion.

'I have caused you to suffer,' said Muawiya.

'No, you haven't.'

'I have caused you a lot of suffering.'

'I tell you you haven't! How could a man like you cause me to suffer? Of course there's this annoying business with the insurance company —'

'I have caused you more suffering than you realize. You are generous, so you don't know how much suffering I have brought you. You do not like being with me now, for example. That is why I want you to forgive me.'

'There's nothing to forgive, I tell you.'

'Ah.' Muawiya sucked the last of the chocolate from his fingers. 'When my ambitions are realized I shall show you what a friend I can be. You English do not understand friendship. I will teach you what friendship is. You will stay with me in Egypt. I shall have a big house in the country and we shall go duck shooting. Are there ducks in England — for shooting, I mean? We should have silver flasks of whisky to keep us warm before the dawn. The whisky will be specially imported by me. I shall make a fortune. First, though, I want the English to make me a hero. Imagine me getting off the aeroplane at Cairo, looking thin, after my experiences in a British prison.'

'They'd probably treat you very well.'

'You are not a politician, Mr Hillingdon. They will never forgive Colonel Nasser for what he has done. My sufferings would not have so much value, though, if the Embassy hands me over. It would make my trial respectable. People in Egypt would say: "Ah, then even the Embassy thought he was guilty." No, such a trial and punishment would be worth nothing.'

Muawiya produced a new-looking wallet in yellow leather from an inside pocket. It was so thick he held it like a book and when he opened it the unfolding bulk of notes gave out a leathery creak. 'Here is two hundred pounds, Mr Hillingdon.' A rubber band enclosed a wad of five-pound notes, and these Muawiya now lifted out and wagged in Hillingdon's face. 'I accept all the responsibility for the smash to your car. I was a fool. This money will help you get a new one.'

'Where does this money come from?'

Muawiya withdrew the wad and looked at Hillingdon in surprise. 'You don't think I stole it! I have thousands of pounds. Why not?'

'I'm not taking it.'

'Politics is one thing, friendship is another. It is well known that England and Egypt hate each other. That does not mean that you and I hate each other. It is important to me that you forgive me. I cannot live without your forgiveness. Look!' His voice had risen. 'If you do not take this money I shall tear it up and throw all the pieces in the wind.' He paused to measure the effect of this promise which had, in fact, deceived neither of them. He pushed the bundle of notes once more into Hillingdon's hand. Hillingdon put them on the seat between them.

'You do not forgive me?'

'No.'

'Very well.' Muawiya snatched up the notes and jumped to his feet. His nostrils widened with passion. He stood over Hillingdon with one hand raised, fingers wide apart as though about to confer a ceremonial curse, and Hillingdon felt the man's anger like a surge of cold blood about the heart. 'Then we are not friends. We are to hate one another for ever.'

Hillingdon said nothing. He felt like one of those prisoners he had read about, the tough ones who refused to be brainwashed, who stuck it to the point when they were annoying the torturers, and who knew they now had only to hang on, not scream too much, not soften, not forgive anybody, and soon they would be left alone in a quiet cell. He saw that Muawiya had picked up the money and stuffed it back in his wallet. Now that the fellow was openly angry he seemed, paradoxically, less alarming.

'And what about those whisky distillers?' Muawiya demanded. 'Are you going to slide out of that too?'

Hillingdon closed his eyes.

'It is a bad thing, sir, in the state the world is for a man to turn his back on friendship. The way the world is we can't afford all this bad feeling. Let us be careful and know what we are doing. We must all love one another, sir.'

There were tempters behind every tree. Only Muawiya was speaking but Hillingdon knew perfectly well that they were all backing him up, snuffling to themselves and gesticulating. It occurred to him that prayer would be beneficial. He liked that point in the old stories when the Christian saint is tried to the point of despair and then makes the sign of the cross, withering and utterly confounding the demonic legions that hemmed him in. He was not a saint, of course. He was not even a Christian, he knew far too much for that! But there was a source of Power and Knowledge to which he could raise his thoughts.

He put one hand to his eyes and groaned quietly.

Muawiya could be heard drawing in his breath sharply. 'I trust you are not ill?'

Hillingdon waved his free hand. No, no, he was not ill. In some way he did not understand he was surviving the ordeal. He *would* have understood if only he'd not let Perry take Helvetia for a school of English and handed it over instead to the Warburg Institute. It would never have accommodated the whole institute, of course; but they could have used the house as an annexe. The sight of the books and the research workers would have concentrated Hillingdon's mind; his scattered, unorganized knowledge about demonic possession would have been rolled into a pill. Perhaps that was too much to hope for. He had been lucky to think of those characters who had stood up to brain-washing, because until he had done so there had been real danger of his capitulating and saying: 'Of course I forgive you and love you,' words that reeked of perdition.

His thoughts raised so much tumult that he did not hear Muawiya walk away. When Hillingdon opened his eyes the fellow had vanished. The realization gave him a quite unexpected throb of horror. Then he turned his head and saw the silver-grey suit flickering against the trees. As Muawiya walked down the avenue, diminished, became an anonymously walking figure, so remote as to be not even male or female, so the whole magical landscape was deflated. There was not so much as a whiff of sulphur.

He didn't get much change out of me, Hillingdon thought. Suddenly he noticed a young man climbing the grassy bank towards him and waving. It was Tim, Mrs Blainey's son.

★

They went into Jack Straw's Castle for beer and sandwiches. After his conversation with Muawiya, Hillingdon was mildly stunned, and the refreshment came less as ordinary nourishment than stimulant to recovery. Nothing but a stroking of hands and face by Mrs Blainey would have served so well. But he would not tell Tim which way the Egyptian had gone. Tim was annoyed with Muawiya for worrying his mother and he wanted to go after him, take him to a police station and get the prosecution over and done with, in Muawiya's own interests as much as anybody else's. Hillingdon did not like the suggestion at all. He did not know why but he did not want Tim to go chasing after Muawiya. He was still sufficiently jangled not to want any further action for the time being. Let's sort it all out. Let's see what it means. Hillingdon would have liked to go and sit somewhere safe — Hampstead parish church would do — and take stock of the victory he had won. He was convinced it was a victory but he did not know what over.

'I sent him about his business.' Hillingdon ordered another pale ale for Tim and a bitter for himself.

'I still don't know what's happened. I went into the house and Mother said you'd gone off with him, she didn't know where. It was just luck I saw you sitting on that seat. Well, I mean, he's got no clothes, nowhere to go, no money —'

'He's got at least two hundred pounds on him.'

'Two hundred pounds!'

'Said he'd got thousands.' Tim looked so much like his mother that Hillingdon could not help but like him; the blue eyes, the fresh complexion, even the same round-mouthed air of being in need of care and attention. Incensed by the way the Egyptian was imposing on his mother, the boy had come rushing out with all sorts of wild impracticable notions in his head, and Hillingdon thought it was truly fortunate he had been there to avert the evil.

It occurred to him that evil was a kind of perpetually poised lightning. He, Hillingdon, had been a lightning conductor. If he ever went back to that seat on the heath it would not surprise him beyond all bearing that grass failed to grow in the immediate vicinity. In his mind's eye the area was scorched and smoking.

'You know, I really must thank you for the kindnesses you've shown to Mother. She'd hate to admit it but she's pretty lonely really. She needs company and I can't tell you how happy I am, the way you call on her now and again. Does she ever say insulting things to you?'

'Insulting?' Hillingdon was surprised. 'No. Never!'

'She's a funny woman. I sometimes think the more she likes people the more she's rude to them, occasionally. So if she ever does — '

'She says what she thinks. I like that. She's not interested in certain things I'm interested in and she said so. But that's not *rudeness*.'

'I'm glad to hear that, because she gets so lonely sometimes I think she scarcely knows how to behave to people. She's a darling, of course, but she's utterly selfish.'

'Selfish!' Hillingdon was not too doped to feel irritated. 'D'you think it right to criticize your mother? I don't like that kind of behaviour. My mother ruined my life, but I wouldn't dream of criticizing her to somebody like yourself, almost a stranger. Now *there* was an utterly selfish woman, if ever there was one. Until the day she died the only life of my own I was able to lead was when I worked in the Ministry of Food during the war. But it isn't right for a son to attack his mother. Your mother's a bloody sight too good for you! When people get to her age and to my age they naturally think young people should give way to them. They think, all the time, about dying. Constantly! I suppose I might last another twenty years.'

'I didn't mean to annoy you.'

Hillingdon's heavy face was flushed with heat and drink. The whites of his eyes were blood-washed. He looked as though he hadn't slept for months. 'I'm not annoyed. It just sickens me anybody with a mother like yours should be so insensitive. What are you doing in Hampstead at this time of day, anyway? You on holiday?'

'I really didn't mean —'

'That's ALL RIGHT!'

They sat silently on their stools until Tim said: 'I'm really very proud of Mother, and I only wanted to say what she couldn't very well say herself — that is, thank you for looking in and doing so many odd jobs.'

Hillingdon thawed. 'I didn't mean to flare up like that. Fact is I had rather a time with this Egyptian.'

'What happened?'

'He told me he'd hate me for ever, that sort of thing. I wouldn't want anybody else to go through an experience like that. D'you know he actually tried to murder poor Perry in Egypt?'

'I knew you were trying to find out what actually happened. But do you *really* think —? I mean, he was brought to this country by the British Council.'

'Being up on that seat with him,' said Hillingdon, 'it was like being tempted by Satan.' He belched into his hand and felt better now that he had succeeded in expressing something of the terror of his experience.

'Tempted?'

'Yes.'

'What to do?'

Hillingdon looked into his beer. That was the question. In what way had he been tempted? He didn't know exactly. All he knew was that he had been subjected to a nearly intolerable test from which he would have been released the moment he accepted the two hundred pounds and become really chummy with the fellow.

'It was just a way of speaking. There's something wicked about that man, let me warn you, and I couldn't go into this very well without a lot of occult theorizing – and you're like your mother, too much of a rationalist, to listen to that.'

'Perhaps we'd better go back and tell Mother what's happened. She's got this worry about Elaine too.'

'What's that?'

'Elaine's husband has been ordered back to Egypt and Elaine won't go. As a matter of fact that's why I am here this morning. They've had some sort of a row and Yehia can't get out of the Embassy – '

'No, no.' Hillingdon lifted a hand. He insisted on paying the bill and they walked into the sunlight. The traffic wound past. On the other side of the diesel fumes the white railings wobbled in the heat; and beyond them were the scored flanks of the heath, the many kinds of green in the continually shifting foliage of the trees, and that remote exclamation mark in water-colour, the factory chimney. The strangeness had faded. No black serpent seemed likely to wind up from the Vale of Health and engulf them. The carnivorous plants had been tugged underground by the roots. No upas tree would be found in the grove. But the scene was one which, for Hillingdon, had received an imprint. He could not look upon it without a shudder. If his life was not judged satisfactory this scene would undoubtedly occur in one of the landscapes of hell that had been contrived for him. He saw himself repeatedly climbing the grassy bank to the wooden seat and reading, never-endingly, the red flaunting MANN'S BROWN ALE. He raised a hand and said: 'I can't bear any more complications.'

They crossed the road and walked slowly down the hill, saying very little until Hillingdon began murmuring that events were becoming too much for him and that he needed a holiday. He thought he might go abroad for a month until this Egyptian business had blown over. And not only the Egyptian business. Hillingdon confided that he had been forced to terminate Perry's lease and that the Helvetia School of English would therefore not be opening for the new term. There were bound to be unpleasantnesses which he would do well to avoid. His solicitor would see to everything.

'What will Mr Perry do?'

'He's a very capable man. Please don't worry about Perry. It's me you ought to be worrying about. What am I going to do with this great house on my hands?'

'Does Perry want to go?'

'Of course not.'

'Then why – '

'The fact is I can't stand foreigners. What I'd like to do is hand the house over to a learned society. Matter of fact, it was to ask your mother's advice on this that I was calling to see her this morning. But I can see now that what I want is a holiday.'

Tim said he did not think it wise to travel abroad at a time like this. He took a pessimistic view of the Government's handling of the Suez crisis. This military build-up in Cyprus. It was appalling that the Government was even contemplating military intervention. An attack on Egypt would be worse than immoral; it would be a mistake.

'You don't know what you're talking about.' Hillingdon saw the look on Tim's face. 'Oh, I don't mean to be rude. I mean just what I say. You couldn't possibly know what you're talking about. Nobody outside the Government could. Have you ever had experience of checking facts for yourself? My mother and I once climbed to the top of West Wycombe church. You know the one? It has a ball on top. All the guide books say the ball is made of copper. It isn't. My mother and I established that it was wooden, and we wrote all round, correcting people. But do you think anybody took any notice? The guide book still says the ball's made of copper. Nobody knows anything. How do we know the Russians aren't encamped in the Sinai Desert? No private person knows what considerations the Government has. Governments know. The Vatican knows. The Vatican knows everything.'

'If we attack Egypt,' said Tim, 'I shall resign from the British Council.'

'What has the British Council got to do with it?'

'Nothing, but it's a government agency and it's the only gesture I can think of.'

'You might just as well cancel your subscription to *The Times*.'

'*The Times* is coming round,' Tim said seriously. 'It's getting quite critical. But surely what you were saying just now doesn't mean you believe a man has always to back up the Government in whatever it does?'

'Not in everything, but usually in foreign policy, because every action is based upon information.'

'I don't believe this,' said Tim, 'and what's more I think that if there were a lot of people about like you we'd be on our way to totalitarianism.'

'That's the second time today I've been called a fascist.'

'I'm sorry, I didn't mean — '

'Quite all right! We've got to believe in the goodness of the Government or we should go mad. I think you underestimate the power of authority to influence opinion. Take the Hundred Years War, for example.'

They were waiting to cross Heath Street. Although Hillingdon spoke freely he was not considering very closely what he said. He was wondering whether he could bear to go back to Mrs Blainey's house and be cross-examined about Muawiya and the way he had been got rid of.

'What about the Hundred Years War?'

'Well,' said Hillingdon, 'the English behaved atrociously, but if you'd been alive at the time you wouldn't have thought so. Government propaganda was quite effective.'

'But my point is, that if the English behave atrociously it's up to the individual Englishman to protest.'

'There's so much secrecy in public affairs he can't be sure what he's protesting about. That's what I mean when I say that unless we believe in the goodness of Government we should go mad.'

'But the Opposition is informed and they're strongly against any attack on Egypt.'

'It's all a blind, so that if the intervention doesn't come off there'll be a general election and a new Government with clean hands.'

'You don't really believe that?'

'I believe in nothing but the wisdom of the Government.'

At the corner of the narrow street leading to Mrs Blainey's house Hillingdon paused. 'Do you think your mother would marry me?'

Tim looked at him incredulously.

'Do you?' said Hillingdon. 'I wouldn't like to ask her if you thought it was a waste of time.'

He could see the colour returning to Tim's face. He was annoyed with himself for having given the lad such a shock. That's what came of talking about one thing when your mind was really engaged with another.

'I should think it would be a waste of time,' said Tim coldly, and he walked off, leaving Hillingdon drawing a hand down across his flat cheeks, first his right and then his left, and remembering that he had been talking of people going mad. He could not remember in what connection. Why should he have spoken about madness? He began to relive his experiences with Muawiya and found significance in words he'd previously not thought important. And not only words but actions. Why a banana, for example? Why not an apple? An apple?

With no hesitation at all Tim went to the sideboard and helped himself to a whisky and water. He drank it straight off, and was lifting the bottle for a second time when he looked up and saw that his mother was watching him. She had come very quietly into the room and was looking first at her son's face, then at the bottle, then at Tim again. After a momentary hesitation he lowered an inch of Scotch into the glass and topped up with water. He lifted the glass to his lips and looked at her with his whisky-drinking frown. The taste of the stuff always made him frown. But it was worth it. Whisky helped him to breathe more deeply; he was all air at the front between belly and shoulders.

'Muawiya's cleared off. I caught up with Hillingdon on the heath. You've had your lunch? You didn't wait for me?'

'Elaine's not come yet.'

'She hasn't?'

'No.'

'But hasn't she phoned or anything? What's the time?' He looked at his watch and saw that it was quarter past two. The watch frightened him a bit. He knew that his mother had expected Elaine at one o'clock, and when he had spoken to

Yehia on the telephone just after eleven that morning Yehia was agitated because he had quarrelled with Elaine (also over the telephone) and now he could not leave the Embassy, he was on duty; Yehia had said: 'For God's sake get hold of her, Tim, and talk her into a sensible frame of mind.' The difficulty was that Yehia did not know where she was at that moment. She had telephoned from a call-box at Piccadilly Underground. Tim went straight round to the flat off Charles Steet, thinking that Elaine might have looked in, but the porter said no, Mrs Yehia was away and he certainly had not seen her that morning. There was nothing for it but to go up to Hampstead and see whether his mother had any information. He was angry with Elaine for telephoning Yehia when he was immersed probably in some frantic diplomatic tangle to say that she had finally decided not to return to Egypt with him; it was perfectly natural for Yehia to lose his temper. When Yehia had spoken to Tim about talking Elaine into a sensible frame of mind he had not meant, however, persuading her to go out to Egypt. There was enough worry in his voice to indicate that he meant talk her into a little cheerfulness. He went so far as to say that even if he did return to Egypt it would be for a few months only and he was confident of being posted overseas soon — if not to London itself, at least to Europe or America.

Another reason for Tim's annoyance with Elaine was that her quite irrational refusal to live in Egypt seemed to make the tension over the Suez crisis just that much harder to bear. In a time of gloom and crisis quite small happenings take on the import of symbols. He saw her as a flag showing which way the wind was blowing. She was uncompromising and idiotic, and he found himself thinking that meant the Canal Users' Association, Nasser, the United States, Soviet Russia and whoever else had a finger in the Suez pie would be uncompromising and idiotic too. When Elaine's behaviour could have implications as large as these it was perfectly natural to be annoyed with her.

'Do you mean you've not had lunch?'

'I really don't think we ought to wait any longer, Tim. We were only having cold meat and salad, anyway. You can eat Elaine's. Though why she hasn't let me know she didn't intend coming in I can't imagine. I hope nothing has happened to her.'

'I ate some sandwiches with that fat man. I say, Mother, I hope you don't encourage that chap about the place too much.'

Mrs Blainey led the way into the dining-room and called for Alice to come in and rearrange the chairs; whereas Elaine and she would have sat at right angles to one another Tim and she would sit at opposite ends of the table. By the time this whim had been humoured and Tim had repeated that he was not hungry but did not mind sitting down to keep her company she seemed to have forgotten the remark about Hillingdon.

'You are drinking too much, Tim. I could smell the beer as soon as you came into the house. And then two whiskies. It isn't so much the drunkenness I mind, but it shows in your features, my dear — you'll go all porky and bloated.'

'But, Mother —'

'Let's not say any more about it, Tim.'

'It isn't very often I do any drinking. I've had a very difficult morning.' He thought of Hillingdon once more and was about to attack him again when his mother broke in.

'There's nothing like drink for ageing a man. If you begin to look like a man of forty I shan't own you.'

'But I don't —'

'Your poor little face is all flushed. If you look forty it won't be any good my telling everybody I'm forty-nine, will it?'

He laughed, leaned across the table and kissed her. She sat for some moments with her cheek held up for the kiss and he allowed his fingers to caress her throat. 'Did you know that fellow Hillingdon had designs on you?'

'What?'

'He asked me whether I thought you'd marry him.'

'And what did you say?'

'I said I thought not.'

'Did you now?' She broke a roll and explored the white bread with her thumb. So far she had eaten nothing. The salad bowl was in front of her. Alice had already helped her to tongue and gone to the kitchen for water. Mrs Blainey smiled and went on gouging the roll until all the white bread had been worked on to the plate and she was left with a hollow crust, which she looked at uncomprehendingly for a while and then closed her fingers upon it. 'Did you now? And why did you say you thought not?'

'But Mother —'

A look of sudden concern appeared on her face. She looked at her son. 'It wasn't that you thought I was too old to marry again?'

'Look, I'm sorry I started this conversation.'

'But do you?'

'Of course not. But there's something about this man Hillingdon I don't like.'

'I must say he's very useful and obliging about the place.'

'If it's that you want I can be useful and obliging too. You've got Alice. You know perfectly well I'm always ready to —'

'You're jealous.'

'Perhaps I am.'

At last Mrs Blainey began to eat. It was easy to see that she was pleased and amused by what he had told her, and as he watched her quick movements and the way she glanced at him when she thought he was not looking Tim began to smile too. He was grateful for her refusal to be annoyed. If she had told him not to be impertinent, the rebuke would have been no more than he deserved. She understood him too well. Come to that, everyone seemed to understand him too well. There were times he felt naked; no, worse than that, transparent like one of those tropical fish, glass fish, who swam about in a tank displaying a palpitating brain, stomach and gut for all the world to see. His psycho-physical constitution must be fairly elementary, he thought. Up there on the heath he had been thanking Hillingdon for the way he had befriended his mother; down here, after a couple of beers and two whiskies he was blackguarding him. It would not have surprised him to know that his mother was aware of the way he had thanked Hillingdon, and that Hillingdon, at this very minute, knew he was being attacked.

'Anyway, that's not what I'm here for. I ought to be ringing Yehia to say I can't find Elaine, but I don't like doing it because he'll –'

'There she is.'

'What?'

'I said there's Elaine. She's just gone past the window.'

'Oh!' Alice went to answer the doorbell and Tim thought it was fortunate he had not started on the tongue; it was unlike Alice to buy more than was immediately necessary, and if he had eaten what was set before him Elaine would have had to go without. And serve her right, too, he thought, turning up for lunch an hour and a half late. He decided he was going to be angry with Elaine. First of all she depresses poor Mahmoud so much he has to telephone for help and now she is late for lunch! He had no sympathy with her. In the debate over whether or not she would return to Egypt with her husband he was entirely on Mahmoud's side. He was, in truth, almost sobered by the relief of knowing that Elaine had not done something hysterical, thrown herself in the river, or simply disappeared (which was what Tim mainly feared) so that Mahmoud would have to refuse to return to Egypt in order to look for her. Relief was replaced by anger. For the first time Tim realized how much pressure Elaine was putting on Mahmoud to make him choose between her and his duty. Surely she could not seriously have thought he would choose her, particularly now, during an Anglo-Egyptian crisis? Even if Mahmoud *was* anti-Nasser in his sympathies (and Tim did not know that he was) this Suez business would rally him.

'I'm *dreadfully* sorry! Oh, hallo, Tim! What are you doing here?'

She looked surprisingly self-possessed and pretty, Tim thought. He was taken by her dress which was made out of a pinky-brown material covered with sprigs of white; fresh, summery. He looked at her dress and looked at her face which was slightly pink from hurrying. It was a little like a clown's face, he thought, if one could think of a clown's face without at the same time thinking of the grotesque. She was *very* pretty. But she had this wide mouth, eyes set wide apart, and a long upper lip which could have been picked out in white, like a clown's mask. He did not even hear what her excuse was for being late, but it seemed to satisfy his mother, for within a matter of moments they were eating and chatting about a fur sale in one of the big stores. Harrods. That was it. Elaine had been in Harrods looking at the furs and not noticed how the time was passing.

'Why didn't you telephone?' said Tim rudely.

Frankly, he just didn't believe this story about Harrods. He could not understand why she was in such good spirits when, from Yehia's account, she ought to have been suicidal. She ate the tongue, the salad, all the bread she could lay hands on, and then Alice brought her an iced lager. She was inscrutable. If he was a glass fish in an aquarium she was — well, like nothing in the fish world at all. She was just a woman. Tim began to feel more and more helpless because he suspected that his mother did not believe this story about Harrods either; and, somehow, he knew that Elaine knew. But this undercurrent of scepticism did not seem to impede the general splutter of conversation in the slightest. He wanted to hit the table with his fist. He would have liked to throw a plate on the floor.

'By the way,' she broke off to say, 'I spoke to Mahmoud this morning on the telephone.'

'So did I,' said the glass fish.

'It looks pretty definite that we'll be going back to Egypt.'

'We?'

'Mahmoud and I. Within the next three weeks. The exact date depends on when some substitute can arrive from Washington.'

Glass fish stared. 'You've made up your mind to go to Egypt?'

'Tim, dear!' She sounded pained. What the hell gave her the right to be pained with him? he thought. 'Of course I'm going to Egypt. If Mahmoud returns, what else can I do? I can't pretend that I like it, but — ' and she shrugged. This was almost insulting.

'Oh but my dear!' Mrs Blainey put her spoon down.

'Does Mahmoud know that you've made up your mind to go to Egypt?' Tim heard his voice rising.

'Well — '

'When I spoke to him he was in a state because he said you'd had a quarrel. That's why I'm here. You asked what I'm doing. I'm here because Mahmoud said you'd had a quarrel. He was terribly worried. There he was stuck in the Embassy, and he asked me to track you down.'

'No, we didn't have a quarrel, Tim.'

'Elaine!'

'Oh do shut up, Tim, will you, there's a darling,' said his mother unexpectedly. 'If Elaine says they've not had a quarrel she ought to know, didn't she? Go and get the coffee, there's a good boy. Well, so you're going to Egypt! I wouldn't, myself, not while that black man is in power.'

'Nasser isn't black.'

'You know what I mean. Tim, *for heaven's sake!*'

Tim went to the kitchen and found that Alice had not yet made the coffee. He had leisure to sit and think about the lack of consideration with which he had been treated. He had known Elaine longer than Yehia had known her and still flattered himself that if he had been ten years older they would never have married. He was the oldest friend they had in common, and now here he was in a situation where one or other of them had deliberately lied to him. For no reason. It was quite baffling.

He was still waiting for the coffee when his mother came into the kitchen, carefully closed the door behind her and started to scold him. 'Tim, I never thought you could be such a prig.'

He stared at her.

'Now go in to Elaine at once and apologize.'

'What for?'

'Why, for shouting at her and being so rude. I said you weren't yourself. But of course she can see you've been drinking. I think you ought to have a strong black coffee and go straight in and apologize.

'*What for?*'

'Don't shout at *me*, Tim. You're behaving in a very odd way. It wouldn't surprise me if I discovered you'd made up that story about Mr Hillingdon, too.'

He did not know whether she was joking or in earnest. He followed her into the sitting-room where Alice had already taken the coffee. Elaine and Alice were talking about the colour of the roses in a bowl — they were strawberry-coloured, yes, that was exactly it — and when Mrs Blainey sat down the conversation turned to the effect of certain soils on the depth of colour in a rose.

Tim stared at Elaine until she blushed. 'My mother seems to think I owe you an apology. Well, I don't know what for, but I'll apologize if you like. I'd better get back to work. As it is I've wasted a whole morning.'

He kissed his mother and, before anyone could protest, had gone. He picked up his hat in the hall and shot out of the front door. What could he do to make people take him more seriously? Perhaps he could do something to his appearance. A lot of fellows were wearing beards these days. He swung down Heath Street formulating and reformulating the terms of his resignation to the British Council.

Later that afternoon he rang up Yehia.

'I say, what's all this about you and Elaine having a row? I saw her at lunch-time and she not only denied it flatly but said she was going to Egypt with you.'

He was accustomed to the note of caution in Yehia's voice when they spoke on the telephone so he was not surprised when for some moments there was no stronger reaction than a remote, contemplative grunt.

But he was startled that Yehia should change the subject entirely.

'Tim! Can you hear me?' He must have been whispering into the mouthpiece.

'Yes.'

'We've just heard that Khaslat is speaking in Hyde Park at seven o'clock tomorrow evening.'

'What?'

The line was cut.

CHAPTER FIVE

PERRY bought an evening paper at the Tottenham Court Road Tube station and read how Mr Menzies had no change out of President Nasser with his plan from the Lancaster House conference to manage the Suez Canal for him; Mr Menzies was already flying back to London. Perry ran his eye down the football results. It was quite impossible to carry in his head the way he had filled in his football pool, but there were one or two results which he recognized to be significant: Chelsea, for example, had lost at home and he had taken them to be a certain win. Unlikely that the pools would solve his problem that week. What *was* his problem? he wondered. He walked through to the Central Line platform and caught a train to the Marble Arch.

He did not want to speculate too much (the times were not propitious; he would have liked to believe in the existence of nothing that wasn't immediately in view), but take the case of this old lady knocked down and injured on a zebra crossing in Hammersmith. The incident was reported in three lines in the bottom right-hand corner of the front page and, so far as Perry could see, it was the only street accident reported. He checked all the columns before the train arrived at Oxford Circus. According to the *Evening News* there had been no other accident. No fatality in Regent Street. Piccadilly traffic had been uninterrupted. All day the taxis, the trucks, the buses had rolled along the

Strand, all over London the flow had continued, and a lunatic newspaper proprietor could perfectly well have filled his journal with a list of the places where there had not been an accident.

As Perry rode up to Marble Arch, to watch Muawiya's arrest at Speakers' Corner he reflected on the number of street accidents that had failed to occur that day and felt he was hovering on the edge of a great truth. The unfortunate old lady's accident was good news when one remembered its implication: that all the other old ladies in London were safe. Take his own case. There had been quite a crowd on that Tottenham Court Road platform and it was not beyond the bounds of possibility for him to have been pushed on to the electric rail. He visualized himself lying there as the train came nearer and nearer and eventually cut off his head. Well, it had not happened. He was alive. Mary and Christopher were also alive. From the position which his new grasp on normality afforded him the well-being of himself and family constituted news of the most bracing kind; and Perry looked his fellow-passengers and at the advertisements — Nobody Deserves a Glass of Hall's Wine as Much as You Do — with slightly widened eyes.

If only one could hold an imaginative balance between what was happening and what was not happening then, surely, one would have achieved maturity. That was another thing. He was not at all sure that he was what the analysts would have called Mature; or even what Mary, in her new frigidity, would call Mature. He saw now that a man's true stature depended on his ability to hold the actual and the possible in harmony. He might have died at birth. Everything in sight, every breath he took, was a bonus. He climbed the steps at Marble Arch thinking of the moments in history worse than this present Suez crisis.

Where did this particular evening at the Marble Arch feature on the scale of normality? More traffic than could conveniently get in and out of Park Lane at the same time was trying to do just that, and it was a good five minutes before he had finally passed the even trickier traffic hazards of the park gateways and joined a small crowd listening to a young woman who warned them against the use of artificial manure. Like so many food reformers she looked rather ill, he thought, but nevertheless he took one of her pamphlets and passed on to the Salvation Army who were in excellent voice that evening, beating out a hymn with such vigour that men and women, eager to join in, were snapping their fingers at the bonneted girl who gave out the books. Water dripped from the rain-sodden trees. Clouds that might have been beaten with a whisk and washed on their sunward margins with yolk of egg floated east into an autumnal murk. The sun itself palpitated like a bloodless heart over the Bayswater chimneys. A couple of hundred pigeons, bright-eyed and inquiring, ran about with clockwork precision and took to the air in dozens when startled. The air was damp and unrefreshing as though stored for a long time in a limestone cave. Perry looked at his watch. It was seven-fifteen. He had already seen enough of Speakers' Corner to know that even if Muawiya had honoured his promise and arrived he was certainly not speaking.

'This is very terrible,' said a voice in his ear. 'Sir, Professor Perry, sir, I would never have put forward this idea if I had known what a dreadful place this is.'

The speaker was wearing a very hairy German-looking hat with a feather in the band, dark glasses and a belted tweed overcoat that was red rather than brown.

'No one cares,' he said. 'No one *really* cares. I have been listening to them. It is all a game. If I got up and spoke about the Egyptian point of view they would treat me as an entertainment. Really, sir, it is insulting to ideas.'

'I didn't recognize you,' said Perry who, by this time, had realized he was in the presence of Muawiya.

'This is my disguise. At the correct moment I planned to throw it off, but now I don't know!'

'Throw it off?'

'Oh yes! When I am arrested it is important that the business is properly handled. Now, you see over there! Follow my finger! You see that blue car and those men sitting inside. That is a police car. Those men are from Scotland Yard. They are waiting to arrest me. Now, you see that red MG, that man getting out? He is a Press photographer. I have seen his camera. There are two other Press photographers here somewhere. I have identified them both myself. I am sure there are a lot of newspaper reporters especially from the Afro-Asian Press. I have warned them all. I have not seen the Arab News Agency representative. It is disgraceful. I shall take it up with Colonel Nasser when I return.'

'You're sure this Arab News Agency chap is not singing hymns with the Salvation Army?'

Perry was more annoyed than he cared to reveal. When Muawiya had telephoned to say he was going to speak in Hyde Park he had taken it for granted that nobody else had been let into the secret; but now, it seemed, the Press, Scotland Yard and — for all he knew — Colonel Nasser himself, had been tipped off. It was not the revelation that he was less privileged than he thought that irritated Perry. He had told Muawiya flatly that he had not the slightest intention of making one of his audience at Speakers' Corner. He was irritated because Muawiya had not believed him. He certainly had no intention of *speaking* to Muawiya. His plan had been to keep in the background and watch Muawiya's arrest anonymously. He assumed Muawiya would be arrested.

'This is not a time for jokes, Edgar. I thought this was a place for responsible people, but all they want is a laugh. All these speakers are cranks. It might do me harm in Egypt if it became known that I had spoken with a man on my right hand warning people about the end of the world and another man on my left saying. 'Down with the royal family', or some nonsense. The British royal family is popular in Egypt, after all.'

Perry was silenced by Muawiya's casual use of his Christian name. It was for the first time.

'When I climb on to a chair,' Muawiya said gloomily, 'and begin speaking it will be such a surprise to everyone that a man is speaking sense. Then after a while they will not listen. They will go away. Edgar!' Muawiya's voice hardened. 'You will have to help me.'

'Help you?'

Muawiya walked over to the kiosk to buy a packet of cigarettes and Perry was tempted to escape. If Muawiya was going to be picked up by the police during the next few minutes he would have liked to watch from behind a tree. Helping Muawiya to resist arrest was probably an astute move for the principal of an international school of English, attended mainly by Asians and Africans, but even if this personal consideration bore any weight (which it did not) it was clear that Muawiya was not trying to dodge the police this time. Otherwise, why had he alerted them? Certainly, though, he was planning the kind of arrest that would stir up as much public interest and Afro-Asian bad feeling as possible. But how? On his way back, Muawiya was pausing to light a cigarette. He lifted his head and the lenses of his dark glasses caught the yellow evening light; with head high, so that he could look westward over the trees, he breathed two copious streams of smoke out of his nostrils. His lips were still the bitter line that expressed disappointment with the intellectual standing of Speakers' Corner; but there was such arrogant calculation in the head that Perry thought of Rastignac challenging Paris to mortal combat.

'You know that I've been betrayed by my own countrymen?' He breathed more cigarette smoke into Perry's ear. 'They would have handed me over to your police. It's a mistake they'll pay for. They'll all have to go! They do not understand me. They do not see that they were inviting me to commit political suicide.'

They were about two hundred yards from the blue Humber. A constable in uniform was talking to the plain-clothes driver who now climbed out and stood, stretching his arms and apparently yawning.

'Do you know, Edgar, there is not one speaker here tonight who is discussing the Suez situation. Not one! Is England so indifferent? It had been my hope to find a man saying that Colonel Nasser was like Hitler. I could have attacked him. All very satisfactory. Arrest, photographs, very good Press publicity. But now? I have to speak myself. And you know what? Everyone here is so stupid they will not attack me. I shall say, "Colonel Nasser is the great man of our time," and no one will try to hit me. I shall say, "Mr Eden is a bloody-minded imperialist." Still no good. Some of them might even agree. If I said "Send your soldiers against Egypt and we shall gobble them up!" there would be a few interruptions. But nothing violent! I know these people. I've listened to these speakers for an hour and I've watched the faces of the crowd. They would not attack me, even if I spat at their religion. It is because they have no religion. They do not believe anything. All they want is entertainment. But what I want,' said Muawiya, laying a hand on Perry's arm and looking at him severely through the goggling dark glasses, 'is violence!'

Perry knew that in spite of living in the twentieth century he had never really faced the problem of violence. In spite of two years in the Army — spent safely in India, it was true — in spite of air raids, in spite of Egypt where he had come within a breath of being shot through the body by this same Muawiya who now stood in front of him generalizing about British public opinion and looking a little like the newspaper photographs of the old Aga Khan, dark glasses and all — in spite of newspaper headlines, television, movies, detective stories (possibily because of them) he still, in the depths of his consciousness, doubted violence. No, that was stating it a little too strongly. He doubted whether violence occupied the commanding position on the scale of possible happenings that everyone said it did. The possibility of violence was always present in Muawiya's mind. But Perry did not believe (no, he knew!) that he himself was any the less realistic for believing that compromise, accommodation, 'trimming' were nearer the truth of things. Or so it seemed to him.

'You're not asking me, by any chance, to attack you in public, are you?'

'Yes,' said Muawiya, 'that is exactly what I am asking you to do. After I have been speaking for a little while I should like you to begin threatening me and working the crowd up.'

'What good would that do you?'

Muawiya shrugged. 'It cannot be guaranteed, of course, but if foreign newspapers, particularly in India and Egypt, reported that I was set upon by an English mob and was then arrested for speaking politics in public it would be excellent for my career.'

'You don't think the fact that I was mixed up in it would look suspicious?'

'It is well known in Egypt that you very narrowly escaped assassination and it would be supposed you were getting revenge.'

Perry accepted one of Muawiya's cigarettes. 'You're a scoundrel.'

'There's nothing personal in this, Edgar. We are always the closest friends.'

They walked slowly northwards, Muawiya still talking and

gesticulating. His plot began to seem almost intolerably funny to him. He stopped, with the fingers of his left hand resting lightly on Perry's wrist as though to steady him, while he opened his mouth in the direction of the pale façade of the Cumberland Hotel and laughed with such explosive force that pigeons rose in agitation, faces were turned in his direction, a woman speaker on the Catholic Truth rostrum paused in mid-sentence. The air had darkened. Illuminated buses forged past the Marble Arch. Beyond the park railings the soft drizzle of light from Oxford Street intensified. Muawiya said that he was the first free Egyptian ever to walk in London. All the others, whether they knew it or not, had been in a state of servitude. Even the present diplomatic staff were slaves; they had not understood the scope of the revolution through which their country had passed. But he, Muawiya Khaslat, inhaled the London air through the nostrils of a free man.

'The most difficult part,' he said, referring to his speech, 'will be the beginning. I just pray to God that I am not arrested before I have gathered a crowd big enough for you to work on, Edgar.'

His head was so filled with the larger possibilities of the evening that he showed no nervousness about approaching the police car. He was making for a spot where a number of unoccupied park chairs could be seen. Clearly he meant to use one for a stand. They could perfectly well have walked round the back of the crowd, away from the police car, but Muawiya stalked on, almost splendid in his disdain, garrulous to the last. When he slipped away Perry had the impression Muawiya did not notice.

'Excuse me,' he said to the uniformed policeman, 'but if you're looking for the Egyptian that's him, over there.'

And he turned and pointed. Muawiya was gazing after him in astonishment, froglike in his bulky overcoat and glasses.

'What's that?' said the policeman.

A man wearing a loose-fitting raincoat opened the door of the car and began to climb out. For the first time Perry became aware that a third man was sitting in the back seat. He was leaning forward in order to look at Muawiya and Perry could not remember where he had seen him before. The man caught his eye and smiled.

'And what might your name be?' said the policeman mulishly.

'Did you say that was the Egyptian Khaslat?' Without waiting for an answer the man in the raincoat set off in Muawiya's direction. Perry felt dizzy. Some very significant action was taking place. He could see it but he could not appraise it. Muawiya, for example, who should have been running away was in fact walking slowly towards the detective. Perry could not be sure even that the man was a detective. He had only Muawiya's word to go on, that and the undoubtedly policemanly behaviour of the uniformed man at his side. Judging by the calm way Muawiya was taking the new turn of events was it entirely out of the question that the three men in the car were his accomplices in some scheme more devious still?

Perry dodged round the Humber and, without hesitation, into the line of traffic. A Morris Minor screamed and skidded on the greasy road. A woman's voice could be heard shouting angrily, but above that, and above the hooting and the alternating blare and thunder of traffic, above the distant hymn singing, the wind in the trees, whirring of pigeon wings, came the unmistakable bellow of Muawiya, delivered (for all his anger) with such clarity that Perry could visualize the shaping of his lips: 'You have betrayed me.'

Perry silently marked the language down as unnecessarily dramatic and shot out of the park gate, where he bumped into a man in a grey suit who caught him by the arm, saying: 'Oh, Mr. Perry, fancy meeting you.'

It was young Blainey.

Perry looked back into the park. 'The police have just picked up your protégé. Over there. See that car?'

'What a nuisance! I did so want to see what happened. I got held up.'

Muawiya with his cigarette between his lips was chatting quietly, half sitting on the Humber's wing. The fellow in the raincoat stood with arms folded, apparently engrossed by what Muawiya was saying. The driver and the man in the back seat were leaning over to listen. The policeman was a dozen yards away, rubbing his chin and looking as though he had been told to keep out of the conversation. No one else took any notice.

'How did you know?' Perry asked.

'Yehia phoned.'

'Did he?' Perry was interested.

Back in the park Muawiya was waving his arms about, evidently very angry and shouting his head off. He immediately became a centre of interest but before a crowd had time to gather the man in the raincoat bundled him into the car which immediately excuted a circle before speeding south towards Hyde Park Corner. It came within ten yards of Perry and he had a clear view of Muawiya, sitting erect between two men, without his dark glasses, without his hat, but grim and dignified as a sultan before his subjects.

'Do you know what?' Perry was already wondering which was the nearest pub. 'I feel like hell! I don't know why I feel like this, but I feel like hell.'

By the time they had found a bar Perry said he would vomit if he drank anything; but Tim, looking concerned, ordered him a brandy, and after he had taken a sip the blood warmed and he drained the glass.

'What are you having yourself?' He was conscious of making a fool of himself.

'That's all right. Shall I get you another?'

Perry nodded. The second brandy gave him enough confidence to start breathing normally once more. Brandy was not his drink. Invalid's tipple. He could tell by the expression on young Blainey's face that he must have looked pretty yellow. Brandy was what you'd choose under the circumstances, no doubt. He would have liked a Scotch but was afraid of getting tight. In a crisis like this he needed a clear head.

Blainey was drinking a glass of bitter. 'I must say I'm glad Mr Khaslat decided to give himself up. I suppose they'll deal with the case as quickly as possible.'

'Where would they take him to?'

'There's a police station actually in the park, isn't there? They'd take him there and charge him, I suppose. Then an Embassy official will stand surety and he'll be let out until his case comes up.'

'You mean somebody's got to bail him out?'

'The Embassy will certainly do that.'

'That,' said Perry, 'is something I must know.'

'What I can't understand is how the police got to know his plans.'

'If you're insinuating I told them —'

'Good God, no!'

Perry examined Blainey's two eyes carefully in turn. 'Well, why shouldn't I? Isn't it in the young fool's interest to get him arrested, tried, punished and packed off back home? But I didn't tip the police off. He did it himself. And the Press. From what he told me that crowd was practically made up of journalists and Press photographers.'

'You mean you actually spoke to him?'

'Certainly I spoke to him. We had a long friendly talk. He

wanted me to start a riot. Would you like to come with me to that police station in Hyde Park?'

'Of course, as this case involves diplomatic considerations it may not be dealt with in the ordinary way.'

Perry decided once again that he would be wise not to have a Scotch, and stood up. 'How do you know so much about this sort of thing?'

'I look after a lot of foreign visitors and sometimes they have dealings with the police. Mind you,' he added hastily, 'Mr Khaslat's case is a bit outside my experience.'

'Perhaps you could draw on it and tell me whether a cab can take us to this police station.'

Perry understood that the Marble Arch itself housed a police station of sorts, and the moment he had conceived the possibility of Muawiya being arrested at Speakers' Corner he had also imagined the opening of the door within the Arch and Muawiya being whisked up by lift to desk, charge book, station sergeant and cell. He did not know the Hyde Park station existed, and when the cab dropped them in front of the main entrance he was pleasantly surprised. Were it not for the blue lamp and the sight, through one of the windows, of constables playing billiards in their shirt-sleeves, this dignified red-brick building with a façade of white columns on the ground storey might well have been a girls' school in the country. Among the trees could be seen the gleam of Serpentine water. Lawn flowed away from the beds of geranium and dahlia.

'I hope you're feeling better.'

'I'm all right now,' said Perry. 'Perhaps you'd like to sit in the cab while I go and make inquiries. It seems an awfully long way from London here and I hate to have to walk back.'

'We're quite near Hyde Park Corner.'

'It feels like Shropshire.'

Before walking up the station steps Perry had some confidence that he had come to the right place, for he had noticed a blue Humber parked against a circular flower bed away to the right of the building and although there was no guarantee it was the same one Perry took it for a sign. He chose the side entrance, under the blue lamp, judging himself not important enough to walk in through the double doors, and found himself in a corridor where a man in blue trousers and studded boots was dashing water on to the floor out of a tin jug. As Perry appeared he picked up a brush and began sweeping.

'I'd like to see the officer in charge.'

'Yessir.' The policeman — he was little more than a boy and he had blue eyes — looked at him thoughtfully. 'The sergeant's in there.'

Perry opened a door marked OFFICE and found himself in a room with a desk of handsome Victorian mahogany, some prints of the 1820 Aylesbury Steeplechase and a worn brown floor-covering that was wiry even through the soles of his shoes. Behind the desk an open door afforded a view of the hall, notice-boards, a plaster bust of a man with curly hair; and he could hear the click of balls from the billiard room and a radio softly playing 'Gold and Silver'. The young policeman in the corridor had been wrong about the sergeant. He was nowhere to be seen. But as Perry was on the point of retreating the third man out of the Humber walked in — the familiar grey eyes and rugger full-back's build — carrying a green booklet which Perry recognized as an Egyptian passport. He assumed it was Muawiya's.

'Oh, hallo!'

'Good evening,' said Perry.

'This is Mr Perry,' said the rugger player, introducing him to a middle-aged man with thin grey hair brushed close to his skull who had walked in at his heels. He wore three pips on the shoulders of his blue uniform. 'Mr Perry, Mr Rawlinson.'

'How'd you get in here?' said Rawlinson, staring.

'We could very well have given you a lift over from Marble Arch if only we'd known.' Todd waved towards a chair and slapped the passport on the desk. 'Why don't we all sit down?'

'I was asking him how he got in here.'

'Oh yes.'

'Well, I walked in,' said Perry. 'If you've got Mr Khaslat here, and he's been charged and so on, I'd like to stand surety for his appearance in court.'

Rawlinson sat at the desk, opening and shutting drawers, and eventually found what he was looking for. It was a stapling-machine. He stapled some sheets of paper together and tossed them into a steel tray. All this time Todd — the only one of the three standing — was rolling himself a cigarette.

'It's just a personal opinion, of course,' he said, 'but I should have thought the authorities could not possibly have found a better surety. The trouble is that Mr Khaslat is in such a temper he doesn't want to be bailed out. He says the time he spends in custody will count against his sentence and he'll get home all the quicker. I told him he was unlikely to get a prison sentence.'

'I still don't know who this man is,' Rawlinson complained.

'Mr Perry is Principal of the Helvetia School of English and he has known Mr Khaslat since Khaslat was his student in Egypt.'

Rawlinson nodded. 'Well, that's all right, if you say so. As far as we're concerned, Mr Perry, you can take the fellow away with you, but he's already told his own Embassy he's staying in custody. They were perfectly ready to guarantee his appearance before the magistrate.'

'They've come completely round,' said Todd vaguely.

'May I see him?'

'This is all a lot of bloody fuss about very little.' Rawlinson spoke with unexpected vehemence and pressed a button. 'Anybody would think he was some dangerous spy, the fuss there is. Yes, there's no reason at all why you shouldn't see him. A very hysterical type, if you ask me.'

The sergeant whose chair Rawlinson appeared to be usurping appeared through the doorway.

'Bring Khaslat in here, will you, Pedge?'

While they were waiting Rawlinson leafed through the passport. 'You were in Egypt, were you, Mr Perry? So was I. I did five years with the Cairo City Police in Russell Pasha's time. When I think of what that man did for Egypt, and the ingratitude of the bastards — not only this new mob, but Farouk, Nahas, the lot! — I get so angry I wish Hitler had managed to take over their country for them during the War, just for one year. That's all! One year and then get chased out again. But in that year he'd have shown them a thing or two.' Rawlinson finally closed the passport. 'Russell was a great man. I saw him stop a riot single-handed. Do you know what?' Rawlinson smiled and showed a set of even, yellow, teeth. 'Old King Foaud, Farouk's father, was a wonderful man. I've seen him on a white horse charging the crowd with a drawn sabre. He understood the Egyptians.'

Perry was struggling to put Rawlinson into perspective by thinking of all the police captains who did not think that Egyptians were bastards when the door opened for a second time and Sergeant Pedge appeared ushering Muawiya into the room, who now that he was unburdened of his hat and overcoat was seen to be wearing a neatly cut lovat tweed suit with a blue spotted handkerchief peeping from the breast pocket. Perry never understood where he obtained all his clothes — whether he had brought them all with him (but wasn't his luggage inaccessible in the Egyptian Embassy?) or whether he bought them off the hook when he wasn't appearing at debating societies or dodging the police.

'Mr Khaslat,' said Rawlinson before he had time to put a foot over the threshold, 'your friend here is ready to stand surety for you, and under the circumstances I think this is the best course for you.'

'Professor Perry is not my friend,' said Muawiya coldly, and he would have turned and marched out of the room again if Pedge had not hurriedly closed the door.

'It may be some time before you appear before a magistrate,' said Todd. He offered Muawiya a cigarette but Muawiya ignored it. 'I am quite content. My incarceration will not go unreplied.'

'Unremarked,' Perry corrected mechanically.

'Oh sir!' Muawiya's aloofness was suddenly dropped. Tears appeared in his eyes and his voice was husky with emotion. 'How could you have treated me so?' He walked round the desk and seized Perry's hands in his. 'When I think what I do for you, saving your life many many times, so that people say I am in the pocket of the English. I cannot understand such cruelty in you.'

'Don't talk such rubbish —'

'You deny I save your life?'

'I'm talking of the present situation. Even your own Embassy —'

'I do not regard the men there as representing my country! They are not worthy!'

The accumulated stress was too much for Perry. Here he was, in the middle of his life, with a frigid wife, a landlord who was threatening to end his lease before the end of the next calendar month and so wipe out the Helvetia School of English and his livelihood, tired of his own identity, bounced from one unpleasant surprise to another in the full knowledge that if only he were more like Waldo or this police captain the surprise would be less. He lost his temper.

'You can sit in a prison cell until kingdom-come for all I care; but at least I won't have you sitting there in the belief that I'm responsible. You're in trouble because you've broken the law. You smashed up the property of a man who was trying to do you a kindness, and you've so little conscience in the matter that all you think of is making some sort of political capital out of being arrested. Frankly you nauseate me.'

Muawiya's eyes widened. 'Edgar, how can you speak so!'

'Who gave you permission to call me by my Christian name?'

'But we are old friends.'

' — you being pinched for a criminal offence and pretending it's got some political significance. I've always known you were a crook, but in the past I did at least see something engaging in you. If you're at all typical of the kind of people who are going to run Egypt in the future then God help Egypt.'

'You do not understand politics, Edgar.'

'Are you coming home with me, or aren't you?'

'Yes, of course,' Muawiya said quietly. 'It is very nice of you, Edgar, to bail me. If these gentlemen are agreeable I am ready to come with you at once.'

Perry turned to Rawlinson. 'I expect you'll want me to sign some papers or other.'

'You can stand surety for this man's presence at Marlborough Street Magistrate's Court when summoned to the extent of five hundred pounds. In the meantime we'll hang on to his passport.'

A quarter of an hour later, Todd accompanied Perry and Muawiya to the taxi. By this time it was night and the park lamps illuminated the trees in exaggerated green. A bed of geraniums was quite black. Tim Blainey, who had been strolling up and down with the cab-driver, advanced to meet the little party.

'As for you,' he said to Todd, 'I take it you're no longer interested in that job?'

Todd was puzzled for a moment. 'Oh yes! I feel I owe you an apology, coming to see you on false pretences like that. As a matter of fact I botched it rather, didn't I?'

'You certainly didn't take us in, if that's what you mean.' He followed Muawiya and Tim into the taxi and gave the driver the Helvetia address. 'This is not the last you'll hear of it. You may be a decent sort of chap in private life, I don't know, but in your official capacity you stink. I shall raise your trespass and false representation with my Member of Parliament.'

'Thank you very much, sir,' said Todd, grinning and waving as the cab moved off.

The drive to Hampstead Garden Suburb took just over half an hour, and when they arrived Perry discovered that neither he nor Tim Blainey had enough for the fare. To his mortification he was forced to borrow a pound from Muawiya and this seemed to give the Egyptian some reassurance that the world still needed him, for he roused himself a little from the silent gloom in which he had travelled and said nobody liked or even respected him. He said that Mrs Perry, in particular, detested and despised him and he could not believe she was willing to let him sleep under her roof. Encouraged by Perry's silence he said that he doubted whether she was the right wife for him, even as long ago as when he had first met her, on her visit to Egypt. Perry, Muawiya insisted, needed a more sympathetic and gentler wife.

'Shut up, will you!' And to Blainey: 'You coming in? Come and have a drink, anyway.'

The front door stood open and a single twenty-five-watt bulb burned in the hall. Perry began shouting for Mary as soon as he walked in, but there was no reply: the house, in fact, seemed deserted, and this disappointed him. He had been prepared for Mary, Waldo and Hillingdon constituting a horrified reception committee. Then he remembered it was Saturday, Ilse's evening off, when Mary would probably be having supper in the kitchen. In passing he gave the gong in the hall a thump with the back of his fist and took his two guests into the study, where he was pouring out whisky before the reverberations had finally died away.

'You can clear off, for all I care,' he said to Muawiya.

'Clear off?'

'You don't have to stay here unless you want.'

Tim carred Muawiya's whisky over to him and he drank it at a draught without waiting for the water. Perry looked interested and asked whether he made a practice of drinking in that way. Muawiya ignored the question and Tim tried to start a conversation about the Lancashire cotton industry, but he abandoned the attempt when Perry challenged him.

'I saw this bit in the paper about Japanese competition,' he explained.

Perry said he was not interested in the cotton industry.

'If you were an Egyptian,' said Muawiya, 'you could divorce your wife very easily and marry somebody more congenial.'

'Will you stop talking about my wife?'

Perry had been increasingly uneasy by the silence that hung over the house. He walked through to the kitchen and found that supper was laid for two, but untouched; cooked ham, salad, Caerphilly cheese, cold sherry trifle, and two bottles of Worthington. He picked up a tomato and ate it on the way back to the hall.

'Mary,' he shouted.

He climbed the stairs and saw, from the end of the landing,

that their bedroom door was wide open. He went into Christopher's room. The boy ought to have been in bed and asleep by this time, but the bed was still made up as Ilse had left it that morning. From overhead came the creaking of floorboards as weight was shifted ponderously from one foot to another. Perry went to the stairwell and shouted, but the footsteps continued as deliberately as before. Perry's shout had brought both Muawiya and Tim into the hall.

'I can't find my wife.' The words sounded quite idiotic and the fact that he could have uttered them worried Perry even more. He began to descend the stairs. 'It's very queer. Christopher isn't in bed either.'

Whoever it was up in Hillingdon's flat now seemed to be running about. Perry did not know why Muawiya should come up the stairs to meet him — he was becoming too tired to think — and it struck him they were on the brink of one of those extraordinary happenings, like old ladies being knocked down on zebra crossings, which were reported in the newspapers.

'I expect they're all up in Mr Hillingdon's room,' said Muawiya, smiling.

Perry was scandalized. 'What? Oh, rubbish!'

He found that he was considering the events of the evening, from the moment he read the football results to the seemingly never-ending ride in the cab right up to Muawiya's moral collapse (for that is what it was, agreeing to be bailed out) in great detail but so rapidly that the review was over and done with in the interval between lifting his foot and setting it down on the first of the flight of stairs leading up to Hillingdon's flat. What struck him about the events of the evening was their surprising ordinariness. It was as though he made a practice of walking up to Hyde Park every Saturday evening, witnessing the arrest of a friend, bailing him out in spite of protests and bringing him all the way home. Even Muawiya's conduct seemed remarkable. The extraordinary had not begun until a few minutes ago. The absence of Mary and Christopher was so un-normal that he was frightened. He was all the more frightened when he shouted up the stairs. 'Oh, is that you, Hillingdon? I suppose you haven't seen my wife?' and there was no reply but heavy breathing and the creak of a stair. There were two flights of stairs between the floors and if there had been a mirror on the landing half way up they would have been able to see who was coming down from the top. But there was no mirror; only a large uncurtained window framing black night.

By now Perry was convinced that the man on the second floor was a burglar, and he was just calling down to Tim, telling him to dial 999, when Muawiya pushed past and began climbing to the landing. This annoyed Perry. Muawiya was considered to be so morally deflated as to be incapable of anything but penitence and sulks; but Perry supposed he ought to have been warned there was still fight in the fellow by those impertinent remarks about Mary.

'Come back at once,' he said sharply.

Muawiya had gained the landing and was looking up the second flight of stairs, his eyebrows soaring with astonishment.

'But Mr Hillingdon – '

'What's the matter? Is he ill?'

Perry hurried up the last few steps, but before he reached Muawiya the Egyptian gasped and clapped a hand to the left side of his neck. What appeared to be a black thorn, about two inches long, with a blob of cotton wool at one end fell on a step just below Perry's eye level. Muawiya was expelling air like a pricked balloon and still lifting his exaggeratedly astonished face towards the unseen Hillingdon.

Perry picked up the thorn and wrapped it in a handkerchief.

'Blainey, go and telephone for an ambulance, there's a good chap.'

'What's happened?' Instead of doing what he was told Tim came running up the stairs. He and Perry reached Muawiya's side, one on each hand, almost simultaneously.

Hillingdon, wearing an open-neck shirt and white flannels was sitting on the top step with one end of what appeared to be a heavy broomstick in his right fist, exactly as though he had just removed it from his mouth after sucking it. The weight of the other end of the broomstick was taken by a three-foot wand, secured to the stick by a little thong. They could see now that the stick had been bored, like a gun.

Hillingdon's face flickered, as though he were trying to suppress a smile.

Complaining of a headache he had left Mrs Blainey's house abruptly that afternoon. He had no headache, in fact. Mrs Blainey could not have known that he was lying; so that her indifference, he concluded, was indifference to what for all she knew was considerable suffering. Impetuously he had said headaches were a matter of almost daily martyrdom for him; at times he was quite stunned with pain. No drugs could relieve it. She had nodded, said she hoped he would soon be better, and continued talking to that Mrs Yehia. Even Alice had scarcely a word for him when he went to collect his plastic raincoat from where it had been dripping over the sink. Hillingdon had the impression these women did not respect him as much as they should.

His sense of pathos was increased by this wretched plastic raincoat. It was still damp from a shower. He put it on over his blue blazer and white flannels and thought what a depressing sight he must make; a middle-aged — no, why deceive himself? — an elderly man dressed for a game he obviously could not play on a showery, windy afternoon when it could not have been played anyway. Tennis. Well, perhaps people would imagine it was bowls. He walked slowly down the hill thinking that the great mistake one could make was in being too transparent about one's intentions. With Mrs Blainey he had not been mysterious enough. He had been altogether too obliging.

Scarcely had he made himself comfortable in the wing chair than she had said in her light, teasing way — as though the matter were trivial and could be quickly disposed of — that she must absolutely insist that he changed his mind about ending Mr Perry's lease on his house. Mrs Perry had been to see her that morning to explain all the circumstances and ask for intervention. Mrs Blainey (hard to think of her as Margaret now) spoke like one conscious of her authority. So remote from her calculations was the possibility of a refusal that she did not even bother to put to him the kind of question he would have had to answer with a yes or no. She said he was a good, sweet man, but no one would have said he was powerfully imaginative and he could not possibly have realized the consternation into which his decision had thrown the Perry household. It was pleasant, too, to meet a woman like Mrs Perry so devoted to her husband's interests. She had come along quite without his knowledge.

Hillingdon was able to escape without saying how he would act on her plea — or, rather, instructions. He escaped practically without saying anything at all, so little necessary were any words of his to a conversation with Mrs Blainey. He did not know whether he could ever go back; certainly, he would never visit her again on the old terms. He was in revolt. Let her move her own furniture about, and if fuses needed repairing — well, that was a job for an electrician. Hillingdon stood in Heath Street, looking up at the ragged clouds uncovering and covering again the patches of open, pale blue sky. No doubt a great deal of a woman's time was spent in establishing power over a man and then using it. But that it should have occurred to Mary Perry that she might use *another* woman's power over him; or what she thought was power! It was insulting.

He counted the coins in his trouser pocket, hoisting his plastic raincoat to get at it. If the number of coins was even he would be able to visit Mrs Blainey's house again just as though nothing had happened; if odd, she would insist on using her imagined authority. He counted ten coins. He began to see that the person to be angry with was not Mrs Blainey at all but Mary Perry. This woman had thought she had spied out his weakness. He is completely under the thumb of Mrs Blainey, she had said to herself, and therefore Mrs Blainey is the person to appeal to. Acting on thoughts like this, Mary Perry had made it impossible for Mrs Blainey to *avoid* asking him to renew the lease. If the next vehicle to pass him was commercial of some sort and not a private car he would walk straight back and apologize. He had now crossed Heath Street and was walking up the hill past Christ Church when, to his astonishment, a black and white bird flew out of one of the trees in the churchyard and made off towards the heath. It was a magpie. He had no idea magpies were to be seen in such a built-up area. One magpie meant sorrow. He walked on, more apprehensive even than when he had sat listening to Mrs Blainey's request.

He reconsidered the word 'apprehensive'. Would it do? It was more accurate than the word 'angry'. He was much more worried than angry. Mary Perry was intelligent, and if she had supposed that he would do just what Mrs Blainey told him he had better look out. During his mother's lifetime it would have been natural for somebody to approach her, to enlist her support, if they wanted to change his mind. But his mother had an authority that was naturally conferred by blood. Mrs Blainey was a stranger.

A second magpie flew out of the trees, swung with a curious pendulum movement over the road, and slipped away in the direction taken by the first. Coming to the trees on the edge of the heath it climbed steeply and tumbled sideways. Hillingdon watched, his mouth hanging open. Perhaps it was one magpie for joy and two for sorrow. Confound the birds, why didn't somebody shoot them, appearing like that and confusing him! He was hungry too. It was unusual to enter Mrs Blainey's house without being offered refreshment; but on this occasion he had taken not so much as a cup of tea. He wanted more than a drink. He wanted food — fruit of some kind. A banana would have been very nourishing. He had heard bananas were good for the bones.

The ground fell away quickly to the Vale of Health. Down there was a pocket of air protected from the wind and it was thickening into mist. Autumnal mist lay in the bowl of grass and earth. Through the veil peeped housetop, treetop, a wishy-washy sepia line that was a wooden fence. If he followed the path Hillingdon would descend into the mist, pass through it and presumably climb out of it again on the far side. This was what he was not prepared to do. Slipping and cursing, he followed a contour above the mist and looked down into what it contained. To the ordinary eye the prospect might have looked Chinese; the roofs, wall angles, the pine tree, sketched lightly with an eloquent emptiness between. If Hillingdon had slipped down into the mist he would have known he was so much in love with Mrs Blainey that he would have to return to her house and say Perry's lease had been extended.

He was not going anywhere. He had no appointment to keep. Perhaps the effort required to stop himself slipping down into the mist was sufficient to explain the state of sweating anxiety into which he had got himself. He paused, partly to recover breath and partly, by an imposed immobility, to affirm that he was under no obligation to hurry. If he pleased he would stay on that very spot for ten minutes. To pass the time he searched in all his pockets for food. Perhaps an odd square of chocolate was tucked away.

The final climb to the seat demanded so much effort that his legs trembled and he found himself screaming silently into some cranial cavern: Let me stop! Let me stop! He caught at the long grass. But there was no one on the seat. He stood looking at it for some moments, swaying a little, and giving sighs of relief. This part of the heath seemed deserted. He seated himself and looked, first of all, at the mud and grass stains on his trousers; then at the point where the red sign should have said MANN's BROWN ALE. To his despair the sign was invisible behind the mist. This unexpected development had a darker meaning than the magpies. He could not see what he had hoped to see.

The westering sun threw enough hard, yellow light over the edge of Hampstead to send enormous shadows of bush and tree spinning to the east. Hillingdon wanted to lose his shadow. In spite of his fatigue he stood up and walked to the edge of the declivity where his shadow would fall on darkness; or so he thought. Enough mist must have been rising from the Vale of Health to thicken the air on the level he stood so that the sunlight hung in an infinitely dispersed flush, the merest hint of an old rose cloud, between him and London. Before he turned and hurried away he saw, or thought he saw, his enormously elongated shadow heading indeterminately over the abyss. He did not return to examine the phenomenon. He had read about climbers in the Alps encountering just such visions. Whether his floating shadow was real in the sense that the Spectre of the Brocken was real, or whether he had imagined it, was of no great importance. He had felt the sign inwardly. He was profoundly and psychically shaken. If, before boarding a bus, he managed to avoid seeing a four-legged creature it would be a sign of grace, but the thought had no sooner entered his head than a girl in jeans came along the track exercising two large amber dogs — boxers who writhed their jaws at him as they passed.

At Golders Green he would have liked to take a cab up to the house, but no cab was to be seen and he set himself to the long climb past the Crematorium with only an occasional pause for a backward stare at what, in contrast to the street lighting, was the deepening green of the sky. On a gatepost was a metal tab inscribed with the words NO HAWKERS, NO CIRCULARS, BEWARE OF THE DOG, and he immediately saw how they applied to him. He imagined himself some itinerant salesman, not perhaps of any ordinary commodity but like that young man who had called the other day selling the Encyclopaedia Britannica. With his little sheaf of pamphlets Hillingdon went calling at the house that did not want hawkers. They did not want him. They rejected not only what he had to sell but Hillingdon himself as a person. They did not like such a heavy man bringing dirt into the house on his shoes. His conversation was not of a kind they enjoyed. He had not been at school with anyone they knew. Hillingdon sighed deeply after the imaginary encounter and walked on till he came to an empty plot where electric cabling descended from the sky to a featureless, red-brick construction, shielded from the road by concrete posts, wire fencing and a notice that read KEEP OUT. DANGER. Never in his life had he felt so sorry for himself. It was out of life itself that he was now being warned. What did they want him to do? Destroy himself?

During all the years he had passed in and out of his own gateway he had never previously noticed the warning he could now make out with the help of the street lamp opposite: PRIVATE DRIVE. DO NOT TURN. He looked at it blankly. By examining it closely he could see that the metal notice was held in place by two screws. The heads of these screws were rusted. Even details like this, then, had been considered. Their requirements were not met by putting a new notice there without warning. The notice would have to appear old, so that he would torment himself with the question 'Why do I see it this evening for the first time?' In this way its meaning was underlined. *Private*. His life was very private. No one had been admitted to his confidence. Do not turn. Do not evade. In fact *you cannot evade*, shirk, your duty, your fate, your destiny. Hillingdon walked rapidly up the drive, glancing from side to side into the shrubbery and thinking of those big yellow dogs he had met on the heath and the warning they had let drop from their twisted mouths: 'You are in danger of losing your secret. The working of your mind is understood!'

As he entered the hall Mary Perry was replacing the telephone and turning towards Christopher who was sitting on the stairs. Hillingdon knew that the first words she spoke to him would be of particular significance. He would not speak first. His remark would only condition her reply.

'Oh!' Suddenly to see him standing there, and in silence, was undoubtedly a little shock to her. She looked at the mud on his white trousers. Being a woman she would attach a great importance to cleanliness. Her own appearance indicated a great fastidiousness: over her dress she wore a biscuit-coloured linen smock with strings that tied up at the back.

'The mud is nothing,' she said, 'but the laundry won't find it so easy to get rid of those grass stains. What have you been doing? Playing football?'

'Football?' He had always thought of her as a twittering sort of woman, not to be taken too seriously. He even allowed her to call him Napier, though he never called her Mary in return.

She ought to have been selling knick-knacks in a store and laughing with the customers, not trying to run a big house like Helvetia and be school secretary into the bargain. Perry was exploiting her. Hillingdon felt sorry for her but he still did not think he could excuse her presumption. The mud is nothing, she had said, but the stains would be more difficult to get rid of. What did this mean? What stains? Could there possibly be some implication that his association with Mrs Blainey had in some way been degrading?

'You leave this house at once,' he cried, 'you and your little boy! It will be as much in your own interest as mine. I am going up to my room to change. By the time I come down I must insist that you are gone.'

Mary looked at him as though waiting for the laugh. Hillingdon had not understood as much himself until that very moment so he could scarcely be anything but indulgent to her own imperceptiveness. 'For various reasons which I won't go into I am in personal danger. Anybody near me shares that danger.'

'What *are* you talking about?'

'As for you, Mrs Perry, you've been used. I don't believe you could ever have thought of going to Mrs Blainey without prompting. You couldn't have known so much about me. No, I don't mean prompting from your husband. I warn you,' he said, climbing the stairs, and giving Christopher a pat on the head as he passed, 'that you must be out of this house by the time I return. For your own safety.'

All the time that he was bathing he wondered what other meanings lay behind her remarks about mud and stain. He ran the water so hot that as he lay with his head on the rubber pillow that he had fixed to the bath for just this purpose he found it impossible to look through the clouds of vapour to the window and walls. He might have been floating in boundless space. Naked, he floated between the planets, fair game for whatever demonic agencies had decided to persecute him. The attack did not come. He closed his eyes and found himself once more on Hampstead Heath, looking at his gigantic shadow floating on the mist. But now that he had more opportunity to examine the shadow carefully he saw that it was not his own. It was that of the Egyptian, Muawiya. He swiftly clambered out of the bath, dried himself and dressed in a clean open-neck white shirt, clean white flannels and sandals.

Back in his room he would have liked to read but the words of whatever book he took up seemed to have no meaning he could disentangle. He bitterly regretted that he had never had the foresight to commit to memory any of the chants he had recently come across as set down by the Renaissance philosopher Lazarelli; these magical chants could procure the beneficent intervention of a planetary spirit. Hillingdon sighed and dragged himself about the room. He looked at some of his curios: the mummified cat, the shrunken head, the masks, totem pole, the primitive weapons. He accidentally knocked a hole in the kayak with his knuckles.

At the first sound of movement in the house he happened to be handling a blowpipe. The darts were kept in a small leather flask attached to the head of the pipe. He knew perfectly well how to prepare the darts for flight. Removing a pad of cotton wool from an aspirin bottle he attached enough of the wool to the base of the dart as would hold it firmly, with an almost airtight barrier, in the mouth of the pipe. Not that even a curare-charged dart would be very effective against the supernatural. To his disappointment the contents of the curare gourd had dried to a powder. He smoothed the powder pessimistically on the dart and saw how it immediately fell off again. The dart itself still preserved, however, some dark coagulated traces of the drug.

He had many times practised the use of his blowpipes and knew his competence to propel a dart anything up to eight feet. He did not doubt in the least that the face to appear in the line of fire would be that of Muawiya.

As luck would have it Waldo came up the drive, smoking his pipe and with a knapsack of books from the London Library, just in time to see Muawiya being carried out to the ambulance on a stretcher. Muawiya was saying that he was perfectly all right and that even if he did have to go to hospital for examination he was quite fit enough to walk to the ambulance.

'The trouble about these native poisons,' said one of the stretcher-bearers, a man in a white tunic and a cloth cap, 'is that they strike you down when you least expect it. If I was you I'd take it easy. You see, they affects the breaving. Leastways, some of 'em do. We probably ought to be a-rushing of you up and down to keep you from going into a coma.'

'What's happened?' Waldo demanded of Perry who was anxiously watching Muawiya into the ambulance.

'Hillingdon shot him with a blowpipe.'

'Good God! Why a blowpipe?'

'The police are in there now. One of them's got a straitjacket.'

'Poor Hillingdon. Are you sure he's not just tight?'

'Excuse me, sir,' said a sergeant to Perry, 'but we've searched the house and the grounds pretty thoroughly and there's no sign of the lady or the little boy. So that's good news, isn't it, really?'

'Good God!' said Waldo.

Once Muawiya on his stretcher had been slid into the ambulance nothing could prevent him jumping off it. He would have jumped out of the ambulance altogether if Perry had not stopped him. 'If you don't get back in there I'll hit you. D'you think I want you to drop dead on the premises.'

'O.K., Walter,' shouted the second stretcher-bearer to the driver. He jumped up into the back of the ambulance. Before shutting himself and Muawiya in he gave Perry a wink and said: 'That's right, sir. You 'it 'im. It all comes out of the National 'Ealf Service.'

The ambulance shot up the drive and into the street.

'The dart,' said Waldo. 'Did it stick in him? I mean, did you have to pull it out?'

'Of course not, you fool. It's only a little thing, just big enough to scratch. I should think Muawiya's perfectly all right, but there was no sense in taking any risks. It's a bloody scandal, though, not sending doctors out with ambulances.' Waldo was going to speak but Perry stopped him. 'Oh look, there's Mary and Christopher, thank God!'

Mary's custard yellow raincoat caught the headlights from the police car as she turned into the drive, holding Christopher in his jersey and jeans, by the hand. She hesitated until she saw Perry running towards her and then allowed herself to be dragged along by Christopher who was shouting to his father: 'Daddy, we were out in the dark and could see all the stars.'

Perry picked him up and took Mary by the arm. 'Thank God you've come,' he said. 'Poor Hillingdon's gone off his rocker and shot Muawiya with one of his filthy blowpipes. I don't suppose any harm's done really, but he's gone off to hospital for a check-up.'

'He told me to get out of the house.' Mary began to sob. 'He told me to get out of the house before he came downstairs again, and take Christopher with me.'

'Let's go indoors by the back.' Still clutching Christopher

Perry steered her along the path that would bring them to the dustbins. 'The police are busy with Hillingdon in the front.'

Mary stopped crying and blew her nose. 'How awful. He's quite mad. His eyes were so big. I was terrified. And his voice. It was so hoarse. He said he was in danger and anybody that was near him would share it. Edgar,' she said, after they had entered the kitchen and could see each other in a good light, 'do you mean to tell me that that Egyptian was here, in this house again?'

'Don't let's go into that now, dear. Let's get Christopher into bed first.'

Putting the boy to bed was not much of a task, especially as the boy was almost asleep on his feet, but Perry hovered around almost incoherent with solicitude. Had Christopher had his supper? Where had they been for the last couple of hours? As soon as Mary had kissed the boy on his forehead and turned out the light Perry almost dragged her from the room and held her tightly in his arms.

'I've been quite terrified,' he said. 'The police have been looking for your body for the last half-hour.'

'Do you have to be so morbid? If I don't have a cigarette I shall scream. Edgar, you're *hurting me!*'

They went into their bedroom and Perry thrust a packet of cigarettes at her. Only when she had lit one and taken a couple of appreciative draughts did she remove her raincoat. She sat at the dressing-table, examining her face in the mirror, drawing at her cigarette with a degree of passion that he had rarely seen her exhibit. She began to comb her hair — still without uttering a word — and for the first time he noticed that her hand was trembling. He wanted to throw himself on his knees at her feet.

'Well, what's happening?' she said at last. 'Are they taking him away?'

'I suppose so.'

'I mean, is he violent?'

'I don't think so.'

She could not possibly know how much he loved and yearned for her. The sudden strength of his feeling subdued the other happenings of the evening to comparative unimportance. If Muawiya had been lying on the top landing in a curare trance, if Hillingdon had thrown himself from his bedroom window and Waldo been run down by the ambulance as it turned into the drive, Perry would still have sat with his wife in their bedroom, burning to kiss and comfort her. It was, he felt, a moment when he was as near reality as he would ever get; the evidence of violence somewhere in the offing, on the other side of a wall, on another floor, in a recently departed ambulance; and he himself, caught by femininity as a poet is caught with words, frustrated to the point of idiocy but kept living and breathing by repeated hints of an astonishing fulfilment. Mary — it was quite possible — might suddenly want to be kissed.

'I'm going to the bathroom to be sick,' she said. When she returned a few minutes later she said she had never been so angry with anyone as she had been with Hillingdon. Not being quite sure that he had gone out of his mind she had taken his conduct for ordinary rudeness. But now she couldn't help feeling sorry for him.

'I expect they're a long time because they haven't got a strait-jacket big enough,' she said.

Perry wanted to be reassuring. 'As a matter of fact strait-jackets have rather gone out of use, I believe, like leeches. Mind you, they're as likely as not to be a bit behind the times in this part of London. Whenever I go to the solicitor's the chief clerk offers me a pinch of snuff.'

'I do wish you wouldn't joke about such frightful things, Edgar. At times I almost wonder if you understand what is happening. Now perhaps you'll tell me what that Egyptian was doing in this house.'

'Mary, darling.' This time Perry did get down on his knees. He kissed her right wrist and leaned on her right thigh. 'Don't you love me any more?'

'Really, Edgar, at a time like this, what a way to talk.'

But nevertheless she allowed him to kiss her. He caressed the back of her head and kissed her eyelids. He lifted her skirt and kissed her nylon knees. Trying to undo the white belt that effectively divided for his exploring hand the top half of her body from the lower, he found that he was emerging from a grey dream. Anything, absolutely anything, became possible. The range of possibilities presented to his consciousness had opened like a giant concertina; cannibalism, mass-murder, a jump from the Eiffel Tower, the extreme of self-sacrifice (giving your parachute to a friend who was without one as all four engines burst into flame), even poor Hillingdon downstairs being taken away by the police to the loony-bin, all these became quite ordinary and even absurd. The absurdity of life! That was the phrase he was looking for. He stood up with the intention of lifting Mary in his arms and carrying her to the bed.

'You don't care tuppence for me really,' she said. 'If I died you'd be married again in six months.'

He knew that she was not teasing, and he knew that she was right in a dim theoretical sort of way. During those few minutes he felt capable of loving all the women who had ever existed, all of them sincerely and, taking them in turn, the one exclusive of any other. Perhaps that was another way of saying he was, in Mary's calculation, capable of loving nobody. But this was a mere playing with words. By loving he meant not excited surrender to the mind and body of the moment, but an ardour approached with all the experience that living together for years and years had brought. This was the moment he and Mary were sharing. It was wicked to say that he did not care tuppence for her. He cared for nothing else.

'It's true, isn't it?' she insisted.

'What is?'

'That if I died you'd marry again in six months.'

'Now who's being morbid?' She was right though. He even thought of Miss Gunter. No, it was out of the question that he should marry Miss Gunter. She was too young for him and, anyway, was under Waldo's spell. Probably, too, she despised him for his drinking.

'I think we're being rather hideous really, Edgar, up here like this when downstairs the police are putting Hillingdon into a strait-jacket or giving him a tranquillizer, or something.'

'Blast Hillingdon.'

'What does curare do to you anyway?'

'And blast curare too,' he said tenderly. They held the kiss for a full minute. Hearing a car drive off Perry said there was nothing to stop them undressing properly now and going to bed; that was certainly the police car and its departure meant that the risk of the bedroom door opening to admit a detective-inspector had now passed.

'Mr Perry!' he heard someone calling from downstairs.

'You'd better go, darling.' Mary gave him a dismissive kiss on the nose and began rearranging her clothes with the kind of firmness he knew could not be argued with. He drew on his jacket, tightened his tie, and ran a comb through his hair.

'Oh, by the way, darling. Muawiya was pinched this evening so I had to go along to the police station and bail him out.'

He did not wait for Mary's comment but opened the door and hurried downstairs to the study, where he found Tim Blainey,

Waldo and a police sergeant standing with expressions of exaggerated calm upon their faces. Perry looked about for signs of damage but found none.

'My wife and son are all right, I'm glad to say. He scared them out of the house, which was a good thing as matters turned out.'

'We'll be wanting Mrs Perry's statement later,' said the sergeant. 'We won't bother the lady now. But I'd be very glad if you and this gentleman – ' nodding at Tim Blainey – ' would be kind enough to come down to the station and make a statement. I've got my proper clerk down there, d'you see?'

'How did Mr Hillingdon go off?'

'Oh very well, sir, I think you might say.' The sergeant might have been referring to some public ceremony. 'A bit drawn out, perhaps. We could very well have done without a lot of the details. But very well on the whole, sir, I would say.'

'What do you think will happen to him?'

'Unfit to plead, sir, that's what they'll find him, but that's only my opinion, see?'

'Unfit to plead.' Perry tried to concentrate on Hillingdon's plight. 'Poor old boy!' He also wondered how his lease would be affected.

Waldo was in charge of Helvetia while Tim Blainey and Perry were down at the police station and visiting the hospital. The result was that when they returned there were three journalists and two Press photographers in the house. The Press knew all about Muawiya's arrest. At least, they knew he had been arrested, charged and released on bail. They also knew who was standing surety for him, and as Waldo did not the conversation he had with the news desk of the *Sun* caused him such stupefaction that he said: 'I am happy to inform you that this Egyptian is no longer in the house. I won't conceal from you the fact that he was here. But he has been taken away after a shooting incident involving a blowpipe and poisoned dart.' He put down the receiver thinking he had closed the matter so far as the Press was concerned.

'I tell you he's not here,' Waldo was shouting at the journalists when Perry and Blainey arrived. Waldo had said he would regard the first man to put his foot over the threshold as guilty of a trespass and take action accordingly. The journalists stood in the front porch, a naked electric light bulb swinging on a cord over their heads. Waldo was a good ten feet up the hall, well away from the wide open door, as though to emphasize he was not threatening them with force; his ascendancy (as he saw it) was entirely moral. 'So if you want anything out of him you'd better go along to the hospital.'

'But what's this about a blowpipe?'

'That is an entirely different matter.'

'I understand Mr Hillingdon's got his room fixed up like a sort of museum,' said one of the journalists. 'We'd most awfully appreciate it if you'd let us go up and take a photo.'

'Certainly not,' said Waldo.

Perry pushed his way through. 'My name is Perry, gentlemen, and if you'd like to step inside I'll tell you whatever is reasonable, but we've got a kid asleep upstairs, so please be quiet.'

It took half an hour to get rid of the journalists. Perry was firm about not letting them go up to Hillingdon's flat and they took his refusal good-humouredly when he confirmed most of the information they already had about Muawiya's arrest. He said very little about the blowpipe. A dart *had* struck Muawiya, but who was responsible and just what sort of prank he thought he was up to, Perry could not say.

'Mr Hillingdon is assisting the police in their inquiries,' said a fellow with a flash-bulb held over his head.

'You could safely say that,' Perry agreed, and the flash blanched everyone.

His thoughts were with Muawiya rather than Hillingdon. After an hour at the police station, during which time they identified the blowpipe and dart, watched them wrapped up and labelled, dictated statements which were carefully written out in long-hand by a police clerk, asked (and were refused) permission to see Hillingdon, a police car took them through some ill-lit and leafy avenues and between a pair of brick piers supporting a stone ball each to a cavernous door. Lights snapped on as they walked up the steps. The word CASUALTY was printed in red on a white panel.

They found Muawiya wearing blue pyjamas and sitting in the night sister's cubicle smoking a cigarette. The sister herself was not to be seen. Muawiya explained that she was in one of the wards, working on a patient; a very nice woman who had given him permission to come out here and smoke because, she said, judging by what the doctor had told her Muawiya didn't have long to live and she was ready to ease his last hours in this world.

'She is an Irish sister,' said Muawiya.

Clearly, there was nothing the matter with him. A piece of plaster had been stuck on his cheek and he had been given an injection.

'They wouldn't let us see Hillingdon,' Tim remarked.

Muawiya laughed so scornfully that Perry asked him what he had in his mind.

'You are all so funny.'

'I hope you're not suggesting that Hillingdon is funny.'

'No, no. He is a sensible man. I respect him. But what I think is funny is the way you say "Oh poor Hillingdon, he is gone mad." You think he is mad, don't you? I have been sitting here and thinking about him. He is not at all mad, if you ask me.' He stubbed his cigarette and spread his right hand. 'But let us not talk about this. There are other subjects. It was nice of you to come and see me.'

Perry, too, did not particularly want to talk about Hillingdon. Once assured of Muawiya's well-being he was quite ready to go home, but Muawiya had begged them to stay just a little while longer, he was so lonely, and returned to Hillingdon's behaviour as though it were the one subject guaranteed to hold them there.

'Sh!' He raised his finger. 'I thought she was coming back.' He offered Perry and Blainey cigarettes and threw the empty packet into the corner. 'You see, I understand Mr Hillingdon. We are really the most excellent friends. Although I have not known him so long as you, Edgar, I hope I do not annoy you in saying that he is a better friend. One day he is coming to stay with me in Egypt and we shall go duck shooting. We are deep, deep friends. Only politics come between us.'

'What sort of politics?'

'He is very anti-Egyptian. In just the same way I am anti-British. That is all patriotism and politics. He tried to kill me because of it. Perhaps he has killed me. Who knows? Nobody in this hospital seems to understand this poison at all. Maybe I am dead in the morning. All politics! In our hearts we love each other.'

Perry and Blainey had exchanged glances.

'You don't think he was acting a bit queer tonight?' said Perry.

'Queer? No! Why should it be queer? Violence is not queer. It is natural.'

'My dear Muawiya, surely even you can see that the poor chap has had some kind of mental breakdown.'

'Mental breakdown! Edgar, dear sir, Mr Blainey! Believe me, sirs, I do not want to argue about this. It is not important. But since you have raised the matter I must talk. Mr Hillingdon is quite all right. He is a good man. If he were here now I would shake his hand. Because a man acts on his beliefs surely you do not say he is mad? Why should we be so hypocritical? Why do you English always make excuses and refuse to face the truth? Why do you have so many double thoughts? If England attacks my country because she is greedy over the Suez Canal it will only be under pretence of doing something else. You will not give names to things in England. Or you give them the wrong names. When a man commits some terrible crime you say he is mad and in need of care and attention. No, I say. Kill him!'

'Hillingdon does need care and attention.'

Muawiya smiled. 'It is of no importance, sirs. Let us not talk further. What the authorities do with Mr Hillingdon is more your business than mine. All I want now is to return to my country as quickly as possible, before the war starts.'

The hospital was ten minutes' walk from the nearest Tube station according to the porter, and in twenty minutes they could walk all the way to Helvetia. No cabs about. Perry and Blainey walked under black trees that occasionally shivered water on them, moving from one street lamp and its island of light to the next, and looking over walls, through shrubbery, up drives to the gleams between the curtains and the occasional brilliant interior, the blue wallpaper and the red, the mirror-loaded mantels. For a long time they had said nothing, and when they did talk it was not, to begin with, about Muawiya or about Hillingdon but about the political crisis. Blainey said he thought the French were particularly dangerous because they had taken such a beating and now regarded an attack on Egypt as a way of boosting their own morale.

'Why aren't there more people like you and me?' Blainey tried to sound humorous; instead, he sounded wistful. 'If there were people like you and me at the head of affairs there'd be none of this international squabbling. Would there?'

'Yes,' said Perry.

'But neither you nor I would start a war!'

'Yes, you would. A man who becomes a head of a Government becomes a different person.'

'But —'

'Oh, for God's sake! You don't think we've got any superior wisdom, do you?'

Blainey hesitated. 'I don't want to sound offensive but what you've just said is very like something Hillingdon was arguing when I met him the other day. He said that one ought to support the Government in pretty well everything they do, because the Government alone has all the information needed for a correct judgment to be made. Or something like that.'

'And we all know what's happened to Hillingdon. No,' said Perry, 'I'm not arguing that at all. I'm just saying that nobody is very clever, not even you and me.'

A light drizzle began to fall, so gentle that the street lamps lit it up like haze. Nobody else was walking. A church clock was striking midnight and cars hissed on the wet tarmac.

Perry was thinking that it would take a great deal to convince Muawiya there was a pathological explanation for Hillingdon's behaviour. And, in exactly the same way, any military attack on Egypt would be regarded by the Egyptians not as some queer aberration but as an act of calculated policy. *If* there was an attack. Perry would not enjoy a conversation with Muawiya after it had taken place, whatever the outcome. It would be unendurable to have Muawiya arguing, as he had argued about Hillingdon, that they were friends beneath the skin and the dotty attack with the blowpipe had been the gesture of a patriot.

Blainey turned up his coat collar — neither of them had raincoats — and solemnly cursed the weather and the sequence of events that had brought them out in it.

'I ought to have been forewarned about Hillingdon,' he said. 'I could see he was going off his head. He was going to ask my mother to marry him.'

Blainey thought for a while. 'But I warned him off.'

CHAPTER SIX

Now that an appearance at the magistrate's court was inevitable Muawiya agreed to seeing a legal officer from the Embassy as soon as he was discharged from hospital. An interview with a solicitor was arranged. Perry wished him anywhere but at Helvetia, but Muawiya insisted he would not be happy in an hotel.

'All the time, Edgar, you would be wondering where I was and about your five hundred pounds. My sense of obligation to you prevents me from leaving your side. Why should I cause you a moment's anxiety? Really, sir, I am not worth it.'

And Mary, quite unexpectedly, agreed. For two or three days Mary saw Muawiya as the chief hope of a future for the Helvetia School of English, a livelihood for the Perry family and, in particular, bread in the mouth of Christopher. Hillingdon's threat to terminate their lease had thoroughly upset her. She had been sufficiently frightened by the blowpipe not to repress her natural thankfulness that he had gone off his head, got himself shut up and so made any further action to terminate the lease impossible. The police were looking in vain for Hillingdon's next of kin. In the meantime the Helvetia School of English was to carry on. She knew that Edgar was optimistic about the future because he was arguing that Hillingdon's acute paranoia would serve as a lustration wherein all pettiness would be lost; he would emerge, altogether tireless in his philanthropy. But long before the new Hillingdon arose, the school it seemed might well have fallen a victim to the Suez crisis. Enrolled students were turning up to demand their fees back. A Saudi Arabian by the name of Mansoury appeared in a scarlet Allard and said that now the Prime Minister had made this statement in the House of Commons, that 'the use of force could not be ruled out', he had no alternative but to ask for the return of his forty guineas. He was polite and apologetic, but he was going on strike. He thought all the students of Helvetia, the Iraqis, the Sudanese, the Pakistanis, the Burmese, the Malay — all, all would go on strike and demand their forty guineas back. He was not sure about the Turks.

Muawiya bounded out of Perry's study on hearing this and said, speaking in English for Mary's benefit, that it was a long time since he had heard such bad political thinking from an Arab. 'Who would they be injuring, all these foreign students, by not knowing English? Would it be the English? Or the French? Or the Americans? Or the Russians? No, they would injure themselves! These English,' said Muawiya, 'must be sucked like an egg. They exploited you for five hundred years. Now exploit them. Eat their brains. Besides, Professor Perry is an old friend of mine and if he has no students how is he going to live?'

These mid-September days saw Mary in the hall with a chair and a trestle table covered with enrolment papers, copies of the syllabus, prospectuses, time-tables, and receipt forms. Without Muawiya's help she would have been helpless. He sat at her side, addressing the Iraqis, the Sudanese and the Saudi Arabians in Arabic, the rest in English, asserting that as an Egyptian and a man who had actually been present at the Bandoeng Conference — he had reported the conference for his paper — he could assure them they were all doing their duty at this difficult time by carrying on with their studies and fitting themselves to be citizens not just of some corner of Africa or Asia but of the whole world. 'The English have gone swimming in deep water,' he said. 'Now is our chance to steal their clothes.' Without actually saying so he contrived the impression that the Helvetia School of English had been approved by Colonel Nasser himself.

Journalists were granted interviews at the same table and frequently at the same time. The enrolment of students at the Helvetia School of English was seen on the television and cinema screens of the world. A couple of policemen were kept posted at the head of the drive during the hours of daylight to keep out the crowd. Perry, Waldo and Miss Gunter — re-recruited to help cope with the extra work — came and went by the back entrance. Muawiya was in a continuous flush of excitement. The time between Hillingdon's arrest and his own appearance at Marlborough Street Police Court seemed one long public meeting in which he spoke to students, journalists, officials from the Egyptian Embassy, the solicitor, the police, doctors, an expert from the British Museum who wanted to see the kind of wound made by a blowpipe dart, the Perrys, the Blaineys, the Yehias and — of course — Waldo himself who was bilious from a sense of outrage. Waldo did not reply.

Once she had overcome her annoyance with Edgar for bailing Muawiya out, Mary realized it was a hard legal fact that if Muawiya absconded they would have to find five hundred pounds; and they hadn't got five hundred pounds. Muawiya's wish to spare them anxiety over his movements showed that he had some glimmerings of humanity. His presence had to be tolerated and therefore it was tolerated — he slept in a camp bed in the box-room — particularly if he continued to act as the Helvetian public relations officer to the Afro-Asian world.

Mary was, too, reconciled to Muawiya's presence because

217

she felt so guilty about the way she was treating Edgar. He pretended that he wanted the Egyptian out of the house; but she was not deceived. She knew that ever since Muawiya had tried to murder Edgar in Egypt they had shown a warm regard for one another. On Muawiya's side she did not doubt that the regard was quite sincere. Edgar, always wanting to be large-minded and noble, would think it his duty to like Muawiya and no passing irritation would really affect that liking. Edgar could swear as much as he liked but it did not mean anything. He would always be grateful to the man who had thought him sufficiently important to assassinate. He would see it as the most enormous compliment. He was being compared to Julius Caesar or General Gordon. When she heard her husband and Muawiya talking together she had exactly the same bored jealousy as when she heard Edgar with some fellow who had been at the same school with him. She wanted to break in with wifeliness and they always ignored her.

Wifeliness. Yes, she could manage that — the show of possessiveness and the bossing about and the appeal for unnecessary help. This could not satisfy Edgar. At the deeper levels of their relationship she knew that she was a disappointment to him. In her heart of hearts she did not care, much, that she was a disappointment, and the knowledge of her indifference made Edgar appear pathetic, even childish, to her. She could do without him but he could not do without her. Poor, poor Edgar! It was *quite* upsetting when you came to think of it, the way they were married that terribly hot spring morning with the hawthorn bush by the church door looking too crazily beautiful in its smoking, white blossom. The parson making the mistake, *take this woman, Edgar*, while she looked at him sideways and saw how his fat neck was peeping over the top of his tight collar. And now she felt guilty because she could do without him. Not financially, of course. She could not do without the money.

He was all those years older than her too! He was middle-aged. He ought to have dulled over. It wasn't that bed bored her, but people attached too much importance to it. The novels, and the plays, and the films, and the advice columns in the magazines, they all busied themselves pumping up this emotion about sex, and she did not believe that half the people who read that stuff, or watched it, felt themselves really equal to so much effort. No, not a quarter the people. If people were only honest they would get up in the middle of one of those hot scenes and say: 'No, this is setting the standard too high and damaging my self-esteem.' It was not only love. In spite of that man Hillingdon she could not build up as much hate as twentieth-century entertainment seemed to imply was expected of her. She was just too pallid. Perhaps she should never have married. To be a nun, though, you had first of all to be a Roman Catholic and they believed too many things she could not accept. And kissing the Pope's toe!

Edgar was not handsome any more. To see him first thing in the morning, his belly showing over the top of his pyjamas, purpling rings under his eyes, was depressing. When he drew his hand across his chin it sounded like paper tearing. You could see his bald patch, too, perfectly well when he leaned forward as he fished his slippers from under the bed. And the grunting. And the cigarette, lit while he was still in this stupid state between sleeping and waking, filling the bedroom with smoke and making her sneeze. They had to sleep with the door to Christopher's room ajar in case he should have one of his nightmares. Even when she did want to indulge Edgar a bit there was always the thought of Christopher in her mind. He was a sharp little boy. She had never mentioned this to Edgar, but she often worried about the amount of psychological damage they were doing to their son.

Polygamy as an institution was probably put down by men. From the woman's point of view the advantages were all too obvious. If you were one of half a dozen wives it ought to be possible to establish some sort of relationship with your husband that was reasonably in accord with your temperament. Monogamy demanded an all-round competence in the wife she probably did not possess. Mary thought that if she could be chief wife with the kind of authority that the bearing of Christopher, a son, would naturally confer, she would have no rooted objection to Edgar having a strong wife like Ilse to do all the housework with no wages and no day off. He could have a slut, too, for his passions. Mary began to throb with laughter at the thought of Edgar with three wives. Poor little man, she almost said aloud. It was impossible to be jealous of these hypothetical other wives. They looked too much like a good business arrangement.

A sense of the queerness and unfairness of matrimony was a wave that occasionally swept over her. Here was this man, Edgar Perry, forty-five years of age, feeding and clothing her. She had no food or clothes of her own. Her subsistence depended on this man's health and goodwill. The law said that as a spouse she had certain rights; but these, to her, did not seem natural rights. They were imposed from above. Every penny she spent came from this man, and what did he receive in return? In his own judgment certainly not enough. If she were Edgar she saw herself ruling the roost with a great deal more firmness than Edgar did. There were times when she would have set about herself with the hairbrush. But as it was — and to this point she always returned — the Mary-she-was did not need the Edgar-he-was in the way that *he* needed *her*. Hence her self-reproaches. Hence, too, the uninterrupted presence of Muawiya which made Helvetia as a centre of news-interest comparable with Lancaster House itself.

The newspapers and the radio went on and on about this

Egyptian crisis and that only served to make Mary's reflections on marriage all the sadder. It was in Egypt, she saw perfectly well now, that they had been happiest. She had quite fallen in love with him all over again; but then, she had been young and romantic in those days. She had thought Edgar could never love her as much as she loved him. That was why she told him she had a lover; but Edgar had, even then, understood her far too well and disbelieved her. The trouble was, she thought, that men wanted sex right up to the end of their lives even if they lived to be a hundred. There was that old Turk who had a son when he was a hundred and twenty. Women, thank God, were not in the grip of procreation beyond a certain age. She hoped they could look forward to calm. In her own case, with a husband like Edgar, she feared she could not.

Mrs Elaine Yehia, whom at first Mary did not remember, telephoned to say she was the only Englishwoman she knew who had actually kept house in Egypt, and as she, Mrs Yehia, was about to do just that, would it be too much of an imposition if she called and had a chat? She said it was no good talking to Egyptian women about a subject like this; they had such different ideas about everything, from cooking to birth control. Mary said she was glad to talk to anyone. She doubted whether she would be much use. She couldn't remember that housekeeping in Egypt was all that different. She could recommend a good dentist, though. That was one thing she could do.

Until Elaine came Mary went on with her work and thought a great deal about Egypt. She suddenly remembered the hell of baking a cake in a portable oven over Primus stoves. What was the name of that bridge? You could stand there towards evening and watch the sun slipping down into the greasy flood, an immense glow of water, more like a lake than a river. The trees on the far shore were so distant you couldn't see them moving. She imagined herself riding in one of those rickety carriages behind the driver sitting on his bale of green fodder and a horse that broke wind; the smell of hot leather in the sunshine and the ammoniacal bitterness of the horse. Stepping out of the plane from Alexandria, as she had once, into the evening stew of Heliopolis, and gliding by coach down to the city, past street lamps wobbling in the heat, was simple happiness. A boy was burning rubbish on a plot of waste land. The fire floated on the evening like – oh, like a rose-petal. She could have cried with happiness. Please God, let me not be too happy, she had thought. I don't want to be a trivial woman. I want to know what unhappiness is too. Dear Edgar, waiting for her at the terminus, smoking a cigar. She had never seen him smoke a cigar before or since.

'I think you're lucky to be going to Egypt, the winter coming on,' she said to Elaine. They sat in the kitchen, drinking tea and looking out of the open door into the garden where Christopher and his friend from across the road were riding their tricycles.

'Frankly, I'm not looking forward to it, especially at a time like this. But there it is, my husband's been called back to Cairo.'

Mary gazed at her. Those long white fingers looked as though they'd never peeled a potato, which made it all the odder that she had this rather coarse open-air complexion, red, white and freckles where they hadn't been disguised under powder. She could imagine a man, particularly an Egyptian, wanting her. Why was she blushing? Mary had been staring, rather absently, into the blue eyes when she became aware that the woman was blushing. Not out of shame. She wasn't ashamed or embarrassed. The colour had come to her face and, yes, to her lips too, with an effect of happiness – the happiness that had been in her own mind as she thought of Cairo. All right! You love your husband; there's no need to shout it at me. It was difficult, though, to look away from Elaine's face. How beautiful she had suddenly become! Mary could imagine a man taking such a face between his hands and kissing it reverently and gently, not the hard kisses that Edgar gave her. Mary thought of the Egyptian husband — she remembered him really very well now — and thought of him kissing this fair girl.

'Why don't you have a baby?'

Elaine looked startled. 'Well, later on —'

Once she had a son would even she glow for her husband like this? But no, she would never have children. Her husband would always come first. Mary had heard that Egyptians gave their wives drugs, to make them more passionate. Probably lies. This woman would never need drugs. She made Mary feel like a maiden aunt.

'I feel guilty worrying you at a time like this when I know — I mean, this man behaving so oddly and the police taking him. I've just been seeing Mrs Blainey. She's terribly upset because Mr Hillingdon was round there so often. She says they'll certify him and shut him up for the rest of his life when there's nothing the matter with him.'

'Nothing the matter with him?'

'Mrs Blainey says he was perfectly all right when he left her house.'

Mary had heard from Edgar of Hillingdon's wish to marry Mrs Blainey, and it occurred to her that Elaine Yehia had arrived at Helvetia not so much to find out whether Egyptian shops stocked the right kind of toilet necessities but, sent by Mrs Blainey, to discover as much as possible about Hillingdon. Of course Mrs Blainey would have an interest in him and refuse to believe that he had suddenly lost his reason. No woman could believe a man to be tottering on the edge of madness when he was collecting himself to make a proposal.

'He's been remanded for a medical report, that's all I know. No, it isn't all I know. He's as mad as a hatter. He was practically foaming at the mouth. If I hadn't taken Christopher and gone out he'd have probably murdered the both of us. Edgar's seeing him this afternoon.'

'Your husband's seeing him?'

'He's been trying for days without any success, and then this morning the police phoned and said he could go along this afternoon. Napier was particularly asking for him.'

This glowing dairymaid of a woman after her own Egyptian husband, and now that Mrs Blainey, with her cunning slug eyes and the quivering lips, was after Napier with the most complete lack of shame. At times Mary felt she belonged to a different species; to be more accurate, a mutation — the beginning of a new species. It struck her that through all the millennia there had been human beings like herself, and animals too, slightly less obsessed with sex than the rest of their kind but, by the very nature of their difference, unable to propagate the new species in which they would feel more at home. The thought was novel and it confused her. She began to spell it out silently. If the difference had been one of stature there would have been no problem. The little man picked the little woman and they went away into the forest to breed pygmies. But if she went off into the forest with a like-minded man they probably wouldn't breed at all. Nature was interested only in fertility. She found herself rebelling against evolution and particularly the way she saw evidence of pullulating nature in the eyes of this woman, Elaine, and the behaviour of this Mrs Blainey who seemed so determined to snatch Napier at the very gates of the lunatic asylum.

'You can take it from me,' she said, 'he's mentally a very sick man.'

'It's not having relations that seems to make it so much worse.

If you've got no relations Mrs Blainey says they can certify you out of hand.'

'Of course,' said Mary, 'this has been coming on some time. He was actually talking of not renewing our lease. Can you imagine it? We should have had to get out next week.'

'You're not altogether sorry, then?'

'No, frankly, no.' Mary put down her cup and called out to Christopher that it was naughty to hit his little friend on the head with a spanner. 'But perhaps you wouldn't sympathize, your husband having a safe government job. You've got to remember we represent private enterprise. Everybody tries to do us down — the University of London, the Berlitz School, the British Council, the Linguaphone, everybody in this language racket. They're all green about this publicity we're getting. I wonder if one of them put Napier up to this idea of evicting us. Mr Blainey — '

'But this is absurd.'

'He works for the British Council, doesn't he?'

'But they would have no conceivable interest in harming you.'

'Anyway, it wasn't until Napier met young Blainey that he began talking about leases. There's this friendship, or whatever you call it, with his mother.'

'You can't be serious.' Elaine produced cigarettes and they both sucked in smoke thoughtfully.

'But as I say,' Mary continued, 'now that Napier's got himself locked up the danger seems to be passing. Hallo!' She stood up. 'What is it?' A cloud passed and green light from the garden flooded into the room. 'I'm in here, Edgar. What do you want? I thought you'd gone down to see Napier. It's Edgar,' she explained.

He appeared in the doorway and looked round the kitchen with the worried expression on his face she associated with breakfast time and the morning papers. It was unusual for Edgar to be without a tie. His shoes, too, were the laceless, slip-on, brown brogues. That particular suit, the grey thornproof, had not been worn for some time and she supposed its appearance was due to some special Edgarian calculation; then she remembered that, of all his trousers, these were the only ones that did not need braces. Clearly, Edgar was in his garb for visiting the mentally afflicted. No laces or straps which could be seized and used for strangling. But perhaps she was allowing her imagination to run away with her.

'You know my husband, of course.'

Elaine nodded and continued to smoke. The act was as deliberate as that. The cigarette did not merely burn in her hand or between her lips. She was lifting it to her lips and taking methodical draws. She might have been giving a demonstration.

'I'm looking for Muawiya,' Edgar said. 'You haven't seen him?'

The School Principal and the School Secretary, she thought, posing before this Yehia woman as man and wife. The arrangement was utterly immoral when you came to think of it. She made up her mind that they would have separate bedrooms from that day forward. The decision was taken as Edgar and Mrs Yehia were exchanging a few words. No intellectual or emotional struggle. From now on she and Edgar were business partners only.

Through the window he could look up and see a bricklayer working on the face of a building, some sixty feet above the ground. Beneath the bricklayer were windows and red brick; above, a framework of steel. In white overalls and a cap to match, he was standing on a platform and steadily laying bricks in one of these frames. He was silhouetted against steel girders, white clouds and blue sky; and as Perry and Hillingdon talked Perry found it difficult to stop looking at this bricklayer. He seemed to know exactly what he was doing, and this seemed a rare and attractive state of mind.

He was relieved to find Hillingdon looking so normal. He seemed a little thinner in the face, a little lighter on the bones, but, if anything, more intelligent than Perry had ever seen him. He was wearing his suede shoes and grey flannel suit. He looked straight into your eyes when he spoke, was obviously sharply alive to his situation and its implications. There was even colour in his cheeks and his eyes were clear. As often as not Hillingdon had a dozy, slightly aloof, manner as though he were no more interested in you than politeness demanded. But now he might have been a rather sharp lawyer interviewing a client.

'I asked to see you because I can trust you.' He glanced at the policeman who was sitting at a desk in the corner and dropped his voice. 'I know perfectly well that I've behaved like a bloody fool, resisting arrest and all that. It's natural for an innocent man to resist arrest. But that's not the point. They gave me some injections and now I'm going to be transferred down to some place in the country for observation. I've got to see a good solicitor. Unless they see I've got myself looked after legally there's no knowing what might happen. My solicitor is a man called Burniston, but he's no good. He's actually been here and said how shocked he was. Shocked! He's my mother's solicitor, so you can be sure he's a fool. Now, you've got to hire me a solicitor who isn't shocked. D'you see?'

'I don't know any solicitors.'

'Dammit, you can go to the Law Society, or whatever it's called. You must get somebody who'll issue a writ of habeas corpus. I haven't gone out of my mind. I'm not mad, d'you understand me?'

Perry privately decided that before he took any action he would have a word with this man Burniston on the telephone.

'Apart from that, is there anything else you want? You're looking pretty fit.'

'I want to get out.'

'Books, for example. How are you off for reading?'

Hillingdon placed his two hands flat on the table and put some of his weight behind them. The table creaked. Perry looked away from the bricklayer. Hillingdon's fingers caught his attention. Some of the nails were broken and the tips raw as though he had been trying to tear down a brick wall with his bare hands.

'But I don't think,' said Hillingdon, 'that the State can afford to let me survive.'

Perry saw that the bricklayer had stopped and was lighting a cigarette. By watching him Perry felt he was maintaining some small grip on reality. He tried to think what the bricklayer would see if he looked in their direction; two men, sitting on either side of a table, one of them leaning back and swinging his foot.

'What do you mean? I don't understand.'

'When I am disposed of I can no longer be a centre for dissent or opposition of any kind. Mind you, I would give my oath to live the life of a retired and private gentleman. My ambition is broken. Let them have the kingdom!'

The door opened and a young man in a white jacket appeared. Simultaneously the policeman rose from his desk, but Hillingdon rose too, saying: 'No I don't need you yet. Let me finish what I am saying.' And, taking Perry by the arm, and walking with him up and down the room he really did contrive an impression of deposed royalty, braver and more self-possessed than the Hillingdon Perry remembered.

'This Egyptian,' Hillingdon was saying. 'What's his name?'

'You mean Muawiya?'

'He intends to assassinate the Prime Minister. This is what I wanted to see you for, to tell you this. Just how he will do this I don't know, that is not my affair. You know perfectly well that he is capable of it. I know what his intentions are. He is so stupid and proud of himself he couldn't help dropping hints. All right,' he said abruptly. 'You can go now.'

Perry said that he would come and see him again as soon as possible and that in the meantime he would certainly look into the matter of having more powerful legal help, but Hillingdon seemed to have lost interest and stood with his hands behind his back looking out of the window.

On the way out of the building Perry, still feeling dazed, was shown into an office where a large man with pink hanging cheeks, and eyes set impossibly wide apart, said they were sending Hillingdon to a supervised sanatorium for a while in the hope that this trouble would clear up, as it might well do after a year.

'A year? What exactly is the trouble?'

'Paranoia symptoms.'

'I see,' said Perry and five minutes later he was walking along a tree-lined road, enormous silver scabs hanging on the trunks of the trees, and looking over the low wall that separated the path from a canal. It was an area of large, nineteenth-century houses, simple as children's drawings, set in sodden shrubberies. A couple of boys were playing jacks on the pavement and Perry stopped to watch for a few moments; he hadn't seen the game played since he himself was a boy. The pleasure of watching was surprisingly intense. Momentarily he recaptured a tang of his own childhood. Nobody else was about. There were some parked cars down the road. Perry looked at the boys, counting with them under his breath, and then walked quickly on, living over and over again the quarter of an hour or so he had spent with Hillingdon, and more particularly the experience of watching that bricklayer light his cigarette and go on with his work, and all the girders and the clouds and the sky behind him. Paranoia symptoms, he thought. They could happen to anyone.

At Golders Green he dropped off the bus as it slowed to take the corner, bought an evening paper and read an account of French troops arriving in Cyprus. He would have walked home but for seeing Waldo come swinging along the pavement, head well forward and neck quivering like a chicken's, his shoulders drawn back by the rucksack of books. He was on one of his treks from the London Library. Just what were all these books about? Perry realized that it must be years since he and Waldo had seriously discussed anything that wasn't politics or hadn't an immediate bearing on the running of the school.

'Hallo there!'

Waldo looked into his face and stalked on.

Perry caught him up and laid a hand on his arm.

'All right,' said Waldo. 'I saw you. What d'you want?'

'I've just been to see Hillingdon.' They were standing outside an Espresso coffee bar. 'Let's go in here. I'd like to talk to you.'

Waldo hesitated. Ever since Muawiya had come to stay at Helvetia he had refused to speak to anyone except Mary — whom he probably regarded as a fellow-sufferer — and took his meals in ostentatious silence. The arrival of Miss Gunter angered him not only in itself but because his self-imposed silence prevented him from telling Perry what he thought of her return. But he would be glad to hear news of Hillingdon. There still remained a great deal he would like to know about the happenings that led up to Hillingdon's arrest. So far as he could see Hillingdon had not behaved unreasonably. After all, Muawiya *was* Muawiya. Hillingdon's might be a case raising serious issues for those concerned with the liberty of the subject.

'I don't like coffee in the afternoon.' Nevertheless, he allowed himself to be drawn into The Old London, as it was called, where he sucked frothy coffee through his teeth and looked with growing incredulity at the decor: a profusion of castor-oil plants and, the length of one wall, a reproduction of Vischer's panoramic view of London at the beginning of the seventeenth century. Waldo looked at the pink and black mosaic floor, the pink and mosaic table-tops, and the pink — the exact tone of pink — varnish on the nails of the waitress. He picked out the Globe Theatre and the heads of traitors on old London Bridge. 'The waitress is wearing trousers. D'you see that? I'll swear this place wasn't here yesterday.'

'It's been open two years.'

Waldo stared round. 'Very original. I like it. Continental. Those coffee machines are Italian.'

'Do you mean to say you've not been in an Espresso bar before?'

'Are there others?' He produced a tobacco pouch and a contraption for making cigarettes. 'How's Hillingdon?' He dropped his tongue into the contraption like an ant-eater with an ant-hill, twiddled his fingers and produced a flabby white worm with tobacco foaming from each end. When finally he lit up the tobacco flared and threw out sparks. Ash and tobacco strands fell on to his waistcoat. A fan overhead drew off some of the smoke and discharged it into the street, but enough remained to soften, like a gauze curtain, the harsh lines of Waldo's face.

Perry looked at him with tired affection. Good old Waldo! They had know each other for ten years and still Waldo did not call him by his Christian name. He would have hated him to start now. This particular minute Perry felt he would start sobbing if Waldo took it into his head to call him Edgar. He might start sobbing anyway. Dear, beloved Waldo! What a complete idiot you are! And how completely lacking in self-pity!

'The fellow said symptoms of paranoia and they're putting him in a sanatorium. He might be better in a year.'

'A year!'

'That's what this fellow said.'

'I don't like it, Perry. I don't like it at all. When the law and medicine get together they can do anything. Look, I'll have a word with Lucas-Tooth' — Lucas-Tooth was the local M.P. 'He's quite a reasonable chap and bound to see my point of view. But what did Hillingdon *say*?'

'He said "Let them have the kingdom."'

'Let them what?'

'Have the kingdom.'

'But what does that mean?'

'He said "I would live the life of a retired and private gentleman. My ambition is broken. Let them have the kingdom."'

Waldo made himself another cigarette. The rollers of his machine squeaked agonizingly. Another lick of the tongue, an enormous thrust forward of the bunched eyebrows, a savage nip of the thumb at one end of the white worm. Flames licked at his face. He might have been an idol in a pantomime. 'Do you know what? I think that sounds serious! If he said that he must be out of his mind!'

They stared at one another.

'You're not going to speak to Lucas-Tooth, then?'

'If Hillingdon really is balmy I don't want to bother, do I? Use your head!'

The waitress in navy blue slacks came and removed the cups and Perry thought: yes, let them have the kingdom! Let them have the power to do with it what they liked! Let them threaten and bomb! As for me, I abdicate. Here, in front of me, is a mosaic table-top of black and pink. Opposite is a human countenance fifty-five years old, hairy and lined. Over there, a panorama of old London and the waitress is watching her grotesque reflection in the polished flank of the coffee machine. If the faculty of memory suddenly deserted him, if he knew nothing of Helvetia, Mary, Hillingdon, Suez, the interior of this coffee bar would be to him the limits of the known world. This was not the abdication Hillingdon had in mind when he said 'Let them have the kingdom', but for about ten seconds it granted Perry a steadying calm; and then the bubble burst — he knew that Waldo would start to grumble about Muawiya's presence at Helvetia; while he waited for the words to come he watched once more the bricklayer lighting that cigarette against a backcloth of clouds and blue sky.

Let whom have the kingdom? Perry wondered.

He ought to be getting home to phone Hillingdon's solicitor — what was his name? He would remember it in a minute. But instead of giving this as a reason for going he said he was worried about Muawiya. He made a joke about it. If Muawiya disappeared the Perry family did not eat for three months.

'Then you won't eat. That's what you want, isn't it? Dammit, it's a wonder you don't play the complete host and offer him your wife as well.' The thought of Muawiya so maddened Waldo that he pushed his chair back and lifted his voice. Perry watched the oscillation of his Adam's apple and wondered why Waldo's taunt about Mary had not annoyed him more than it did. What greater insult could be offered a husband? And Waldo meant it. He meant the words to hurt. The juxtaposition of Mary and Muawiya, even in the mind's eye, was plainly horrifying to Waldo. Then why, Perry wondered, was it not horrifying to him? Perhaps he was out of love. I will live the life of a retired and private gentleman, he thought. Let them have the kingdom.

'You can pay for the coffee.' Perry leaned forward and uttered the words with unnecessary force in Waldo's ear, then rose to his feet and walked out. He knew that Waldo would think his insult had driven him into the street and pay up with a good grace. A few flecks of rain appeared on the pavement, being absorbed by the porous stone almost as soon as they fell, and he walked on quickly. A placard at the news-stand had the one word SUEZ printed in heavy type, and below, in nineteenth-century copperplate: *Russians in Egypt*. The trolley-bus cables sang. Perry crossed the road at the traffic lights and set himself to the hill that would take him past the Crematorium with its smoking chimney.

'Muawiya!' he called as soon as he entered the house.

Hearing Mary's voice he went into the kitchen and found her with Elaine.

'I'm looking for Muawiya,' he said. 'You haven't seen him?'

The attic window was shut and the room seemed airless. The pink plastered walls rose at an angle of forty-five degrees to a cracked ceiling two feet wide. Between this ceiling and the tiles he could hear birds running about like mice. Most of the junk in the room seemed unfamiliar so, no doubt, it was Hillingdon's. There was the old cabin trunk, though, with EDGAR PERRY painted on the sides, standing on one end beneath a load of *Punch* volumes going back to the eighteen-eighties, a battered violin case (empty) and a fish tank so old that the green mould of age seemed to have eaten into the glass itself. A coloured print called 'A Street Scene in Paris, 1775' lay face up on a suitcase. The first time he had seen this print it had hung on the wall of his bedroom when staying with his grandmother. Seeing it again gave him the same kind of magical translation as when he had stopped to watch the boys playing jacks on the pavement. There was the handsome young hussar smiling at the impossibly well-dressed milkmaid under a tangle of beautifully drawn shop signs; a great metal jackboot, a golden grasshopper, a pestle and mortar. He really ought to have the picture glazed and taken downstairs. Lifting the lower window he found that the sash-cord had broken. He supported the window with one of the volumes of *Punch* and stood for some moments looking over the rooftop opposite to the Hampstead windows that were so angled they fired in the yellow sun.

Muawiya's camp bed stood against a small cliff of tea-chests full of heaven knew what. The bed had been neatly made, an enormous white pillow peeping at the end of a candlewick counterpane, and as it was unlikely that Muawiya himself could have been so orderly Perry supposed that Ilse had been in. A Victorian leather hat-box supported a reading-lamp at the bed's head, and at its side was an Arabic picture paper with a picture of a smiling Negro on the front. There was also a battered copy of Edgar Rice Burroughs's *Tarzan of the Apes* and a new, as yet plainly unread, copy of the Lewis and Maude Pelican *The English Middle Classes*. Perry saw that the blurb declared it was from the middle classes 'most of the nation's brains, leadership and organizing ability' came. So Muawiya planned not only to fight the enemy but to study him as well!

Anyway, the fellow was nowhere in the house that Perry could find.

Muawiya's clothes were displayed on hangers which had been hooked over the tea-chests. The grey suit with the silky glitter had half a dozen ties draped round its shoulders. The tweed suit, the one he had been arrested in, was also on show. A camel-hair coat in a style popular about five years before crouched on the back of a chair. Seeing so much of his gear in evidence Perry wondered what Muawiya was actually wearing. As he wondered he tried to lift the lid of one of the suitcases with his toe. To his surprise it rose easily.

Soiled linen mostly. A tin box contained chocolate biscuits. There were more books, a paper-back crime novel in English and some Arabic books that looked like fiction too. Perry found an empty Thermos flask and shook it. But the case contained nothing more dangerous than an electric razor in its leather case; made in Western Germany, he noticed. The other piece of luggage consisted of a soft camel-hide grip; it was secured by a thong running through metal rings to a small padlock which, to Perry's surprise, was unlocked. He withdrew the thong and turned out shoes, soft white paper used for padding, a camera —

'Edgar!'

Muawiya stood in the doorway. He was wearing the wide-sleeved, collarless gown of the Egyptian peasant. One bare foot was advanced from beneath the hem and his right hand was raised, an almost hieratic gesture, to emphasize his surprise. He waved the hand slowly backwards and forwards as though to efface an unwelcome vision. 'Edgar, what are you doing with my bag, please?'

'Searching it. Where have you been? I looked all over the place for you. Didn't you hear me calling?'

'I was in the bathroom praying.'

'Praying?'

'Certainly.'

Perry satisfied himself that the grip contained nothing of interest and stood up.

'Come here.'

Muawiya came and stood directly in front of him with a remote but patronizing smile upon his face. Perry slapped him gently under the arms and at the waist.

'I was looking to see if you'd got a gun, or something. It

suddenly occurred to me. I thought you might have a gun in your luggage and I wanted to take it away from you in case you were tempted to do any damage.'

'A gun! Me?' Muawiya looked horrified. 'You think that I, your guest, your friend — '

'No, I wasn't thinking of myself. I was thinking you might have a go at some public figure. The Prime Minister, say.'

'Sir Anthony Eden,' said Muawiya slowly. 'Sir Anthony Eden. What is this dreadful suspicion?' He raised his voice. His naked throat seemed to thicken. 'I am a guest of your Government. They have paid my expenses. Well, I laugh at them for their simplicity. I am not indoctrinated. I come in my own interest and the interest of my country. This is no secret. I tell everyone. I spit in the face of all your culture and William Shakespeare. But so long as I am a guest of the English I behave as a guest. I shoot nobody!'

'Anyway,' he went on, 'you think if I had a gun I would leave it in an unlocked case?'

Perry gave the grip a push with his foot. 'Don't raise your voice at me. Yes, I think you'd behave in whatever way you thought best.'

'You call me assassin.'

'Yes, yes, yes, I call you assassin! I know damn well you're an assassin. It's only by God's providence you haven't got my blood on your hands.'

Muawiya brought his hand round sharply against Perry's cheek. The force of the blow turned Perry's head to the right. The combination of anger and astonishment numbed him. He held his head stiffly averted until pain began to flow into his cheek; but before he had time to look at Muawiya again, the Egyptian was kneeling at his feet, apparently sobbing. Perry tangled the fingers of his left hand in Muawiya's hair and lifted. The face rose slowly until it was level with his own. He had been wrong about the sobbing. The eyes were dry. They looked at him, though, as if they had never seen him before. The two men looked at each other as strangers might look at each other; a couple brought face to face in a crowded Underground train. Never seen before and never to see again.

'I'm sorry I looked in your bags. It was quite wrong. I apologize.'

Muawiya lifted his hand and disengaged Perry's fingers from his hair. 'You are very welcome to see into my bags.' He spoke with obvious insincerity.

'We're going through a bad patch politically. Almost anything seems possible.'

He was still angry with Muawiya and all the angrier for knowing that the fault was his own. An Egyptian had struck him, an old pupil had struck him; and, to make matters worse, he, Perry, had apologized to him.

'You would like me to leave your house. I will go to the police and release you from your obligation.'

'I won't hear of it.'

This was not what had been intended. He wanted to beg of Muawiya, 'What has happened in this room, let us forget it', but it was impossible to put such a plea into words. Why had it happened? Perry did not know whether he was angry with Muawiya, himself, the Government, or Fate itself. He was in a mood to hit back at Muawiya. If he really wanted to avoid trouble he ought to send Muawiya packing immediately. They ought never to meet again.

'Yes, Edgar, I think it best if I go.'

'I won't hear of it, I tell you! I've apologized, haven't I? Dammit, what more do you expect?'

Muawiya sat on the bed and began drawing a pink nylon sock on to his knobbly foot. 'I thought we were deep friends. But we cannot be friends, Edgar. Do you know who will be my friend? Mr Hillingdon. One day he will come to Egypt, you see, and we shall have such good times together, duck shooting. There'll be whisky in my silver flask.' He drew on the second sock and sat admiring his feet which now looked as though they had been painted in rosy dentifrice. 'You and I cannot be friends. You are too nervous and you upset me.'

Perry went down to the hall where he met Waldo who had lowered his rucksack of books on to a chair and was reading an evening paper.

'They've built up enough gear in Cyprus for the biggest amphibious attack since D-day, according to this paper. Well, something's got to give, somewhere.'

He thought Perry would have been pleased that he was speaking once more.

'Nothing's going to give. We're all too blasted stupid.'

Waldo picked up his rucksack. He drew in his breath sharply, his nostrils vibrating slightly, to indicate that he was one to notice when a friendly gesture was ignored.

The night before Muawiya made his appearance at Marlborough Street Tim Blainey was staying with his mother. He had borrowed a car, a Consul tourer, from a fellow at the office, and as the morning was sunny and warm he drove with the hood down, feeling like the hero in a musical. At half past nine he picked Perry and Muawiya up at Helvetia and swung the car down past the Crematorium singing, quite silently, 'Beautiful Copenhagen'. The Consul should have been full of girls in bathing-costumes. The sun rose from the wet road as from a mirror and Tim had to drive with half-closed eyes, ruining about five hundred feet of film by his calculation. They would have to shoot the scene again. He drove through Hampstead, calling over his shoulder (both Perry and Muawiya sat in the back seat) and making gestures with his left hand.

He said that his mother was taking advice from an old friend of his father's, a fellow called Clem Brough, about the Hillingdon case. He had explained to his mother that Brough would not be a bit of good because he was an academic lawyer (he taught Roman Law at Oxford) who was in no position to interpret the Common Law handling of lunatics. But she said: 'The law's the law, isn't it? I'd be ashamed, if I was a lawyer, only to know the law of a people who are dead and gone.'

'What kind of law are they going to use on me this morning?' Muawiya asked. He was wearing his lovat tweed suit and a pink tie. His well-oiled hair shone in the sunshine. As they rode along he clicked his finger-joints thoughtfully, looking from side to side as though calculating (it seemed to Perry) whether even now it was not possible to cut and run. After their row Perry did not think Muawiya would think twice about costing him five hundred pounds. 'English law.' Muawiya answered his own question. 'Well, Zagloul Pasha suffered under it. Gandhi suffered under it.'

'Not for dangerous driving, driving without a licence and using a motor vehicle without insurance in respect of third-party risks,' said Perry. 'You're lucky they haven't charged you with pinching the car as well.'

Perry left Muawiya outside the court-room talking with his solicitor and the counsel the Egyptian Embassy had insisted on briefing for the case. It was first on the list. Perry did not know whether this was fortuitous or whether a diplomatic word had been said to have the case disposed of quickly, before the Press and the public in general realized what was happening. Perry and Tim — who knew he was to be called as a witness —

did not, it seemed, wait long on their benches at the back of the court-room before the magistrate entered; the extraordinary number of uniformed policemen had risen and settled like so many bluebottles, and Muawiya was walking to the wooden bar below the clerk's desk and looking confidently around him. Perry was sorry that he had not shaved that morning. The blue stubble made him look like a Victorian burglar and might easily add a couple of months to his sentence. Perry looked around, silently labelling a few of the more obvious characters: the man from the Egyptian Embassy, the man from the Foreign Office (pure guesswork this!) and, yes, Todd himself in a smart lavender grey suit, sitting on the solicitor's bench with his eyes closed.

Muawiya pleaded not guilty to the charges and counsel for the prosecution, a pleasant-faced man in a spotted black jacket, rose to say that unfortunately one of the chief witnesses for the Crown was not available as he had left the country. In this way Perry learned for the first time of Yehia's departure. Although expected, it had come more suddenly than Tim, for one, had thought. He whispered in Perry's ear. They both wondered whether Elaine had gone with him.

'Well, you'll have to do the best you can then,' said the magistrate when the circumstances had been explained to him. Perry suddenly formed the conviction that Muawiya would be acquitted. He knew nothing of the legal process. He could tell that Muawiya would get off by the expression on the face of that man in the spotted jacket: there was only one word for it — ritualistic. He blinked sleepily and looked at his witnesses as they came, one by one to the stand, as though he had been putting questions to these very same people for the past five years: the police driver who had chased Muawiya from Hampstead to Park Lane; Tim, who described the incidents in his mother's house that led up to Muawiya's jaunt, and a bearded young man who claimed to have seen the car drive into the park railings, all came up for his dispassionate examination. Counsel for the defence was by no means dispassionate. He was the palest, thinnest, man Perry had ever seen and he was able to establish, with the rapidity of a professional quiz-master, that no one could claim he had seen Muawiya get into the car, drive the car and finally get out of the car. The most they could claim was that they had seen a car.

Muawiya was called to the witness stand and took the oath on the Koran.

'It is quite true,' he said, 'that I started the car and even drove it a little way to make room for the car of my friend, Captain Mahmoud Yehia of the Egyptian Army, who would certainly have agreed if he had not been recalled to Cairo on a matter of national importance.'

'But what is not true,' he continued, after he had been warned to keep to the point, 'is that I drove far or dangerously. Why should I? It does not make sense. I am a stranger in London. It would have been madness for me to drive. No, these accusations are not true. The car must have been stolen. That is the only good explanation.'

The magistrate was so surprised that he intervened.

'Stolen by whom?'

'That is for the police to find out, sir. I would give them all the help I can if they would ask me.'

'You say that you left the vehicle and that someone else came and took it away?'

'I do not know, sir. Truly I cannot remember.' Muawiya clasped his head in his hands and turned it stiffly from right to left. 'Perhaps what these gentlemen say is true. Perhaps I drove through London. But my mind is clouded. How much more likely it is that I left the car and walked back to my friends.'

'But if you walked back to your friends why did they not see you?'

'Sir, you will think me silly but I am in England for the first time. This is a great city and I am frightened. When I thought how angry my friends would be to discover that I had allowed this man to steal the car, drive it away, at sixty miles an hour, I lost my head completely. I was ashamed and hid my face.'

There was silence in the court-room and the magistrate studied Muawiya's face carefully.

'You realize the significance of the oath you have taken?'

'I am telling the whole truth.'

'Your claim is that you do not remember what happened?'

'Yes, sir. It is for the police to prove it. I will give them all my co-operation.'

Muawiya's line of defence took Perry by surprise and, judging by the expression on the defending solicitor's and counsel's face, it took them by surprise too. If Muawiya had been English (there was no doubt at all), he was lying. But being Egyptian? Perry was not so sure. As Muawiya answered more questions put by counsel Perry gazed at his curiously candid face. It was an early-Tudor face, thickening under the blue moss of beard, eyes that gave promise of sinking. But it was not in any way furtive. On the contrary, the smile, which bent the lips and lifted the dark eyebrows over the flashing eyes, had an innocence that was almost girlish. If Muawiya was trying to deceive anybody it was because he had first of all deceived himself.

Muawiya gripped the rail in front of him and leaned forward in his eagerness. He answered all the questions with an arrestingly wide-eyed care that demonstrated his anxiety to get at the truth, whether the truth was to his advantage or not. If he did indeed drive dangerously then let someone come forward who could actually say he had seen him doing it? Had anyone seen him after the crash? He meant, seen him sufficiently well to identify him. On the other hand, had anyone seen him walking in Hampstead? It was in the interest of all that these questions were disposed of. Would it not help if the owner of the car were asked to give evidence?

The white court-room light fell from the glass roof on magistrate, clerk, counsel, solicitors, policemen, witnesses, spectators and the accused with an impartiality comparable to the impartiality with which Muawiya, by tone and bearing, was inviting the Court to consider the evidence.

He was given permission to leave the witness stand and resumed his position in the well of the court where he sat, calmly for the most part, but occasionally cracking a finger-joint by way of confessing the strain to which the trial was putting him. He listened to the evidence of the other witnesses and to the magistrate's summing up with the grandeur of one who has had a compelling vision, and succeeded in some measure in imposing it upon an audience. He was the greatest Method actor of them all. For him the play had become the reality. The account, as he had just given it, of the confused state of his memory had passed into sober history. He would be ready to answer for it on the Day of Judgment.

Perry awoke to the realization that the magistrate was criticizing the prosecution for an inadequately presented case. No material witnesses had been produced, he said. The view that the owner of the car was incapable of an appearance was not acceptable in spite of the medical evidence offered. In the circumstances the magistrate had no alternative but to dismiss the charge and award costs against the police. He had a few words for Muawiya: he had on this occasion been very fortunate indeed to escape a penalty of some kind. Let him remember that motoring offences were viewed seriously in England. If he intended staying for any time he would be well advised to have instruction at a good driving-school.

Muawiya was talking to his counsel and solicitor in the tile-decorated entrance hall when Perry and Tim Blainey joined him. The white-faced barrister was leaning sideways as though caught in a personal gale. 'He finally decided to put his foot down,' he was saying. 'He's had a succession of badly presented charges and he decided to make an example. Said he'd stagger 'em from Scotland Yard down. Well, you're lucky, sir. I knew I'd get you off, of course.' He shook Muawiya by the hand and, his gale becoming too strong for him, he was borne out to the street. Perry congratulated Muawiya on the verdict and realized the moment Muawiya opened his mouth that he had done the wrong thing.

'Edgar, this is dreadful! I was not imprisoned!'

'Did you think you would be?'

'But I shall be the laughing-stock of Egypt! Everyone will mock me. They will say: What! you avoided the police for so long and then when they caught you they let you go because you were not important enough. You were too trivial. They wanted to be rid of you.'

A grey-headed man, an Egyptian, spoke to Muawiya in Arabic and immediately switched to English. 'Come back to the Embassy with me now, please.'

'Go away!' Muawiya shouted at him. A policeman moved in their direction, and Perry took Muawiya by the arm and urged him towards the door. 'You do not understand the temper of modern Egypt, Edgar. I will not dare show my face there.'

'Come at once to the Embassy, please,' said the Egyptian official. 'I have a car waiting.'

'Leave me alone!' They were standing on the pavement in

the sunshine of Marlborough Street. 'This will cause me the loss of all my prestige. It is intolerable! I cannot live!'

About thirty or forty people had gathered round, some of them Press photographers who were snapping Muawiya, Perry and the Egyptian official impartially. A spectacled man in a raincoat wanted Muawiya to accompany him to Fleet Street: the Features Editor would like to discuss a series of articles. Autograph books were thrust forward. Perry pushed Muawiya into the car and told Tim to drive just anywhere he liked provided it was away from this mob. Tim swung the car round in front of Liberty's Tudor façade, but by the time the Regent Street traffic lights had changed to green the Embassy official was on their tail in a hired Daimler. The uniformed chauffeur had the face of a whippet.

'I want,' said Muawiya unexpectedly, 'to see the pigeons in Trafalgar Square.'

'I can't park in Trafalgar Square,' said Tim.

'You drop us in Trafalgar Square,' Perry directed, 'and go off and find somewhere to park.'

The Daimler could not park either, and as Perry and Muawiya walked among the pigeons they occasionally looked up and saw it cruising round and round the square with the Embassy official peering out at them. Muawiya bought a packet of peanuts and fed the pigeons. They perched on his shoulder pecking at the packet while Muawiya, still stiff-faced with despair, looked up at Nelson's steady drift across sky and cloud. The wind dashed fine spray from the fountains over him but he ignored it. 'I have wasted my life,' he said. 'It is meaningless. I have enemies. They will never let me forget my humiliation. All this time I have been in England and I have done nothing but hide from the police! For what? For nothing? It is the police, not me, who are in trouble.'

The sunlight picked the blues and greens out of the gunmetal grey of the pigeons' plumage. Perry was astonished to see so many pigeons. There must have been thousands. The tapping of beak and claw set up a wiry crepitation. Once in the air, startled by a child, they emitted tiny leathery creaks. They were not in the air long. Round the column, perhaps, and then they would be back where they started from, heads on one side or nodding backwards and forwards from the effort of walking.

Muawiya admired the size of the lions and patted one of the paws. The yellowing leaves of the plane trees drifted against the silver buildings. By the blue and gold clock of St Martin's it was half past eleven.

One of the licensed photographers came up and said it would not take a moment — seven and sixpence and they would have three postcard-size photographs on good paper within seven days. He was sorry the developing and printing would take so long, but this was his busy season.

No, said Perry. But Muawiya insisted. He led the way round to the south side of the column and made Perry stand on his left hand, with a peanut on each shoulder and one on the crown of his head to attract the pigeons, while they gazed down Whitehall.

'What is that tower?' Muawiya asked.

'Well, it's the Houses of Parliament. That clock is Big Ben.'

Muawiya nodded with satisfaction. 'We are at the heart of the Empire.'

'We don't call it the Empire any more.'

'Never mind,' said Muawiya. Like Perry he now had pigeons on his shoulders. He extended his arms so that they could promenade. 'I think of it as the Empire. Is it far to Buckingham Palace?'

The redness of buses. They came up Whitehall, passed the

Foreign Office, Downing Street. Slowly they expanded in the sunlight.

'Let us walk to Buckingham Palace,' said Muawiya.

He gave the photographer a ten-shilling note and told him to keep the change. The trees in the Mall were still as green as though it were high summer. Children ran over the grass towards the lake screaming with laughter. Perry was surprised to see the obvious pleasure Muawiya was taking in their walk. The gloom brought on by his unexpected acquittal had lifted.

'I have always imagined London like this, Edgar. This part is very like the Zoological Gardens in Gizeh, isn't it, frankly? But it is not Gizeh. It is London, and here I am walking about in it. You know, the English and Egyptians will be friends. I am suddenly confident of this.'

They paused opposite the Duke of York steps and Muawiya asked who the man was on top of the column; and that gold woman in a helmet in front of that building? To the north, the sky was a patiently unfolding whirl of blue and white.

'What makes you think we shall be friends?'

'The judge was afraid to punish me. He knew I was guilty but he had to let me go.'

Even Perry was taken aback. He stopped. 'Don't talk like a fool.'

'I am not talking like a fool. You know very well I ought to have been put in prison. I had a reasonable expectation of being put in prison. Do you think I would have taken the car and driven through London at night, endangering my life, if I had not thought I would be put in prison?' Muawiya was smiling; under the blue fuzz his face broke into curves. His brown eyes were large with a dew that might easily overflow. 'I have a reputation to think of. It would have been impossible for an Egyptian in the public eye, like myself, to come to London at a time like this without getting arrested. It would have been very compromising. Particularly as I was a guest of your Government.

'Of course,' he said, 'it means that I have wasted a lot of time. If I had known British justice would be afraid to punish me for this offence I should have given myself up immediately. No doubt I should have sacrificed a lot of publicity. But I would very quickly have made good publicity in another way. Frankly, Edgar, I have not been very clever. Smashing your Hillingdon's car, it was nothing. It was not political enough.'

'Then what should you have done?'

'It would have been a mistake to kill anyone. British justice might hang me, even though it was afraid. I don't know. *Something*. Are we near Lancaster House? I could set it on fire, perhaps.'

At a shout they turned and saw Tim bring the car to a halt some thirty yards up the Mall.

'He says the magistrate let him off because he was afraid of upsetting Colonel Nasser.' Perry led the way into the back seat. 'As I understand it, Muawiya claims that this fear has the entire British nation in its grip. As a result no force will be used to open the Canal. This means that we shall all be friends.' He settled back on the leather which was hotter to the touch than he had expected. There was real warmth in the lemon sunshine. 'We also had our photos taken.'

Tim took the car slowly towards the Palace. The Embassy car with the whippet-faced driver was twenty yards behind.

Muawiya laughed boisterously. 'Edgar, you are not quick to notice when I pull your leg. I am always joking. Even when I seem to be at my most serious, Edgar, you must remember the possibility that I am having a good laugh. I do not mean that you English are *afraid* of Colonel Nasser.'

Perry leaned forward and tapped Tim on the shoulder. 'Take us to Lancaster House. We want to set it on fire. Oh, but we shall need a small incendiary bomb. Where d'you get incendiary bombs from? I suppose we could try the Army and Navy Stores.'

Muawiya was not going to allow himself to be thrown. He patted Perry on the knee. 'Did you see the Secret Service man in the court? I expect he passed a note to the judge.'

'To the Army and Navy Stores,' Perry cried.

'Excellent,' said Muawiya. 'An excellent joke. But do you know what I sense about your country? All Arabs, all Africans, all people in Asia are waking up. And you are busy saying to them: Look, we are not imperialists any more, we are just good chaps with a different-coloured skin who had a good start in life.'

'Well?'

'This is very good. It is all hypocrisy, of course, but sometimes hypocrisy is useful. It prevents a man from behaving badly. Edgar, that is why I think we shall be friends. England is still faced with this difficulty of convincing everybody she is full of nobody but good chaps, if you see, and she is not going to let even Colonel Nasser stop her from doing it. Suez? What is Suez? That is what England says, and she is all dressed up like Red Riding Hood's grandma. Now is not the time to show that under the little nightcap there is still this big wolf face. That is what the Secret Service man wrote in the note he passed to the magistrate.'

'You think this Cyprus build-up is all bluff then?'

'Certainly it is bluff.' Muawiya threw himself back in his seat, laughing. As they rounded the Victoria statue he sat up and pointed to the Palace guard. 'Toy soldiers! Bluff!' He sighed. 'Now I must return to Egypt. But I shall come again to England. I like your country, Edgar. I feel at home here. I have enjoyed myself. It would suit me well to be Egyptian Ambassador in London. This is not impossible. I should invite that magistrate to dinner and we should have a good laugh together about the traffic laws in this country. I should make him tell me what was in that note from the Secret Service man.'

Tears ran down his cheeks. 'Egypt, my poor country. What suffering you have.'

The busy season of the Trafalgar Square photographer must have been protracted that year. It was weeks before the photos arrived and by that time Perry had forgotten all about them. They came through the letter-box on November the first, the very day the Franco-British ultimatum to Israel and Egypt expired and the radio told them at breakfast-time that Egyptian airfields had been attacked. Perry did not show the photographs to any of the others. His first job that morning was to move his bed into the spare room at the end of the passage and the photos gave him an excuse to sit quietly at the bedroom window for a few moments, like a Slav on the eve of a long journey. It was a long journey, he thought, out of his wife's bedroom for ever.

The photographer, he had to admit, had been competent. Muawiya, grinning, stood with the self-conscious rigidity of one to whom being photographed was a rare delight. He had two pigeons on each of his extended arms and another on his left shoulder. One of Muawiya's feet was pointed at the camera, the other was at right angles to it. As a result he looked, a little, as though he were tensed to throw the pigeons into the air. And his grin seemed to say: This is a wonderful trick. No one can handle pigeons as I do.

Perry himself never photographed well. He was made to look much too fat. Some trick of light made it appear that his belly was hanging over the top of his trousers. It was simply untrue that he was becoming pear-shaped and he deliberated whether, before sending a print to Muawiya, he might not cut himself out of it. Then he remembered the bombing of the Egyptian airfields and thought it would be some time before Muawiya would be receiving his memento of London.

He went over to his bed and began rolling the sheets and blankets into a bundle. Everybody else he knew photographed well. Why was it that he alone had to look so disgusting? He dropped the bundle on to the floor, plucked the photographs out of his hip pocket and studied once more the middle-aged pathos of the figure that was supposed to represent himself. It had the kind of smooth vacant face he would as a boy have decorated with a thickly pencilled moustache. And not as a boy only! He found a pencil in his waistcoat pocket and went gently to work. If he was going to cut the figure out, anyway, what did it matter? He gave the pencil a good lick.

Hillingdon photographed well! He had one of those heavy bold faces which seemed to impress itself with a noble fidelity on the photographic film. If ever he got to be President of the United States he had just the face for carving on that cliff somewhere. It even looked well in the newspapers. Not only was it a striking face, it was a faithful reproduction. This was proved by the fact that when his cousin in Brighton saw the photograph in the *Mirror* she thought it was of his father. That had a good outcome. In a way that Perry did not understand her appearance on the scene (a blood relation! impossible – she was all skin and bone) made it possible for Burniston to get a magistrate's order for Hillingdon's release from the State institution. He was now a voluntary patient in a pleasant establishment in Hertfordshire which had allowed him to bring along many of his private possessions: the top of the totem pole, the African mask, the glass-eyed tiger skin, and so on. Perry supposed he ought to be grateful to this cousin and Burniston between them because they had worked out some arrangement whereby the lease was renewed for five years. For one thing, this Hertfordshire home was expensive. Five years! That was a long time. Perry had guaranteed to pay the money for all those years. Now there had been this attack on Egypt might not the students melt away?

He held the photograph out at arm's length. By shading the shirt-front he had removed the appearance of a hanging stomach. The moustache, though, was too heavy for the face to carry. It had hanging ends. Perry the Poisoner! That is just what it looked like – an Edwardian murderer snapped playing with the birds. He propped the photograph against the reading-lamp at the head of Mary's bed, where she could not fail to see it last thing at night, picked up the bundle of sheets and blankets and lurched out into the corridor where he met Waldo. At breakfast he had managed to say nothing to Waldo.

This time he did not escape so easily. Waldo held him by the bundle.

'I honestly feel that I can lift up my head in the world again. You know jolly well I'm no chauvinist, Perry, no jingoist, but I'd like to see Nasser's face this morning. He didn't think we'd do it. Another thing! There's no doubt the Russians had the most fantastic depots in the Sinai Desert. The Jews have made that crystal clear. I'd like to see Krushchev's face, too.'

'Not Jews, Waldo, Israelis.'

'Here, what are you carting those clothes about for?'

Perry explained that he was moving his bed into the spare room. When Waldo wanted to know why, Perry was, first of all, tempted to say Mary kept him awake snoring; but Waldo would never have believed him.

'When the devout Hindu reaches a certain age and his family are well established he leaves them and his wealth and his position and goes out with his begging-bowl. Before him is the holy life and asceticism.'

Waldo gave one of his twisted and terrifying frowns. 'What is this nonsense? I think it's very wrong of you, Perry, to lug stuff about like this. After all, there are servants. What if a student came along? You know the Eastern mentality as well as I do. They wouldn't respect you.'

Perry walked to the spare-room door and pushed it open with his foot. He slung the bundle inside and marched briskly back up the passage.

'Give us a hand with the bed, will you?'

There was no need to dismantle it. By tipping it on one side he and Waldo were able to manœuvre it through the doorway and down to the spare room. They placed the head against the hot-water pipes which, even at that time during the morning, were gurgling heavily. Perry threw the mattress on to the springs and was about to lie down when Waldo put a hand on his shoulder and said: 'You and Mary haven't had a quarrel, have you?'

'We've had an evolution.'

'A what?'

Perry was eyeing the rest of the furniture critically. The old-fashioned marble-topped washstand would serve quite well as a desk. He would buy one of those wooden lampholders you screwed to the wall. There were a couple of good chairs. The horsehair sofa under the window would be the place for afternoon naps. With the expenditure of very little time and money the room could be fitted out so well that he would need to leave it only for food and lessons.

'I must have a room of my own,' he said. 'I need privacy.'

'What I really came up to tell you was that there's the young fellow downstairs, Blainey, who wants to see you.' Waldo stalked to the door and paused. 'I should have thought that on a day like this your mind would have been occupied with more public issues. Don't you care what's going on in the world? Thank God there are some people who do care. Mark my words, Perry, what is being done today will have a steadying effect everywhere, and I'm proud to be an Englishman.'

A few minutes later Perry followed him down to the hall where he found Tim Blainey waiting. He could see that the young man was excited. As soon as he had shut the study door behind them Blainey blurted out that he had resigned from the British Council and was wondering if there was any chance of a job at the Helvetia School of English.

'No,' said Perry.

'You've got all the staff you want.' Tim looked disappointed.

'It isn't that so much. I hate to see anybody acting like a fool.'

'But —'

'If I were you I'd go back and withdraw that resignation. It isn't too late, is it?'

'This attack on Egypt —'

'It's bad enough to have people like Waldo Grimbley about the place, without melodramatic characters like you popping up making silly meaningless gestures. This has nothing to do with the Council. Go on, get out of this place before I kick your behind for you!'

The anger came at last. He had thought the very capacity for it had died on him. He marched with Tim, out into the hall, passed through groups of students who were waiting for a class to begin, through the front door and down the steps into the reek of the foggy morning. The fog rose from the soaked ground and sodden bushes. Sounds were muted. Overhead, though, there was a brightness. Higher up the hill the sun might be shining.

'You know it wasn't I who ordered this attack,' said Tim as soon as Perry stopped for breath.

Perry clapped him on the shoulder and apologized. He returned to the house and saw that some of the students had come out on the steps to meet him.

'Inside, the lot of you! At once! You'll get pneumonia. And classes are late anyway. That is, if you want classes – do you?'

They followed him without hesitation to the main lecture room and Perry, taking up position on the platform, looked earnestly and curiously round at their dark faces.

He would have liked to say with Hillingdon: 'I give my oath to live the life of a retired and private gentleman. My ambition is broken. Let them have the kingdom.'

But he understood *them* too well. And, in any case, unlike Hillingdon, he knew the kingdom was not his to give.